THE DARK FIGURE HADN'T MOVED

Gideon tossed the bomb up a few times to check its heft, then in one single and marvelously smooth motion drew back his hand, hesitated, and threw. The bomb landed, and exploded, and the concussion on the otherwise noiseless plain was deafening. Gideon watched patiently for bits and/or pieces of the dark figure to litter the landscape.

And he waited.

Until the dark figure emerged from the cloud and began walking toward them. Slowly. A dark hand up to brush debris from its shoulders, the cowl that covered its head, the puffed and hanging black silk of its sleeves.

"Oh hell," Gideon moaned, and rummaged frantically for another bomb.

"Too late, you miserable little worm," came the voice from the dark figure, the voice of the Wamchu.

Tor Books by Lionel Fenn

BLOOD RIVER DOWN
WEB OF DEFEAT
AGNES DAY

LIONEL FENN

AGNES DAY

TOR

A TOM DOHERTY ASSOCIATES BOOK

AGNES DAY

Copyright © 1987 by Lionel Fenn

First printing: August 1987

A TOR Book

Published by Tom Doherty Associates, Inc.
49 West 24 Street
New York, N.Y. 10010

Cover art by Daniel Horne

ISBN: 0-812-53789-0
CAN. ED.: 0-812-53790-4

Printed in the United States of America

0   9   8   7   6   5   4   3   2   1

For Beth, without whose temporary madness there would be no free lunches, free drinks, or smiles.

ONE

The sharp bark of signals, the crack and grunt of helmeted bodies colliding, the race for position, and out of it all a football that arced gracefully through the clear crisp air, its outline preternaturally sharp against the deep blue of the cloudless sky. The opposition scrambled frantically away from the line of scrimmage when it realized how cleverly it had been fooled, and the receiver, standing alone in the end zone, waited patiently for the spiraling missile to reach him. The home crowd of nearly one hundred thousand screamed its delight at the sight of the winning touchdown soaring toward home. The opposing coach yanked off his earphones and pulled out his hair in great frustrated clumps. The receiver lifted his hands. The crowd rose to its feet and roared encouragement. The opposing coach slumped to his knees and uttered a prayer. The receiver watched in awe as the football dropped lazily toward him. The crowd fell silent in blood-thirsty expectation. The opposing coach closed his eyes.

The receiver dropped the ball.

And Gideon Sunday stood alone on the field with hands on his hips, shaking his head slowly and wondering aloud why, even in his fantasies, he couldn't complete a pass.

"You know," he said, "maybe I ought to take this as a sign."

"It's a rock," a woman's rasping voice said behind him.

"I know it's a rock, but it could be a sign, too."

"A rock is a rock. A sign is a sign. That rock wasn't a sign."

He turned around and glared down at the huge white duck waddling toward him. "Sis, that may be a simple rock to you, but to me it's a sign."

The duck stopped, peered around his legs at the puff of dust rising from the spot where the rock had landed, and shook her head. "It's a rock. If it was a sign, the guy would have caught it."

Gideon brushed a tangle of brown hair from his eyes and raised an eyebrow. "How do you know he dropped it?"

"Because I've been watching you all afternoon. And all afternoon you've been reliving your glory days as a quarterback. Both of them. I know when the guy catches it, and I know when he drops it. That guy dropped it." She moved closer and pecked lightly at his knee. "I'm sorry, but it's not a sign, Giddy. It's a rock."

Slowly, reminding himself that she was after all his sister no matter what she looked like and no matter how often she tried to leech the romance from his soul, he lowered himself to the ground. With a great show of fastidiousness, he dusted off his jeans, adjusted his long, dark, pacch-hide cloak more closely around his shoulders, and sighed. Loudly. Filling the air with a melancholy prelude to figurative self-immolation that would have sent his sister racing for their tent had he not, at the same time, clamped a gentle hand about her neck.

"Sis?"

"What?"

"I'm homesick."

"And I'm a duck. We all have our troubles, brother."

He ignored the lingering bitterness in her voice as a natural reaction to a love lost forever because the man who had prompted such affection to blossom in her downy bosom had not stuck by her after their last efforts to return her to her rightful form had failed. Since the man, a blacksmith with the brawn of his profession and the brains of a horseshoe, had never rated very highly in his estimation anyway, Gideon was not as bereft as his sister. Good riddance to bad rubbish, he thought, though he did not speak the sentiment aloud for fear she would nip his legs off at the kneecaps. She might be down, but she was still in possession of a rather volatile temper that made occasional good use of her present configuration.

"Besides," she added, twisting her neck free and squatting beside him, "you're not homesick, you're in love. Disgusting, but true."

He sighed again.

Ivy.

The very hint of her name sent a curious effervescent tingle through his veins and an equally curious flush to his raggedly bearded cheeks.

Ivy of the sweeping blonde hair and deep green eyes, of the gentle hands and quiet demeanor, of the figure that gave him nightly, and once in a while afternoonly, palpitations.

"And it beats me all to hell why you just don't go up there and see her and get it over with."

"Because," he said sorrowfully.

"Because why?"

"Because I'm not sure I'm really ready yet for a long-term commitment."

The duck eyed him in surprise. "What? Who said anything about a long-term commitment, for heaven's sake? You go up there, you mess around a little, you get her out of your system, and you'll feel a lot better."

"Hey!" he exclaimed in gentlemanly protest.

"What's the matter? You think she won't mess around?" She snorted. "Believe me when I tell you, as your sister who is sick of your cow eyes and sighing, she'll mess around."

"Crude," he muttered. "Very crude."

The duck said nothing.

Gideon stared at the ground.

The duck said nothing.

Gideon stared at his hands.

The duck shifted, and said nothing.

Gideon stared blindly into the distance and shivered as a

cool breeze, autumnal in its touch, tousled his hair over his eyes and ruffled the edges of his cloak.

"Well, for Christ's sake!" the duck said.

"All right, all right," he said. "So maybe I'm not all that sure about the love part."

"That's better."

"But I sure do miss her."

"Then why don't we do something about it, instead of sitting around here like a couple of lumps, waiting for something to happen?" She snapped her beak. "The last time we hung around, I nearly got killed."

He would have argued, at least about the lumps, but he knew she was right. They had vegetated long enough; it was time they bestirred themselves into positive action.

"And I'm tired of being a duck."

Gideon did not respond. He didn't dare. Because every time she complained about her condition, and every time he promised to do something about it, he got into trouble. The first time, though he admitted it was before he knew she was a duck in the first place, he had found this new and strange world at the back of his pantry in New Jersey, and had nearly died a thousand deaths trying to rescue her from a sacrificial plucking. The second time, when he knew full well that the white duck was in reality his sister, Tuesday, the former movie star, he had notched another hundred or so near-death experiences while, at the same time and through no fault of his own, battling a pair of beautiful women who had nothing better to do than to attempt a conquest of this new, strange, and utterly ridiculous world.

Since then, he had vowed each night before falling asleep that there would not be a third time.

He also understood that there was nothing more stubborn than a woman who one day wakes up and finds herself changed into a large, albeit attractive, duck, and who desires more than anything to have said transformation reversed before she pines away for lack of a decent steak and a good man's strong arms.

He stood decisively and faced into the wind. "Tuesday," he said, "you're right."

"Of course I am," she told him. "This duck stuff is a pain in the ass. Do you have any idea what it's like to have a pair of lips that can chop wood in a pinch?"

He strode quickly off, toward a tall, conical tent pitched on a low knoll some hundred yards away.

"Do you know what it's like," she shouted, "when your womanly urges are screwed up because you're covered with a permanent goddamned boa?"

He whistled once, shrilly, and grinned when a large caprine creature wandered into view.

"Gideon, are you listening to me?"

The beast was long-haired, long-tailed, and as tall as a husky long-legged horse; its hooves were rather nastily clawed, and on its head was a pair of oversized ram's horns that had, in the past, done a great deal of damage to those who thought it was only a tranquil, dim-witted lorra.

"Red," he called as he approached the tent, "we're going up to see Ivy. We're leaving as soon as I pack a few things and change my clothes."

Red, who in the manner of his species seldom got excited over much of anything except food, nodded absently and returned to his grazing, the ground-length silky hair that gave him his name rippling as the breeze gusted into a chilled, damp wind. He moved only once—when the tent collapsed and Gideon's thrashing threatened to upset his digestion.

When Gideon finally battled through the folds to the open air, he dragged behind him a large burlap sack that bulged intriguingly. His cloak was gone. His pearl-buttoned shirt had been changed from a blue tartan pattern to one of dark red and darker green. His jeans had been tucked into a pair of smooth leather boots. And around his waist was a thick leather belt, attached to which was a thick leather holster in which had been placed a greenwood weapon that resembled a superbly hewn and sensuously smooth baseball bat.

"Ready," he announced.

Tuesday circled twice overhead and landed neatly at his feet. "Good for you. Someone's coming."

He looked eastward, toward the halfhearted low walls of the city of Rayn nearly half a mile away, and saw a tiny figure racing toward them. "I wonder who that could be?" he said.

Red purred his ignorance.

The figure tripped, fell, picked itself up, and started running again.

"Don't talk to him," the duck pleaded. "It's probably bad news."

"What bad news? Maybe it's . . . lord, maybe it's a message from Whale! God, Sis, maybe he's finally found the right spell!"

Tuesday grumbled something too low for him to hear, though not low enough to convince him it wasn't a fowl obscenity. His sister had too often placed her hopes on Whale Pholler's abilities to change her back into the svelte beauty she claimed once to have been, and each time his abilities had proved not to be up to the task. He tried. He tried terribly hard and very earnestly. But when all was said and done and the smoke cleared from his efforts, he was a better armorer than he was a magician.

The figure tripped, regained its feet, and kept on running.

"On the other hand," Gideon said quietly, "maybe the Wamchus are at it again."

Red snorted, and his eyes turned vaguely black.

Tuesday stretched out her great wings and batted her brother soundly about the shins. "Don't say that!" she hissed.

Gideon only shrugged and stepped out of her way. His reference to the villain who had attempted with his three wives to subjugate the populace of this world was not made lightly. The man in question had been too quiet for too long. He had also, during Gideon's last perilous adventure, lost two of his spouses. He could not, then, be expected to take such a defeat without some thought of retaliation.

Wamchu lived in the world's Lower Ground, called Choy by those who dared give it a name.

Gideon was currently staying in the world's Middle Ground, called Chey by those who wished to distinguish it from the Lower and less hospitable Ground.

Ivy lived on the highest level, the Upper Ground which was hardly ever referred to by name since, when you wanted others to know where you were going or where you were from, all you had to do was point up.

The figure tripped into a cartwheel, landed on its back, and sat there shaking its spike-haired head. Its eyes blinked heavily. Its hands checked for broken limbs and contusions of a debilitating nature. Then it rose to its feet and walked the rest of the way.

"I'll be damned," Gideon said. "It's Jimm."

Tuesday groaned and turned to waddle into the tent, saw the ruins and groaned again, and sat on them. She was not Jimm Horrn's greatest fan, though he had on more than one occasion saved her life with what few combat skills he had. What she could not understand was how a young man like that could dare claim he made his living as a thief.

Jimm took the slope of the rise slowly, puffing and blowing and generally making it clear to anyone who cared to look that he was out of breath, out of condition, and long since out of caring whether he delivered his message or not.

Gideon shook his hand, Red butted him playfully, and the thief dropped to the grass, where he massaged his cheeks and forehead. "That's a long walk," he said. "Well, maybe not all that long a walk, but certainly you couldn't make it in five minutes, could you?" He smiled. "I have a message."

Gideon nodded solemnly. "From Whale, I assume."

"Right." Horrn toyed with the buttons of his leather vest. "I don't think you're going to like it, though. Well, if you're really bored, maybe you will. I don't know if I could ever be that bored, though."

"Kill him," Tuesday said.

Horrn looked alarmed.

"She's kidding," Gideon assured him as he sat beside him and crossed his legs.

"No I'm not," she insisted. "He's got bad news. Kill him before we find out what it is and have to do something about it."

The young man gingerly brushed a hand through his sandy, spiky hair and cleared his throat. "I have to tell you. Whale says I have to tell you."

"Then tell me," Gideon said.

"I'll kill him, if you want," Tuesday said.

"Shut up, Sis."

"It's the Wamchus."

Gideon considered the wisdom of his sister's sage advice, but the look on Horrn's face stopped him from taking out his bat and pounding the hairy spikes into the man's brain.

"What," he said, "about them?"

"Well," Jim said nervously, "Whale said something about getting a message from Above."

"Funny you should mention that," Tuesday muttered.

"He says that there's some kind of trouble up there."

Tuesday made a sound remarkably like a duck imitating a goat's bleating. Red gave her a puzzled look.

"He says the Wamchus have brought an army into the Scarred Mountains and are getting ready to take over the world."

"Again?" Gideon said before his sister could.

"Well, he hasn't actually taken it over before, you know," Jimm said stiffly. "Not really. That is, not all of it."

"Jesus!" Gideon said suddenly, and leapt to his feet. "My god—Ivy!"

Horrn nodded. "Yes. Whale says the message was from Ivy, and Ivy says that if you don't get up there and help her real soon, she's going to die and never see you again."

Gideon whirled to face north, to face the mountain range on the horizon, a range so high its top was obscured by a permanent cap of clouds.

"Tuesday," he said, "I have to go."

"You were going anyway."

"He was?" Horrn said, amazed.

"He's in love."

"He is?"

"With Ivy."

"Ivy?"

Gideon's hands folded slowly into fists, and the wind whipped around him, roaring to his ears. Clouds from the south scudded darkly overhead, and there was the distinct touch of snow in the suddenly colder air. From the woods to the left came the mournful cry of a baying hound. From the city to the east came the high skirling wail of a dirge of pipes. And from the north he could hear the cries of men forging themselves into fighting machines, women weeping over the loss of lovers and children, animals shrieking in pain, birds circling over piles of bloody fresh carrion.

Shit, he thought; all I wanted to do was mess around.

TWO

"If you think," Tuesday said grimly, "I'm going to fly all the way the hell up there just so you can save the life of some hussy, you've got another think coming."

Gideon slipped down off Red's back and rubbed his palms together, massaged his nape, scratched at his chest, did four swift knee bends to loosen his legs, and looked reproachfully at his sister.

"There was a wise man," he told her, "who once said that he who flinches from his duty will soon flinch from the blade of an avenging angel."

Tuesday closed one eye and stared at him. "What wise man was that?"

"I don't know. He's dead."

"From taking his own advice, no doubt."

Gideon raised a sarcastic eyebrow and turned to examine the object of the duck's protest.

It was the foot of the northern mountain range.

Ordinarily, having climbed over mountain ranges, he would not have heeded his sister's threats. This, however, was not ordinary. Nor was it so much a range, he noted, as it was a single gigantic upheaval of Chey's northern frontier, which, at its plateau above, held another world at least as large as this one. It's going to be a bitch, he thought as he walked toward it, and remembered how he had gotten down it in the first place—by falling off the edge. But at that time, a certain residue of Whale's magic had enabled him to glide effortlessly through the air, and into Chey's largest inland sea.

That he had survived the journey reasonably intact was less a commentary on Whale's powers than it was a sign that he didn't want to die.

Now he had to go up.

Straight up.

There were no foothills, no gentle pastoral slopes he could take at his leisure, no trams or cable cars he could ride in and view the panorama spread so awesomely around him.

Straight up.

Two days after they had left Rayn and the plain, the grass and road ended and the range began.

"I don't think it'll be too hard," he said after a while.

"Then why didn't Jimm come with us?"

"Because Whale needs him."

"And why didn't Whale come with us?"

"Because he's the mayor of Rayn and has duties to perform."

Tuesday quacked, flapped her wings, and condemned with sour effectiveness the magician's progeny to a lifetime of baldness in a hatless desert.

Gideon stepped back and looked up, one finger rubbing the side of his nose. He could see no plants or small trees to grasp, nor were there any nooks and crannies he might be able to use as natural foot- and handholds. He had no rope. He had no hot-air balloon. And, unlike his sister, he had no wings.

"What do you think, Red?"

Red lifted his head and appeared to study the situation, his left front hoof clawing an idle trench in the ground. Then, with a snort and a purr, he began walking northwestward, leaving the others no choice but to follow since he was also carrying the tent and food on his back.

"Does he know what he's doing?" Tuesday asked as she panted to keep pace with her brother.

"It looks like it."

"You wanna bet he's faking it?"

"Would you have bet you'd be turned into a duck when you left home that night after refusing that offer to do the nude scene with the dolphins?"

"That," she said primly, "has nothing to do with this. That was a clear matter of artistic judgment. Besides, dolphins have cold noses."

Red wandered on, eyeing the vertical slope and grunting to himself.

"I didn't know that," Gideon said.

"That's because you've never been goosed by one."

"You were goosed by a dolphin?"

Red looked back, looked ahead, and kept walking.

Tuesday told him she didn't want to talk about it, that the memory was painful enough without him dredging up memorable sidelights to the last night of her career. She fell into a pout. Gideon, sighing, reached down and pulled her out, kicked some dirt into the pout to cover it in case other travelers came this way, and refocused his attention on the lorra, who was bulling through a screen of heavy brush, his horns slashing the way clear for his companions.

By midafternoon the sun was high and warm overhead, and he was ready to concede that his sister might have been right. Then Red stopped, lifted his head, and bellowed.

"Now that," said the duck, "is a sign."

"Nice," Gideon said, stroking the lorra's neck.

Here, beyond the now-battered foliage screen, a switchback series of stepped ramps had been cut into the slope's face. They were not steep, though they promised eventual agony for his legs, and they were wide enough so that he would not be forced to walk a tightrope between the face of the cliff and a direct invitation to oblivion.

As he craned his neck, he thought he saw indications of caves farther up, and the sighting brought back another memory—as he was falling toward the lake, he had turned to look at the cliff and had seen a series of caves and ladders which, at the time, had seemed to him an infinitely more convenient way to get to the bottom than the one he'd been using. He began to hope, then, that he'd be at the top in less time than he had feared.

"Well," he said, "I suppose we'd better get going."

Tuesday balked. "What's your hurry? Don't you think we ought to rest for the night? We're not going to get all the way up in one day, you know."

Gideon checked the straps that held the supplies on the lorra's back. "Sis, you know as well as I do that the longer we take, the worse it will be when we get there. Who knows? We may even be too late now."

"Well," she said, "if we're too late, there's no sense in going in the first place, right?"

He looked over his shoulder. "What the hell's the matter with you?"

She looked up.

He looked up. He looked down. "You're kidding."

"If I could, I'd cross my heart."

"But you're a duck!"

"Watch it," she warned.

"I mean, you can fly!"

"You'll notice I don't go very high. And when I do, I close my eyes."

"How can you fly with your eyes closed?"

"A wing and a prayer," she said, and swatted his rump with the former. "I can't do it."

"Then don't look down."

"If I fly, I'll look down."

"Then walk."

She lifted one flat, orange foot.

Gideon slowly lowered his head onto Red's back and considered leaving her behind. After all, she wouldn't be much use to him or Ivy if she was catatonic from fright before they were even halfway to their destination. And, when he thought about it a little longer, he also suspected she wouldn't be much good in a fight. One on one, she was terrific, as he'd already seen; against an army of the sort Wamchu had likely raised, however, she would probably be a disaster.

On the other hand, if he did leave her behind, there was a

chance that one of Wamchu's henchmen might capture her before she reached the safety of the city, and then he would feel guilty for the rest of his life because he had deserted her. And since she was the only member of his family left, duck or not, he didn't think he wanted to be an orphan this late in life.

He lifted his head and swiped the hair from his eyes.

"Well?" she said.

He pointed at the foot of the ramp.

"Shit."

Red's purr sounded very much like a snicker, and she glared at him, glared at her brother, and twitched her tail in a gesture that, had she had a hand, and the appropriate finger, would have been all too clear. As it was, Gideon had to assume, for the sake of her sisterly reputation, that she was merely signaling him to get on with it, stop stalling, let's get it over before my other foot gets cold.

Red followed.

Gideon brought up the rear.

And as they climbed, the afternoon faded into twilight, the sky darkening to bands of purple and rose as a smattering of unfamiliar stars presaged the advent of the faceless moon. The cliff's face shaded from dark brown to nearly black, save where it was irregularly streaked with an odd shade of yellow that more than once made him think of demonic faces leering at him from the depths of the rock.

The going was fairly easy, aside from a few patches of loose stone that almost pitched him over the side forty feet up, and the uneven way the steps had been carved into the ramps so that he never knew where his foot was going to land, and the way Tuesday kept to his right, huddling against his leg and forcing him closer and closer to the edge until he had to nudge her away and then pet her so she wouldn't feel rejected.

The temperature dropped.

Red ruffled his fur, and Tuesday fluffed her feathers.

Gideon pulled out his pacch cloak and slung it around his shoulders, fastening it across the throat by means of a solid gold hook-and-ring in the center of which was a pale green jewel in the shape of a fanged hare. The garment, for all its stiffness, was remarkably comfortable and warm, and he was all the more glad for it when, two hours later, the wind came up, sweeping relentlessly around the face of the cliff with the mournful cry of a midnight owl, pummeling first his back, then his front. His cheeks ached. His ears burned. His legs began to feel as if he were walking a treadmill of slippery pebbles.

There was no sense looking up—the top of the range was still out of sight and, once the sun was gone, even the clouds merged into the black that crept toward them like a vast and sentient shadow.

An hour into the evening the ramp leveled to a broad ledge; in its center was a shallow cave, and Gideon, not wishing to take an unfortunate misstep, suggested they stop torturing themselves and camp for the night. Tuesday was inside before he knew she had even moved, and Red, after realizing there would be no decent foraging, grumpily paced for several minutes before curling up in the cave's mouth. Gideon knelt behind him, arms folded on the animal's spine, chin on his wrists.

"You know," he said quietly, "it's really lovely up here."

Red bobbed his head.

"I remember when I first saw this place—boy, it seems like a hundred years ago. God, I was scared. You wouldn't believe it to see me now, but I was absolutely certain I was going to die without ever seeing you or Sis again. I just knew it. I had, I guess, one of those premonitions, you know what I mean? Like I did when they told me that Sis was dead in that car crash. I didn't believe it. I really didn't. I just knew she was alive. Deep down, so far down inside me I didn't know it was there, I knew for a fact she wouldn't leave me without saying goodbye. Of course, I didn't die, and she didn't say goodbye because she was a duck by then, but you can't be right all the time, right? or else you'd go crazy. Knowing everything that's going to happen in the future, I mean. Wouldn't that drive you out of your mind, knowing all that? Having all that responsibility? Having all those lives, the very world, in your hands? God, that scares me just to think about it.''

Red shifted.

The dark erased everything but the sound of his voice.

"And now here we are. Incredible. It reminds me of the time me and my first sweetheart went to the movies and—"

"Gideon, do you mind?"

He glanced into the cave. "Sorry. I didn't know you were sleeping."

"I'm not. But I want to be."

He turned, using the lorra's side as a pillow, the cloak for a blanket. "You don't have to listen, you know. Red and I were just waxing nostalgia."

"You were waxing. Red was sleeping."

Red snored.

Gideon sighed.

He had stopped counting the number of times he had wondered why everyone seemed to blame their misfortunes on him, and to stick him with the jobs no one else wanted to do. It wasn't as if he didn't have problems of his own. There was Ivy, and there was his sister, and there was the plain and simple fact that, love or not, he was truly homesick. This world, for all its beauty and danger, wasn't his; this world, peopled as it was with some of the most interesting characters he had ever met—aside from his third-grade teacher, who ate raw hamburger for lunch and kept a pet turtle in her drawer— this world, as exotic as it was, couldn't beat his own living room on a Sunday night, when he would settle down in his bathrobe with a crossword puzzle and a glass of moderately poor scotch.

Which was what he had been doing, come to think of it, when this all started.

He wondered who was in his house now.

He wondered how many calls he'd gotten since he'd left, calls from his agent offering him positions on championship-bound teams that needed, just for the season, a seasoned quarterback in case the star sprained a thumb or jammed a toe.

He tried to figure out how those damned Bridges worked—

gateways between worlds, as it had been explained to him, that came and went depending upon the need of the person.

He sat up and stared into the darkness over Red's back, and wondered how that pair of slanted red eyes had gotten all the way up here.

Red eyes he had seen before.

Malevolent red eyes that could belong to only one person.

"Tuesday," he whispered urgently.

"I see them," she answered.

"What should we do?"

"You're the hero, you tell me."

The eyes vanished, and he heard a mocking laugh carried away by the wind.

"I think we should get some sleep."

"What, and be murdered in our beds?"

"Then you stand guard. I'm going to have to be clear-headed in the morning."

"What, and lose my sleep?"

He settled down again and closed his eyes. When his sister called to him, he ignored her; when she called a second time, he rolled over and ignored her; when she called a third time, and added a fairly good scream besides, he sat up, rubbed his eyes, and saw that the sun was already lighting the sky overhead.

He also saw the creature standing on the ledge, a spear in its hand and a gleam in its eye.

THREE

Slowly, not wanting to antagonize the creature into doing something stupid like killing them all and ending forever his dream of returning to New Jersey, Gideon reached for his bat, specially forged for him by Whale Pholler, and cursed when he realized he had taken the belt off sometime during the night. Without moving, he glanced side to side, and saw the weapon off to his left, under Red's tail.

Tuesday waddled up behind him and poked him in the back. "Do you see it?"

"How could I miss it?" he whispered, at the same time telling himself it was only a dream and not to worry, he would wake up any minute now and discover his sister sitting smugly on his chest and nibbling at his nose. Probably, he thought, it was something he'd eaten that his body refused on principle to digest, one of those leafy concoctions Tuesday had whipped up for them last night as they climbed. It was only to be expected; she was a lousy cook, and always had been from the first time she began experimenting with peanut butter and jelly sandwiches on toasted rye and discovered that by adding a touch of pimento and a dash of soft-boiled egg she had hit upon the perfect, if not lethal, cure for a hangover.

"I think it's naked," she said, not altogether shocked.

"How can you tell? It isn't wearing anything."

It was not quite as tall as Gideon, but it gave the appearance of great height nevertheless as it stood boldly framed against the blue of the sky and the green vista below. It was vaguely humanoid, if one, after screaming himself hoarse, discounted the sloping, bleached white, naked skull that had shimmering grey holes where the eyes should have been, the broad skeletonlike torso whose flat polished ribs enclosed shimmering grey hair, and the bony arms and bandy legs that seemed not to have a shred of flesh upon them; and it would have been more than a little corpselike had it not been able to manipulate its facial structure much the way a human does shortly after waking and discovering he's died during the night.

Gideon shuddered.

Red yawned, looked around, saw the thing standing not ten inches from his muzzle and scrambled to his feet, his tail high and whipping, his eyes instantly black. There was the start of a menacing growl before he changed his mind and shook his head as if in disbelief, then backed hastily into the cave and sat on his haunches.

The creature took a step forward.

Gideon and Tuesday each took a step back.

Red began to sample the rare taste of a rock he discovered at his feet.

Suddenly the creature lifted the bone-tipped spear over its head, waved it around in an elaborate circle, and jammed its point deep into the ground.

"I think he's telling us he wants to be friends," Gideon said with more hope than certainty.

"I think he's telling us he can tear us apart with his bare hands."

The creature approached them again, tilted its head sideways and stared at the duck. There was the unmistakable sound of a quizzical whimper in its throat, wherever that was, and Tuesday responded with a whimper of her own, one a bit more definite about what she was thinking.

Gideon knelt and put an arm gently over her back. "It's all right," he said without taking his gaze from the thing. "I honestly don't think it intends to harm us."

"Prove it," she said.

When he looked at Red for support physical or moral, the lorra looked at the roof of the cave; when he looked at his sister, she scuttled away from his arm and squatted between Red's two front hooves; when he looked back at the creature, it held out its hand.

He stood, hesitated, made a wish, and grabbed it.

The creature instantly yanked its hand free and shook it, blew on it; the shimmering grey darkened. "Damn," it said. "What are you trying to do, kill me? For heaven's sake!"

Gideon smiled cautious relief. "I'm sorry. I guess I don't know my own strength."

"Too right by half." It blew on its hand again, then pulled the spear from the ground with a minimum of effort. "Besides, you have a cushion, so to speak, and all I have is this petrified calcium."

It sighed, and Gideon turned his head politely away from the breath that made him think of the mold he used to find on the shower curtain in the middle of the summer before he learned to take baths and examine the rings instead.

The creature drew itself up then and pointed to the right. "Well, let's get going, shall we? This awful wind's going to blow me into toothpicks if I don't get out of here soon." It started along the ledge, paused when it realized no one was following, and returned to put its free hand on its hip. "Well?"

Gideon, with a look to the others to keep them in their place, which by their disgusted expressions they had no intention of leaving in the first place, casually walked over to his belt and picked it up, strapped it on, and let his hand close over the handle of the greenwood bat. The bat no one in this world could lift but him. Immediately, the holster opened and the bat was at port arms, lightly tapping his shoulder as he gauged the distance between him and the spear carrier.

"I think, before we leave, we'd like to know where we're going."

The creature tapped a foot impatiently. "I see."

The bat swung slowly down to point at the ground. "I'm sure you do or you wouldn't have found us, but I still want to know where you think we're going."

"My name," it said proudly, "is Junffer. Jeko Junffer."
Gideon nodded.

Junffer tilted its head again. "Well?"

Gideon, supposing he was caught in some cliff ritual the breach of which might or might not result in the loss of his life, made to introduce himself and the others, but he was cut off by a wave of the spear.

"I already know your names," Junffer snapped crossly. "You don't think I come out to this dreadful place every day, just on the off chance I might run across a stranger or two, do you?"

Gideon frowned. It was bad enough standing hundreds of feet above solid ground, in a wind determined to blow him back where he came from, talking to a skeleton that carried a spear and had clouds for eyes; but how did it know who they were? Was it some devilish lieutenant of Wamchu's, cleverly seeking information for the forthcoming battle? Was it a cold and callous mercenary of some sort, peddling its diabolical combat skills to the highest bidder, which in this case was obviously the Wamchu? Or was it an innocent denizen of the cliff itself, desperately scratching out a meager living on this scoured and naked rock, thinking they were rich merchants he could hold for ransom and thus escape his miserable lot?

"Junffer," the skeleton repeated carefully. "Jeko Junffer."

"You said that already."

"You mean . . . you mean you've never heard of me?"

Gideon shook his head; Tuesday shook her head; Red stood up and walked out of the cave, sniffed Junffer from gleaming bone pate to dusty boned toes and shook his head.

"Well, I'll be damned," Junffer said. He started to walk away, returned and shook his head. "I'm a star, you know."

"Pleased to meet you," Gideon said, and gave the duck a quick kick in the side when he heard her clear her throat. "I've never met a star before."

Tuesday grumbled, and took a piece of his boot.

Junffer rasped a fingertip over his jaw. "You're sure you never heard of me."

"We're strangers here," Gideon explained.

"Ah, I see."

"We're trying to get to the top." He pointed. "We really didn't have much time to . . . to . . . acquaint ourselves with the cliff culture, of which we know nothing."

Junffer nodded. "Well said, human thing. You'll be pleased to know I won't have to kill you."

Gideon smiled his gratitude, and wrapped a brotherly hand around Tuesday's bill before she could take the rest of his boot. Then he ducked away from a particularly fierce blast of wind and suggested, when the dust had settled and the duck was tucked firmly under his arm, that they carry on before disaster struck.

Junffer, whose ribs were whistling symphonically in the same wind, agreed. And he watched as Gideon reset the supply rolls on Red's back, had a word with the duck, which resulted in a promise neither to continue her peckish behavior nor ask stupid questions until they were safely out of the wind, and slipped the bat back into its holster.

"Are you finished?"

Gideon nodded.

"Then walk this way, please."

Not if I live a hundred years, he thought as he pressed against the rock face in an effort to keep the brunt of the wind from toppling him to his death.

Luckily, they didn't have that far to go. Up this ramp, up the next, and at the top of the third they were virtually blown into what he had thought was a cave but learned quickly enough was only the mouth of an extraordinarily long tunnel. Torches in silver brackets on the walls lighted the way, and Red was careful to stay in the center of the floor since he was nearly as wide, and as tall, as the smooth-walled excavation.

Their footsteps echoed.

Gideon, unable to fathom what animated the creature and absolutely positive he didn't want to know and wouldn't ask even if tortured, remained behind Junffer, his curiosity finally swamping his good sense once they had completed their first hour of walking. "Tell me," he said to the skeleton's back, "what exactly is it you're a star of? Television? The movies? What?"

Junffer lifted his head proudly. "Killing." And he stabbed at the air with his suddenly long spear.

Gideon stopped; Red stopped; Tuesday walked around the lorra and quickly started back toward the ledge.

"Killing," Gideon said.

"It's what makes a star these days, don't you think? Lots of killing."

"In . . . the movies?"

Junffer's voice was fading. "Movies? What's that? No, I just kill anyone who hasn't heard of me, and before you know it, everyone knows who you are. God, it's incredible, isn't it. You wouldn't believe the things you can get away with when you're a star. Ask my mother. My father was a star too. As a matter of fact, the last time I saw him . . ."

Gideon had a choice—he could either hurry after his sister and let her berate him deservedly for being such an idiot, or hurry after Junffer to find out more about cliff stardom. His sister was angry. And since there was only one of the skeleton, it stood to reason, however much of it remained, that they should carry on. Red alone ought to be able to handle the creature, should there be any trouble. One swipe of those horns, and Junffer would be dead.

Or whatever passed for it in his condition.

Ivy, he thought, you'll never know the sacrifices I make.

With a call to Tuesday and a warning glance to the lorra, he broke into a trot until the skeleton came into view, just entering what proved to be a massive cavern whose sheer sides were brilliantly white, whose semivaulted roof was starred with torches, and in whose center was a chrome-sided escalator which rose out of a wide hole in the floor. It hummed. The railing flowed like upwardly mobile black water. The steps climbed into the glaring light above. And on each step was a chair upholstered in shades of cinnamon and lavender.

Gideon strode over to a plank which served as a boarding ledge, and looked down. As far as he could see, the escalator gleamed. He shook his head. No. It couldn't reach all the way to the bottom. This couldn't mean he could have saved himself hours of agony, pebbles in his boots, cramps in his thighs, rocks in his head. It was, like everything else, an illusion.

Junffer was leaning against the side, watching with amusement the look on Gideon's face. "Yes," he said at last.

Gideon groaned.

"All the way up," Junffer said with a laugh.

Gideon scowled at Red when the lorra reached him. "Did you know about this? No, don't answer. I don't want to know. I want to think that you would have shown me the entrance before we started." He held up a hand. "No, Red. Not a word. Just let me keep my—"

"Gideon, for Christ's sake, is that what I think it is?" Tuesday flew into the cavern, banked over her escalator, and landed on the ledge. "It is," she said glumly. "And it has chairs."

"I didn't know," he said, with a pointed look at the lorra. Then he turned to Junffer and indicated the steps with a nod. "This will take us where we want to go?"

"Of course. A star never walks, you know."

Tuesday winged to a chair, rode it halfway up, and flew back. "Soft," she said wistfully. "But not too soft." Her eyes narrowed as best they could. "Giddy, you are—"

"Jeko," Gideon said loudly, "you never did tell us how you knew who we were."

"A star knows all and sees all," the skeleton said. "And I have been a star for quite a long time."

"How long?" Tuesday asked.

"Ever since I killed my father."

"Right," she said, and flew back to a chair. "I'm not coming back, Giddy," she called. "You can sit there and chew the fat all you want. I am not coming back."

"You'd better," Junffer called after her. "It's dangerous up there. There are . . . things! Terrible things. That's why I—" He stopped shouting when Tuesday landed back on the ledge. "That is why I came for you. To protect you."

"Who sent you?"

"Do you know Ivy Pholler?"

Gideon's heart stalled, stuttered, revved, and raced. He

gasped a hoarse "Yes," and looked longingly upward. She cares, he thought with a broad smile; by god, she cares!

"What things?" Tuesday said.

Ivy, I'll be there soon. Hang on, my love. I'm coming as fast as I can.

"Oh, dommers, vacs, things like that. You'd never make it without me. That's because I'm a star."

Gideon leaned against the escalator and assumed that the beatification he felt was not unlike the sensation experienced by those who were blessed enough to achieve sainthood without the bother of martyrdom; not, he thought suddenly, that he was in any way comparing himself to a saint. But true love, in its purest and least lustful form, did have that hint of halo about it, that touch of sanctification, that hint of carnal purification that has endeared itself to so many for so long.

He sighed.

He shifted his gaze from his inner vision of Ivy to the outer form of Junffer, and decided that perhaps carnal was too narrow a parameter, though he supposed there were possibilities and eyes of the beholders.

"What's a vac?"

Junffer cracked a smile. "You'll see, little bird. You'll see soon enough."

She turned in a huff. "Gideon, I really think this man—"

"Watch your mouth, bird!"

"Who the hell are you calling a bird, cage?"

Gideon placed his hand lovingly on Red's neck and guided him over to the ledge. Through gestures, grunts, and practical demonstration, he showed the lorra how simple it would be to ride with hind legs on one step and forelegs on the other, rump on a chair to give him support. Red looked doubtful. Gideon kissed his nose and told him not to be silly. Red sneezed, and waited for Gideon to go first, indicating his desire by putting the tips of his horns delicately, but meaningfully, against his chest.

"I am a goddamned star!"

"You are a goddamned—Gideon, where the hell are you going?"

"To see Ivy," he called over Red's head.

"Alone?"

"No, I have Red."

She flew up before he vanished through the ceiling. "But what about the boneyard?"

"He'll be coming," he said blissfully.

"He says he won't unless I apologize."

"Then apologize, Tuesie."

And he would have added to the endearment a sermonette on the Golden Rule, had he not looked up and seen a flurry of winged things pass over the moving steps on the next level. Instantly, he sobered, though not quite in time to keep his arm from being ripped open by a claw.

FOUR

Pain, Gideon thought as he fell to the moving steps and grasped his left forearm just below the elbow, is not what it's cracked up to be.

The gash was a good three inches long and, after a blurry examination of the parted flesh and running blood, he did his best to tie the remnants of his shredded shirt-sleeve around it to stanch the bleeding. He did not call out for help, in spite of the fire that seemed to have caught quite nicely in his veins— the others were too busy with the flying things that swarmed over them the moment they rose above the next floor.

They were dommers, according to Jeko's shrill identification, and exceedingly ugly, about the size of a fat robin dipped in unpreserved buffalo fat, with claws on their wingtips and hooked beaks that sounded like metallic fingers snapping. Their battle cries were loud, persistent whines, and their death throes were, to the objective spectator, somewhere between the collapse of the fat lady in an opera and the writhings of an aged thespian determined to make a permanent mark on the stage.

There were, at a conservative estimate, several hundred of them.

Junffer used his spear with consummate skill, spinning it at such a high speed that it became little more than a deadly

27

blur, which split more than one avian skull and ruined the manicures of dozens more; Tuesday, for her part, darted through the dommers' formations like white lightning, her wings powerful enough to disrupt the things' internal gyros while her beak, used as a club, was equally as effective as Junffer's spear; and Red used both tail and horns to stun and thrust, frustrated not to be able to rise up on his hind legs and give his clawed hooves the chance they craved.

By the time they reached the third level, the dommers were gone, whining their defeat and huddling against the walls like so many quivering blobs of sodden grease.

Gideon had been unable to do a thing. His arm was aflame, and each time he attempted to regain his feet, a wash of dizziness sent him down on his back. Tuesday hunched at his side, demanding someone do something before her brother bled to death. Red was helpless and could only lash his tail about in frustration.

Then Junffer, laying aside his spear, knelt noisily at Gideon's side and untied the makeshift bandage. "Oh, I say," he muttered when he saw the extent of the damage. "That's going to leave a nasty little scar, isn't it."

"Do something," Tuesday pleaded.

The skeleton wiped his hands on Gideon's jeans and leaned closer. "Touchy. Very touchy. If I make a mistake, he could lose that arm. What a waste."

Gideon stared at the cloudgrey in the eye sockets, and laid the blame on impending death when he thought he saw tiny bolts of red lightning flash through them. Not with a bang but a whimper, he thought, and wished he could have been more original, something his sister could quote to the sports editor of the *Times* when she returned to report on his heroic demise.

Tuesday nudged the skeleton's arm. "You gonna admire him or cure him or what?" she demanded.

"Well, he isn't all that good-looking," Junffer said huffily.

"So?"

Junffer sat back, leaning against the gentle whisper of the escalator's moving inner wall. "My dear duck," he said, "I did not get to be a star by saving lives."

Gideon saw an image of Ivy floating before his eyes. He reached out his uninjured arm and tried to caress her face.

Tuesday's feathers puffed alarmingly. "You mean you're going to let him die?"

Red's tail stilled, his hooves scratched on the gleaming metal stairs, and his eyes began to shade from white to black.

"But you were supposed to bring us to the surface," the duck reminded Junffer. "You could get in big trouble if you don't produce what you promise."

They passed into the fourth level, a much dimmer cavern whose shadows ticked and husked, and on whose walls tiny red things crawled.

"I promised nothing. I simply said I'd lend a hand."

Ivy's face drifted closer, and Gideon pursed his lips in anticipation.

Tuesday, facing downward, paced in anger without leaving her place, and finally whirled on the skeleton. "You can't let him die, he's a star!"

Junffer tittered. "How can he be a star? I've never heard of him."

"Where we come from," she said, "he's one of the biggest stars around. If you let him die, a lot of people are going to be very annoyed."

Junffer eyed Gideon as best he could and touched a finger to his chin thoughtfully. "A star?"

"Are you kidding? Hundreds of thousands of people have cheered him on in his lifetime."

"Hundreds of thousands?"

Tuesday remembered the occasional completed pass, and nodded with only a fair bolt of guilt. "If he hadn't come for me, it might even have been millions."

"Millions, you say?"

Gideon smacked the air where Ivy's lips had been, and sighed at the ghostly honey that lay upon his lips. Truly, he thought, I have arrived in my heaven.

Tuesday watched her brother's face grow deathly pale, and worse in contrast to his godawful shaggy beard. "We haven't got much time. Are you going to do something, or what?"

Junffer peered at the wound again.

Red inched closer and lifted his upper lip to expose a row of teeth long and sharp. He snapped them together once, and Junffer stared at him in quick alarm.

Then Gideon raised himself up on his good elbow and smiled at his sister, winked at the lorra, and said to the skeleton, "Blue star, forty-eight, on two, and for Christ's sake don't drop it this time." And collapsed again.

Junffer gaped.

Tuesday told him her brother was delirious.

"Delirious my pelvic girdle!" Junffer said. "That man was talking football!"

"I don't care if he was talking Danish; will you please do something before I become an only duck, for god's sake?"

"But . . ." Junffer clasped his hands over his sternum. "His name is Gideon?"

"Yeah."

"Not . . . not *the* Gideon? Gideon Sunday? Gideon Sunday, the finest third-string quarterback in the entire known universe? *That* Gideon Sunday?"

Tuesday's lower bill sagged. She could only nod.

"And you . . . you're his sister?"

She nodded again.

"But you're a duck!"

She closed her eyes; it was the only sane thing to do.

Gideon, however, upon hearing his name taken in what could only be transporting adoration, unless it was the fever that had taken hold of his brain, opened his bleary eyes and stared at the skeleton. And immediately wished he hadn't.

As they passed into the fifth level, he saw a stream of grey slip from between Junffer's ribs and coil around his open wound; flickers of blue light made his skin tingle, and darts of golden stars made the exposed muscle twitch in electric excitement. Yet he could not turn away as a second and a third extension of the cloudgrey in the thing's torso reached for his forearm, and he could not do much more than swallow when he saw the ragged edges of the gash begin to close, as if the tip of some magical, medicinal zipper had been grasped and was being pulled up toward his elbow.

By the time they reached the seventh level, Gideon's arm was whole again, not to mention his shirt, and he was sitting in a high-backed chair, legs crossed, grinning like an idiot while he told stories of his career to a patently admiring skull. Tuesday, who had wept in her fashion at the miracle she had seen, flew on ahead so as not to ruin her brother's fantasies, and returned in less than five minutes, breathless and afraid.

"So I said to the guy from the network," Gideon was saying, "that I couldn't take less than a mil a year, including endorsements and anchoring. They weren't too happy, I can tell you, but when you're dealing from a position of strength, there isn't anything you can't have." He sighed. "It's a hell of a feeling, one glorious hell of a feeling."

Junffer sighed ecstatically. "That's great, Gideon! I swear, that's absolutely marvelous! Oh, I'm just green with envy, simply green, if you know what I mean. What's television?"

Gideon blinked.

Tuesday stabbed his knee and said, "There are more things up there, Giddy. Big things. Crawly things."

"Oh, not to worry," Junffer said airily as he reached for his spear. "Probably just a herd of vacs, that's all. I'm sure we'll be able to handle them with no trouble at all."

Gideon picked up his bat and looked toward the roof of the cavern. His sigh was rueful. It had been nice there for a while, remembering things that had never happened and making up the rest, not feeling the slightest bit guilty about indulging Junffer's illusions about him, since he had done it to himself hundreds of times when he wasn't being realistic about his chances for survival.

The trouble was, though he didn't feel guilty, he felt lousy instead, and vowed to tell the skeleton the entire truth once they had reached the surface. Of course, Junffer might then be annoyed, and might be tempted to maintain his star status by pitting his spear against the bat. No, he decided, it was best not to destroy an idol. Let the skeleton have his dreams. Gideon would be secure enough in knowing that he would still have his life.

"I really wouldn't stand, if I were you," Junffer said from behind and below him.

Gideon wanted to ask if the skeleton expected him to fight sitting down, but he didn't. He had already seen the gap in the roof, and the things in the gap—the wormy things, the slimy things, the things with hundreds of razorlike projections along their wormy, slimy, writhing pink sides. They were stretched over the opening in a congealed and disgusting web, and when he sat, abruptly, Junffer climbed to the steps above him and set his spear whirling again.

"This is so messy," the skeleton complained. "They really ought to do something about it."

Tuesday wasted no time finding cover beneath Red's long hair, only the tip of one foot and the hint of a bill poking into the open. Red himself had hunkered down as low as he could get, and the silken blanket across his spine fairly rippled in disgust.

"Are they attached to anything?" Gideon asked, pointing the bat toward the wormy, slimy web.

"You want one for a pet?" Junffer said in astonishment.

"No."

"A good thing. They're nasty little beasts. Foul, if you'll pardon the expression, and utterly without redemption on any level except, perhaps, in waste removal."

"What I meant was—"

"Besides, pink is such a tacky color for a creature, don't you think? It makes them look so . . . so undone."

"What I meant was," Gideon persisted, "is that all there is, what we're seeing up there, or are they attached to something bigger, like a body or something?"

"Oh, I see! Oh, I'm terribly sorry. I mistook your interest for affection substitution."

Gideon looked over the side and wondered how many bones would break if he threw Junffer out. Then the skeleton squealed, and Gideon ducked just as the spinning spear made its first contact with the vac web.

It was horrible.

It was like nothing else he had ever experienced, unless he counted his thirty-third birthday, when some friends had taken him to a mud-wrestling exhibition where, on a whim and after several scotches, he had joined the ladies in the arena.

They weren't amused, and proved it; he wasn't amused when he recognized a long-standing and recently surfaced phobia of having his mouth and eyes filled with mud.

It was a shower of flesh and rose-tinted blood and razorlike protrusions and slime and wormy parts, and above it all the shriek of the vacs as their web was shredded and their various pieces were scattered throughout the cavern.

But it was mercifully swift.

Once through the living web, the party quickly noted that the vacs were unable to climb, and were too stupid to use the escalator. The only thing they had to face next was a thoroughly sullied section of their carrier, and the stench that rose from the slaughter below, a stench not unlike that of a battlefield on which hundreds of corpses had been left to rot in the summer after being sprinkled with rose water.

They watched the vacs writhing helplessly, their wormy tips lifting off the cavern floor in search of the prey that had so cleverly outwitted them.

"Big," Gideon muttered.

"Fifteen to twenty feet, the adults," Junffer said.

"Disgusting," Tuesday said.

"Be careful," the skeleton said. "There are mothers down there."

"You said it."

Junffer tsked at the implied obscenity and leaned back, darkened his eyes, and appeared after a while to be snoring. Gideon, however, could not for the life of him shift his gaze away from the next opening, wondering what sort of creature they would encounter next. He asked no one in particular if they had any idea how long it would be before they reached their destination, and Junffer, or some smoky and still alert part of him, replied that there were twelve levels yet to pass through, and he would not speculate on the inhabitants of each since he was, after all, a star, and stars did not concern themselves with petty matters like the little people and their little lives.

Gideon looked down at his sister. "Was I ever like that?"

"You're still alive, aren't you?"

Thank god, he thought. The idea that fame might turn him

into a creature like that made his skin break out in gooseflesh. It had been bad enough hanging on to his already low self-esteem without having to deal with self-worship and pre-demise godhood.

Gideon ate from the scanty supplies still in the pack on Red's back, then stretched his feet out and closed his eyes. It would be wise to get some sleep, he decided, since Junffer, resting or not, seemed to be in control.

He dreamed of Ivy.

He dreamed of home.

He dreamed he had found a Bridge, that brilliant rectangle of light that would take him back to his pantry, to his kitchen, to his living room where the bottle of scotch was waiting beside his crossword puzzle. He also knew the rules—that a Bridge never appeared unless there was a need, and it bothered him even in slumber that the need within was growing stronger.

He had no idea how long he slept.

His eyes snapped open, and he found himself rising slowly above a cavern so huge that the roof was invisible, and the floor was forested by high-growing moss. The air was damp, and a light fog drifted out of the moss clouds that dangled in monstrous clumps from the roof.

He shifted uneasily.

There was something wrong here, something so terribly wrong he decided to go back to sleep and hope it would be taken care of before he woke up again.

Then, in one swift calculation, he realized what it was—the silence.

Absolute and total silence.

Even the whisper of the escalator was muffled.

He looked around wildly, and saw Tuesday huddled next to the lorra, saw Junffer standing with his spear next to his chair. When the skeleton looked down, he put a finger to where his lips would have been and pointed up.

Gideon refused to look.

Junffer pointed again and whispered, "Monster."

FIVE

A *monster?* Gideon asked silently.

Junffer nodded solemnly.

A big monster?

Junffer shook himself to simulate a shudder.

Gideon considered asking another question, but changed his mind. There didn't seem to be much use talking to a skeleton about a monster, especially when that monster was already waiting for them on the next level and was, by Junffer's reaction, something a bit more than a gathering of vacs or a flock of nasty dommers. And considering the way Junffer had handled those two attacks, Gideon was not entirely confident this one would be quite so easily gotten through, all things considered.

The escalator moved on.

Moss hung over the sides and hissed when it was disturbed.

Red lifted his face to the air and sniffed, then growled low and deep in his throat.

Junffer tapped a finger against his kneecap nervously, the grey behind his eyes boiling dark save for an infrequent flash of dull white or pale red. His spear, held butt-down to the steps, trembled in his grip, the tip wavering through a small circle that held no promise at all of a swift and decisive victory.

The opening grew nearer, and quite a bit larger as the moss parted of its own wise accord.

Gideon rubbed a hand over his face, back through his hair, down over the beard that refused to grow with neatly trimmed edges and a definition of character that would mark him as someone special, if not someone who hadn't shaved in a while; he patted his chest to still his heart; he tightened his buttocks in isometric anticipation.

This, he thought, is a stupid way to spend an evening.

He could, were the Fates not so capricious and filled with malicious mischief, still be home. Without a doubt, he could be lying in his bed with the sheet over his face, swearing creatively at the blue jays that had built their nest in the elm tree outside his bedroom window and delighted in giving him weather reports that began an hour before sunup. There was no question that he could not be perfectly, blissfully happy being unemployed and lacking a single viable skill save throwing a football that scarcely anyone could catch when they were supposed to, and sometimes not even then.

At home there was nothing to be afraid of.

At home there were no monsters.

He looked back toward his sister and realized with a start that it was growing dark.

Very dark.

Dark enough, now, to conceal the opening to the next level and thus, with infinite detachment and insidious indifference, the monster that lay in wait for them above.

That's when he heard the breathing, and knew with resigned hysteria it wasn't him, or the lorra, or the duck, or the skeleton.

A slow and steady inhalation, a slow and rasping exhalation that ruffled the moss around the opening's lip and sent a faint, noxious breeze dancing through his hair.

Yep, he thought, that sure is a big monster up there, all right.

Junffer's cloudy insides began to glow, causing the moss to writhe away in terror, dispelling the fog that had thickened and slipped over the escalator's smooth sides, momentarily halting the breathing. Then he touched Gideon's shoulder, pointed upward, and rose.

Gideon hesitated. He failed to see the logic of exposing one's self too soon, despite the possibility that in such exposure lay an element of surprise that the monster might not take into consideration while it was waiting. Up there. Breathing again, with clear, giddy expectation.

Junffer poked his shoulder and gestured angrily.

Gideon groaned silently to his feet and leaned close, squinting against the glow, which had now increased to the level of an infant bonfire.

"He'll see us, Jeko," he whispered harshly. "Can't you turn yourself off?"

"I am a star," the skeleton reminded him.

Good; and I am a walking corpse.

Nevertheless, and not to be beaten at the star game as long as he was playing his last hand, he wiped a palm against his side and began stroking the bat. Junffer looked at him suspiciously. Deep within the greenwood grain there appeared a faint light even as the wood itself grew warm, and even warmer. Junffer looked at the bat. The light rose toward the surface, slowly, slowly, until, just as Gideon's palm was ready to ignite, a cloud of glowing blue separated from the bat. Immediately Gideon cupped his palms around it, shaped it, and lifted it upward, blowing until it hovered ten feet away.

It held that distance as they rose.

Junffer's eyes flashed green.

The opening was revealed as the blue light passed through it, and though Gideon stared until his eyes watered, he could see nothing but the skyward thrust of the escalator and its forlorn, empty chairs.

"Now you've done it," Junffer said testily.

"Done what?"

"Let him know we're coming."

"Well, Jesus, he can see you, can't he?"

Junffer slapped his free hand to his skull and groaned. "But he can't! Don't you know anything, Sunday? Don't you know he's blind to my color?"

The blue light intensified.

"Oh," Gideon said.

"We might have been able to ambush him," Junffer said, his tone one of patronizing disgust. "We had a chance then, but not now. You and your silly little trick have cooked our geese."

"Watch it," Tuesday muttered from under Red's hair.

"So we stand up to him face to face," Gideon said angrily. "Isn't that more honorable than getting him in the back?"

"You want to try it?" the skeleton asked as they reached the floor of the next level and Gideon saw their opponent, leaning casually against the escalator's side, picking its teeth with a sharpened boulder.

Gideon understood perfectly that there are times in a man's life when, surrounded by friends and loved ones, he must make a decision about the proper exhibition of courage, leadership, and qualities so intangible they have yet to be named; he knew also that there was a growing body of evidence proving that the failure of such exhibitions had no effect one way or the other on friends and loved ones, psychologically speaking, in the moment before their hideous deaths.

What it boiled down to was a matter of guilt—either you felt it or you didn't, depending on how guilty you felt.

Thus, standing bravely in the vanguard, he decided that either he'd have to fight the thing, or jump off the escalator—the results of which would be, essentially, the same.

The thing was very much like a giant.

In fact, as his head rose above the floor, Gideon saw that it was exactly like a giant—exceedingly tall, exceedingly hefty, dressed in thonged boots and leather shorts and a puffed-sleeve shirt whose buttons were unable to contain either the continent-spread of its chest or the rain-forest density of its chest hair, in which various things of a disturbing nature crawled about with claw-clicking abandon.

As soon as Gideon was fully above the floor and Jeko's head was poking into view, the giant sighed, dropped the boulder, and picked up a club the size of which would have been daunting to an archangel. Its eyes, virtually invisible beneath brows in which cousins of the chest-hair things also crawled, focused on Gideon's face, then his bat, then the others sliding into view behind and below.

Its head cocked toward its right shoulder in a manner which indicated a measure of bewilderment.

Its club, resting heavily on its left shoulder, jumped a bit in indication of uncertainty.

"We'll have to go for its weak spot," Junffer whispered nervously.

"Where's that?" Gideon whispered back without taking his gaze from the gaze of the giant.

"The small of its back."

Gideon wavered. "But it's facing us!"

They were now close to its waist.

"Then think of something!"

He tried. He considered setting up a diversion while Tuesday took the bat and flew around to the back to clobber the thing senseless, but thanks to Whale he was the only one who could hold the damned thing. He wondered about Red's claws and teeth and horns, how much damage they might be able to do while he took a fast run up the thing's arm and did the bashing himself, but realized that the best he could hope for from the lorra was a scratch in the thing's palm. For a wild moment he entertained the notion of negotiation—spare my friends, and I'm yours—but his parties always had been dull and he figured he'd be dead before he got out the first word. There was, on the other hand, always the possibility that the skeleton had some magic up his marrow, though that was clearly out of the question when Junffer took a step back and huddled cravenly beside the lorra, whose eyes were so busy flashing from angry black to unconcerned white that he was panting. A timely arrival of the cavalry was impossible. An equally fortuitous earthquake, intracavern hurricane, or volcanic eruption was mere fantasy. And the thought of making a last stand on a slow-moving escalator was so humiliating he almost took a frustrated swing at the chest now drifting by, until he caught a glimpse of the things moving around in there, which made him gag and become slightly airsick.

The giant didn't turn around.

"The hell with it," he said, and sat down.

"What?" Junffer stood up. "What in the world are you talking about?"

Gideon looked at him steadily. "I said, 'The hell with it.' "

"That's telling him," Tuesday muttered from beneath Red.

The giant grunted, and shifted the club to its other shoulder.

"But you simply can't let him kill us, Gideon!" Junffer protested. "That's—that's just not done!"

"Look at him," he said.

"Do I have to?"

"I mean, look at the size of him, Jeko."

"A brute," the skeleton sneered. The eyegrey swirled upward. "And talk about needing a bath. . . ."

"We don't have a chance," Gideon said as they came even with the face, and the eyes blinked with the effort to see clearly something so small and so close.

"Hardly the way for a hero to act," said Junffer.

"That's telling him," Tuesday said.

"Look," Gideon said, "if he whistled, he'd blow us off this thing and we'd die. If he sneezed, we'd drown. If he snapped his fingers, we'd be . . ." He shuddered. "It just isn't worth it."

The skeleton blinked as best he could. "But what about Ivy?"

"I'll miss her," Gideon said sadly, noting that the top of the giant's head was in sore need of a brushing. "But I think I'm man enough to understand that she'll have others before long."

"A little late for that," his sister muttered.

Junffer pointed his spear down at the giant's pate. "Well, I, for one, am not going to end my days in disgrace," he announced in a supremely demonstrative huff. "I do have my standards."

"I hope you have a long arm."

"What?" the skeleton said.

"What?" Tuesday said, burrowing out from under Red's

hair and looking down at the giant, who was looking up at them and clearly wondering where it had gone wrong.

They passed into the next level, an extensive garden filled with brilliant flowers, graceful ferns, and the pure scent of Eden. A waterfall on the far side of the cavern dropped in ripples of silver sprays to a rainbow-misted pool around which tiny, deerlike creatures gamboled, innocent of the hell that lay just below them. The air was sweet. The temperature as perfect as anyone could want. The light as gentle on the eyes as a feather drifting from the wing of a passing dove.

"Sonofabitch," the duck said.

Junffer dropped into his chair, arms and legs akimbo, the energy spinning in utter confusion. "How did you do that?"

Gideon carefully laid his bat to one side and wiped his face dry of its sudden sheen of perspiration. He noticed that his fingers were trembling, and his throat was too raspy for swallowing to salve. After waiting several seconds for the reaction to pass, he breathed and grinned.

"What," he said, "do you do every time you see that thing?"

Junffer looked from side to side, and brushed away a cloud of silken butterflies that wound playfully in and out of his rib cage. "Well, I certainly don't make a habit of seeing him at all."

"Of course not. But when you do—"

Junffer lifted a hand. "I get ready to fight, of course. Do you think I'm a complete fool? The spear's up, the legs placed just so, and I dare him to do something to a star such as myself."

"And does he fight?"

"Every time—when he sees me."

"Now suppose," Gideon said, "you just refused to notice him. That you let him know he was beneath your contempt. Suppose you sat down, took out a book, and started to read when you saw him. What would happen?"

"He'd squash the hell out of me, that's what," Junffer said.

"He would?"

"Of course he would, he's a giant! Giants squash things.

That's the rule." Junffer paused. "Why? Did you think that, if you ignored him, he'd ignore you?"

Gideon watched paradise drift away below him. "It had crossed my mind, yes."

"Dumb," the skeleton said. "Not bright at all. Which is to say, giants are stupid by nature, but they're not that stupid, if you see what I mean."

"It worked, didn't it?"

Tuesday waddled up to him and nuzzled his shin. "You mean," she said gently, "you deliberately tried the pacifist routine? You decided, on your own, to put a flower in his gun, so to speak?"

Gideon didn't like the way things were going. "It worked, didn't it?" he repeated stubbornly.

"Well, now," Junffer interrupted, "are we talking about the ends justifying the means here?"

Tuesday turned on him, one eye closed. "Do you mind? I'm talking to my brother."

"Because if we are, we have to define our standards. There's a principle involved, one of—"

"Oh, stuff your damned principles," she said. "This man nearly got us killed!"

Gideon raised his hand.

"But he was thinking of us, not himself," the skeleton reminded her. "Under the circumstances, he was doing the best he could for the greater good."

Tuesday jumped down a step. "Are you saying, *Mr.* Star, that you'd do the same thing now?"

"Not on your life," Junffer said, horrified. "I could be squashed. Messy being squashed, even for someone like me."

Gideon cleared his throat and wiggled his fingers.

"Then what the hell are you talking about?"

Junffer looked at her in disdain. "Principles, as I said. Something you obviously know nothing about. Duck."

"Whose principles? Bones."

"Well not mine, to be sure. I don't have a death wish."

"Excuse me," Gideon said, waving his arm. "My hand's falling asleep."

Tuesday looked over her shoulder. "What!"

"You didn't die. He didn't die. I didn't die. Red didn't die."

"What's he doing now?" Junffer asked.

"Conjugating principles," she answered. "Giddy, what are you talking about?"

"The sun."

"The sun? What sun?"

He pointed over his shoulder. "That one. The one in the sky. I just thought you'd like to know we made it to the top."

SIX

The welcome golden light Gideon referred to was perfectly framed within a large, jagged opening some one hundred yards away, and the air that passed through it was sweet, cool, and almost dizzingly fresh. He took a deep breath, and another, and was about to rise to his feet when he was forced to duck away from a flurry of excitement that passed over his head as Tuesday charged for the exit. Then he scrambled to one side as Red, tail high and nostrils flaring at the scent of homegrown grazing, lumbered in her wake.

Junffer, on the other hand, had dropped into a chair and was busily fastening a seat belt.

The escalator flattened and became like unto a moving walkway.

Gideon looked at the exit, looked at the skeleton, and concluded instantly that there was something someone had not told him, some small detail about leaving the underground that evidently required a certain amount of precaution. When he glanced back at the exit and saw Red gather his legs beneath him and make a magnificent leap toward the sun, he was sure of it.

Junffer crossed his legs and held his spear across his lap, his immovable features stonelike in their resignation to whatever necessary unpleasantness he was about to face.

Gideon, having seen the same expression somewhat more fleshily outlined in a dentist's office, put a hand on the knob of his bat and searched the darkness to either side, expecting one last desperate assault by a horrid and utterly ruthless denizen of the dark who would at the final moment snatch victory from his rasp with, no doubt, a gleeful chortling.

"You'd better get a move on," Junffer warned.

"You're not going?" he said, noting the turbulence that had arisen between the creature's ribs.

"Heavens and earth, no," the skeleton replied, motes of blue lightning sparking his eye sockets indignantly. "Stars do not impress the louts out there. I do have my pride, you know."

Gideon stood beside him and held out his hand. "I'm impressed," he said.

They shook hands, albeit gingerly, and Junffer nodded toward their destination as he tightened the belt another notch. "Now don't waste time," the skeleton suggested. "The end of the road, the pot of gold, parting is such sweet sorrow, and if you don't get a running start you'll probably die. Unless you can fly, of course. I don't know about stars in your world, but in my world stars have no need of such flamboyance. We are a modest lot, in general."

Gideon shaded his eyes and squinted until he saw what appeared to be a rather ominously large gap between the exit and where the escalator seemed to curl under on itself. It took him less time than an apprehensive lurch of his stomach to realize that, in order for the conveyance's furniture not to be demolished at each return journey to the bottom, there must needs be a sizable opening at either end.

Which, at this end at least, explained Tuesday's flight and Red's leap, not to mention the seat belt.

He backed away slowly. "I think I'd better sit down."

"Too late," Junffer said. "One of the reasons I'm a star is because I took out all the other seat belts. It's a grand sight, seeing one's opponents have the rug pulled out from under them, so to speak. The screaming isn't terribly nice, but it doesn't last very long."

Screaming, Gideon thought.

"How wide is it?" he asked.

"The lorra made it."

"The lorra has four legs."

Junffer squirmed. "I can't help you."

"Principles."

"Exactly. As a star yourself, you ought to know that."

Gideon watched the exit grow nearer, the gap wider, the sun brighter, the sky bluer. He felt the muscles in his legs tighten, his breathing become shallow, his arms tense, his teeth gnaw on his lower lips.

"Run," Junffer suggested mildly.

The gap was black, and it was wide, and there was a hissing as the segmented flooring curved under and down.

There was no time left for mental or emotional preparation; within the next few seconds, he would have to break into a headlong gallop or there wouldn't be a long enough stretch for him to gain the proper momentum to make the leap, assuming he would be able to make the leap at all, and assuming that in making the leap he would be able to clear the gap and land safely on the other side.

"Run," Junffer said, sounding a bit nervous himself.

Gideon positioned himself in front of his chair, jogged in place a few steps to loosen his legs, and took a deep breath, the shaky exhalation of which was interrupted by a blinding flash of blue, the smell of singed denim, and a violent stinging in his left buttock, which propelled him forward with an angry bellow.

As he neared the edge, he thought he heard Junffer laughing.

As he reached the spot where the floor began to sink and he had to make a decision as to which foot to push off from in order to give himself the proper height and distance, he felt another, more savage sting in his right buttock, which instantly launched him, a second time, into the air with arms and legs windmilling frantically and with his gaze fixed firmly on a patch of green just beyond the lip of the exit.

With more amazement than skill, he landed upright, stepped back, threw himself forward, and fell prone onto the ground. The air was punched from his system upon contact, and he gasped as his eyes filled with tears, wheezed as he sought to refill his lungs, choked when he discovered his mouth was coated with dirt and a few blades of grass. There was a second when he felt as though he were holding onto the side of a mountain, his fingers gripping the ground and his toes scrabbling for a foothold; and another second when he thought he was going to black out when, in rolling onto his back, his buttocks reminded him of their recently weakened condition.

He rolled back onto his stomach.

He calmed, grinned when he realized he was safe, then stopped grinning when a subterranean rumbling suggested that the cavern giant had finally figured out how he'd been duped and was annoyed enough to find his own way to the surface.

A panicked look over his shoulder, however, showed him nothing but a massive grey boulder slowly sinking into the ground where the exit had been. He watched, fascinated, as the earth ran up its sides, closed over it, buried it, and sprouted instant grass to conform with the other grass that stretched all the way to the hazy horizon.

I will not be amazed, he told himself as he pushed stiff-legged and tight-lipped to his feet; I will simply accept this as one of the amazing qualities of this world, and I will carry on as if nothing has happened. He did not, however, walk over to the spot where he knew he had emerged from the underground, and he did not, in not walking over there, stamp on the ground to see if it sounded hollow.

Luck, or whatever it was that had sustained him thus far, was not to be tempted by doubt or experimentation.

What he did do was throw a salute to Jeko Junffer, then turn around to search for his sister and the lorra, neither of whom he was able to spot immediately on the rolling plain. The one, he decided, was more than likely stretching her wings after so long a dark confinement, and the other was probably gorging himself on the sweet grass of his homeland.

And it was, in a sense, much like coming home, he thought as he sought a familiar landmark. He knew instantly he had arrived on the Sallamin Plain, a vast area that stretched from the inhospitable Blades in the north to a forest, as yet unexplored by Gideon, to the south. A scan of the horizon finally located the distant Scarred Mountains to the northeast, which meant that the edge of the world was behind him, and the village of Pholler was somewhere to the southeast.

And Pholler meant Ivy.

And Ivy meant . . .

He blushed, though there was no one to read his decidedly prurient and somewhat tender thoughts, and turning to his right, began walking, knowing there was a road somewhere in that direction that would eventually lead him to his destiny.

On the other hand, he thought, with both palms pressed just above those areas where Junffer's blue lightning had spurred him on, perhaps "destiny" was too great a word for a man's mere physical longings and his quest for a permanent place in a land to which he was a stranger.

Thirty minutes and a lot of grimacing later, he reached the hard-packed dirt road. His buttocks were not quite so actively painful, and he wasted no time in setting forth eastward, assured by confidence born of experience that he would not be alone for very long. The people of this world had an uncanny ability to pop up at the oddest, and even on occasion the most fortuitous, moments. Though he had been, to be honest, also interrupted by said popping up during other moments that had been notable for their rare serenity, their delicacy of emotion, and their taint of raw lust and virulent promise of chastity denied.

Such as the time when he and Ivy, shortly after their first meeting at Whale's armory shop in Pholler—

A flapping of wings interrupted him. When he looked up and behind, he saw Tuesday swinging over the road toward him, her wings out in a wavering glide that, once she had applied her brakes, ended no six feet from where he walked.

"You have two holes in your ass," she said when he caught up with her.

The sinews alluded to tightened in recognition, and he winced. "I was given a boost." His knees locked until the pain had passed. "I suppose I'll have to get new jeans. Again."

"I don't know," she said. "It looks kind of . . . different. Like you're winking. Of course, I suppose some will say you're being cheeky."

He looked at her, waiting for the laugh, and when it came he felt justified in taking a swat at the back of her head. She squawked, flew a few paces farther on, and settled with a huffy fluff of her feathers.

"Where's Red?" he asked.

A wing extended. "Up there. Eating. You'd think it was his last meal or something."

Poor choice of words, he chided silently, but said nothing aloud as he stretched his neck, trying to catch a glimpse of the hair that had given the lorra its name. Up a rise, down into a hollow, up again, and he saw him, munching on a low shrub and twitching his tail contentedly.

"You notice something?" Tuesday said.

Red looked up, burped, purred, and trotted over to join them.

"Yeah, he needs a brushing."

"No, about this place."

"I recognize it," he said, "if that's what you mean."

"So do I, Giddy, but that's not what I meant."

He looked around carefully, studying the expanse of grass, the trimmed edges of the road, the seductive rise and fall of the land, the sheer grandeur of the sky, the peaks of the Scarred Mountains still some distance away, the dots of black against the blue that indicated flying things that might or might not be of a friendly nature. And when he had completed his survey, he looked at his sister and shrugged.

"Listen," she prompted.

He did. "Except for us, I don't hear anything."

"Right."

He paused, started walking again, and reached out his right hand to stroke Red's flank thoughtfully. "It's very peaceful."

"It's quiet. There's a difference."

A nod. There were no birds crying, no insects buzzing, no wind whispering through the grass.

"It's as if everything's asleep," he said, unconsciously lowering his voice.

"Or dead."

That was a possibility he wished she hadn't raised. Not that he was surprised; she had done that often during her life back in New Jersey and Hollywood—a straight-from-the-shoulder-and-damn-the-torpedos expression of exactly what she was thinking since, she reasoned, what she was thinking wouldn't benefit anyone if they didn't know what it was. Like the time she had tactlessly, though accurately, characterized a woman Gideon had been seeing as someone who had a connoisseur's knowledge of every ceiling in every hotel in every city that had hosted a professional football team. Gideon had been crushed. It was a harsh judgment, and certainly exaggerated, but it definitely explained the woman's constant muttering about when the management was going to fix that damned crack in the corner.

He listened again. "No, not dead. Missing. Absent."

Tuesday nodded. "Maybe we're too late."

He waved her silent and wished to hell she'd stop reading his mind.

"Maybe we ought to go back."

"How?" he said with an impatient gesture behind him. "The only way now is to jump off the edge of the world, like I did the first time."

"So?"

"So Whale was with me and his magic was working then. He's not around now. It's a long way down, in case you've forgotten."

"Not for me."

"We're not talking about you, we're talking about me."

"That's very selfish of you, Giddy," she said softly.

"Don't call me that," he said. "And it's not selfish, it's realistic. If I jump this time, I die. If I die, you don't have a brother. If you don't have a brother, you stay a duck for the rest of your life."

"I can fly down. To Whale. Who'll change me back."

"Who hasn't been able to change you back yet. Besides, Tuesday, it's the principle of the thing!"

"What principle?"

"The principle that a falling body, when it hits the ground, breaks apart and gets smashed."

"Gee," she said. "I hadn't thought of it that way."

To compensate for his desire to convert her into a unique

muff, his feet began to ache; but any thought of riding Red was instantly driven off when he tested his buttocks for signs of recovery. Sitting on the lorra's back would be no pleasure at all.

After an hour Tuesday suggested they sing songs to lift their spirits and make the Sallamin seem a little less spooky.

For spooky it had turned, as a wind came up from the north, lowering the temperature and rustling through the grass, bringing large clouds from the Scarred Mountains whose shadows scuttled over the knolls like things Gideon would just as soon not think about because they reminded him of things he already knew about and didn't much care for.

The songs she chose were spritely, ribald, and ultimately embarrassing, since Gideon could not shake the notion that this duck here was his big sister, who was, in her fashion, a substitute mother, and mothers simply didn't know the lyrics that this one did, not if they wanted to bring their children up correctly and with a sense of propriety.

He refused to join in, even when he knew the words, and Tuesday accused him of blushing.

"I am not blushing," he insisted. "I am red-faced from all this walking."

She laughed, and immediately launched into a chanty about a sailor, a mermaid, a dolphin, an electric eel, and a German shepherd. Gideon caught the eel part, but he ignored the bit about the German shepherd since he was positive it was anatomically impossible anyway. Intriguing, but impossible.

After two hours, she began reciting every part she had had in every movie she had made, or had tested for, or had hoped to test for. It was an enlightening experience for her brother, who hadn't fully realized the true range and breadth of her screaming ability and emotive potential, though the impact was somewhat and sadly diminished because of her duckish limitations. And when she was finished, close enough to sunset for him to caution her about caution in the face of the unknown, Red nuzzled him thankfully and wandered off to forage for supper.

Gideon found them a traveler's clearing at the side of the road, where he discovered some of the nutritious plants he had once disdained. He fashioned a salad on a large and low flat rock, ate without tasting a thing, and finally lay back on the grass to look at the stars. Tuesday nestled beside him and tucked her head under her wing.

Red finally returned and settled on his other side, so Gideon could use the lorra's soft hair for a pillow.

It would have been wonderful, even idyllic, he thought, if it weren't for the familiar red eyes glaring down at him from the dark.

SEVEN

When Gideon woke the following morning, he decided instantly to go back to sleep. Sleep, as he had discovered during his days of terminal unemployment, was a near-perfect method of suppressing, if not actually forgetting, how miserable he was while he was awake. And he was certain, when he saw the dagger pointing at his throat at a distance of less than a hand's breadth, that this was a case of classic misery in the making if he ever saw one.

The weapon itself was, from this angle, imposing—a nine-inch blade of pure, unreflecting black engraved along the cutting edge with what he sincerely hoped were only symbolic silver notches, and a crimson filigree hilt that branched from either side back and around a hand encased in a leather glove as dark as the dagger itself. The point did not waver; neither did it confuse him with any doubt about where it would bury itself should he make a move inconsistent with the owner's perception of survival.

Slowly, Gideon refocused his eyes upward, to see a man whose face was not unlike the side of a mountain that had been carved into human likeness by an artist who had only the vaguest idea of what a human looked like. The brow was square, the eyes marble round, the nose skewed to the left, the mouth skewed to the right, the chin with a daring upward tilt, and the teeth, exposed in what surely had to be a grin, cleverly filed into points that meshed neatly when the mouth was closed.

The luxuriant raven hair that bobbed on the man's shoulders was coiffed in an exact replica of an eighteenth-century French court wig, the rakish hat was a black beret sans plume, and the clothes seemed to have been ripped off the backs of any number of fleeing creatures who were glad to be left with any fur at all.

Gideon was pleased to note his buttocks didn't do more than twinge, despite the fact that he was lying on his back.

"Get up," the man ordered, backing off several paces. The dagger gestured, in case he didn't speak the language.

Gideon rubbed his eyes clear of sleep and noted that the sun was still low on the horizon, and that sometime during the night his pacch-hide cloak had been stolen. He shivered in the chill morning air and groaned silently to his feet. Stretched. Worked his shoulders free of their stiffness. Yawned. But any thought of making a daring bid for freedom was stifled by the realization that the man with the dagger was not alone. There were four others standing in the road, similarly dressed and coiffed, though they had opted for sabers instead of daggers. They snarled at him fiercely. He looked for his sister and the lorra, and found them standing several yards to his left, in the middle of a circle of eight more similarly attired men who had, for the occasion, exchanged their daggers and sabers for bamboolike staffs at the ends of which were star-clusters of rather long blades.

Gideon's cloak was draped over Red's back, and Tuesday was huddled beneath it, only her eyes and beak showing.

With a reassuring smile to them both, he placed his fingers on the handle of his bat and felt the holster slip open, felt the comfortable weight settle into his hand. He cleared his throat and said, "Good morning."

"Who are you?" the leader demanded.

"Who are you?" Gideon riposted, not to be undone by a man who wore clothes that didn't seem to be completely dead.

The man took a step forward and pointedly displayed his dagger. "I am in charge here. Who are you?"

Gideon casually lifted the bat to his shoulder and estimated the distance between himself and the snarling group surrounding the duck and the giant goat. A surprise offensive maneuver would be chancy, and he suspected that if Red had been able to dispatch those men he probably would have done so already. Which meant that those men were likely to be very skilled with their staff-and-blades. Which meant that the odds were decidedly against Gideon and without any socially redeeming qualities, such as living when it was over.

"We . . ." He nodded toward the others. "We're going to Pholler. Who are you?"

The man frowned and adjusted his beret. "Pholler?" He blew a curl out of his eye. "What would you want to go to Pholler for?"

"I think that's my business."

"You thought you thought that was your business," the man corrected with a sneer. "Now it's my business." The dagger shifted, aiming down toward his stomach. "Now, who are you and where are you going?"

"We're going to Pholler," Gideon said.

"Oh, right, you said that already." The man flung a loose pelt over his shoulder, blew at another curl, and glanced at his men. "A little cooperation," he said in a much lower voice, "would be helpful, you know. You are outnumbered, you are a stranger, and I don't think it's very wise of you to play games with me."

Gideon agreed.

"So, then. Where did you come from?"

Gideon pointed westward. "Chey."

The man took a step back, put a fist on his hip and squinted one eye. "Oh really? And how did you manage that, fly?"

"The stairs."

An immediate muttering rose from the quartet, echoed soon after by the octet. The leader stepped back again, pointed west, pointed at Gideon, slapped at a pelt on his chest that seemed not to be quite dead enough for its position, and snorted. "You were on the Trail of Stairs? You?"

Gideon was getting a little fed up with the delay, and felt

his temper beginning to slip. He steadied himself and raised
his head. "Right. We were summoned, and we came, and if
you don't get the hell out of my way, I'm going to knock
your head into center field."

The muttering grew louder.

The leader was taken aback by his defiance and, suddenly
and clearly, had no idea what to do next. Gideon almost
laughed at the man's confusion, but instead suggested they
walk toward Pholler while they straighten out this misunder-
standing. The man in the beret considered the idea for only a
second before motioning to his men, who reassembled themselves into marching guard order—four abreast across the
road behind Gideon, four abreast across the road in front, and
two on either side. Red and Tuesday joined him, the duck on
the lorra's back and uncharacteristically silent. Gideon looked
at her, stroked her back, but she said nothing, not even when
he retrieved his cloak and fastened it around his neck.

"Vondel," the man said amiably as they started off, boots
hard on the road, staffs at port arms, and sabers in their
sheaths. "Chute Vondel. I'm the commander of this sector."

"Gideon Sunday."

Vondel stumbled, looked at him sideways and stumbled
again. "Not *the* Gideon Sunday?"

He nodded.

"Well fancy that. Boy, it just goes to show that you never
know, do you? You're sent out on a mission to do one thing,
and you end up doing something else. It's all very confusing." He checked his men, corrected one's stance, and sighed.
"I really wasn't sent out to escort you, you know. I'm
supposed to search the Sallamin for signs. I mean, that's what
I do, you see. I search for signs."

"Signs of what?"

"The Wamchu."

Gideon recalled the red eyes in the sky and spent several
seconds chastising himself for forgetting the evil tyrant in his
haste to return to the arms of his Ivy.

"Did you find any?" he wanted to know.

"Of course not. He's not here."

They walked on. Gideon managed to get Red purring by

scratching behind his ears, but he was still unable to get a sound from his sister. He was worried; she seemed all right physically, but there was something in the look of her, in the baleful forward gaze of her beautiful large eyes, that disturbed him. He thought he had seen that expression before, but he couldn't put his finger on it, and when he tried she nearly bit it off.

"Who sent for you?" Vondel asked.

"Ivy Pholler," he said.

"Oh my, are you in trouble?"

Gideon frowned. "In trouble? No, I don't think so. Why?"

"Because the only time she ever sends for anybody is when they're in trouble. She's very tough, you know. Very strong."

"Well, I'm pretty sure I'm not in trouble. I take it she's the boss or something?"

Vondel laughed, a high-pitched, pleasant, almost feminine laugh that sent several of his pelts flapping toward his waist before he could slap them back into place. "Not the top boss, no, but boss enough."

"I assume, then, that you'll take us to her."

"Sure. I don't want to get into trouble."

They marched on.

"But it is rather much, don't you think?" Vondel said. "I mean, I'm supposed to be looking for signs."

"But you didn't find any."

Vondel checked to be sure the closest of his men were paying attention to their marching and not to their leader. "Actually, I didn't look very hard. Which is not to say that I don't know a sign when I see one, but a sign from the Wamchu isn't all that hard to spot, if you know what I mean—a lot of bodies here, scorched earth there . . . it doesn't take a genius to know when he's around."

Gideon looked at the odd-featured man. "Is it bad?"

Vondel nodded, and his round eyes lowered their gaze to the ground. "Very bad. The armies are doing their best on all the fronts, but it's difficult to do your best when you're dying. Rather takes the oomph out of your attack."

"The wind from your sails," Gideon said.

"Exactly. The spring from your step."

"Discouraging."

"No, not really," Vondel said. "We're managing to hold our own in most places. But it's the idea of it, you see. One enters the army with dreams of riches and glory, and instead one gets wounds and cold beds. Of course, the alternative is complete and utter subjugation, which is considerably more disheartening than having to spend the night on the ground."

The men muttered their agreement.

Gideon looked across the Sallamin in all directions, but saw nothing to indicate that titanic battles were being fought by thousands of soldiers on a side, or even that small groups of infiltrators were skulking through the stands of trees that here and there broke up the roll of the plain. It was, in fact, extraordinarily peaceful. And puzzling.

"Oh," Vondel said glumly. "You've noticed."

Gideon waited, hoping his silence would answer for him.

Vondel shrugged one shoulder, then grabbed for a pelt before it got away, replaced it and tied its serpentine tail to another just below it. "They really didn't expect to find anything anyway."

"I see."

"It's my first command."

I see, he thought.

"You're right," Vondel said. "It isn't my first command."

Gideon raised an eyebrow.

Vondel seemed to sag as he walked. "Yes, I know. But she was so mad when I made just a little mistake. . . . I suppose it's the moral equivalent of standing in the corner."

Gideon wanted to ask what the mistake was, but kept silent.

They topped a rise, and if there hadn't been men behind him, Gideon would have stopped. Stopped to gaze longingly on the distant rooftops of the village of Pholler. Stopped to imagine that one of those buildings beneath one of those rooftops might well house the woman who had brought him here.

But he didn't. He carried on down the slope, looking at his sister and wondering, and looking at Vondel and wondering.

Then, remembering a certain muscle-bound blacksmith, Gideon looked at his sister again and stopped wondering.

"Sis," he said sternly.

The duck swiveled its head toward him.

"You're talking to a duck," Vondel said, wondering.

The men muttered.

"Tuesday!" Gideon snapped.

She blinked slowly, but her eyes weren't focused.

"Excuse me, but are you really talking to that duck?"

Gideon lifted the duck off Red's back and stopped, and Vondel was just able to halt his men before there was a confusion of bodies that would not have looked at all dignified. Then the men were ordered to take a break, have something to refresh themselves, which they did, muttering, while Vondel stood politely to one side and watched as Gideon held the duck up and forced it to look at him.

"Tuesday, damnit, tell me it isn't true!"

Tuesday's beak fluttered, clacked, and a long swallow rippled down her neck. And finally, softly: "I can't help it."

Red, who was wandering over to the grass for a bite to eat, looked back over his shoulder and growled.

"Well, I can't!" she said to the lorra, and looked back at her brother. "I don't know, it must be hormones or something."

"Ducks don't have hormones," he said.

"The duck talks," Vondel said, his amazement drawing him to Gideon's side. "I heard it talk. Is it battle fatigue?" He blew a curl out of his eye. "Can you get battle fatigue looking for signs?"

Tuesday's eyes closed in what Gideon could only call a languid swoon. "Jesus H," he said in disgust. "You really are something else, Sis, you really are."

"Wait a minute," Vondel said, his eyes widening, a finger pointing.

The duck squirmed, but Gideon wouldn't release her. "Sis, this is too goddamn much."

Vondel seemed to be having trouble breathing, and his face was growing pale. "That's . . ."

Tuesday wriggled, nipped at Gideon's wrists, and finally

broke free to flutter to the ground. "I don't care what you think," she said. "A woman is a woman for a' that, and you can't stop the march of progress."

"I already have," he said, pointing to the muttering men lounging on the grass. "And this is no time to get into this, Sis. We have work to do, remember?"

"Oh my," she said, wings out and spinning. "It's all right for you to get your glands in an uproar, but I'm supposed to be a nun, for god's sake?"

"That's the White Duck!" Vondel shouted.

Tuesday preened.

Gideon whistled to Red and, when the lorra reached his side, asked permission to ride on his back. When Red saw the fuss Vondel was making over the duck, he nodded, and Gideon swung up, looked down, and said, "Y'know, Red, I think we're in bigger trouble than the Wamchu."

"Oh, I don't think so," Vondel said as he knelt to gather Tuesday into one hand while the other skewered an escaping pelt. "I don't think so at all."

With a growl, Red warned Gideon not to ask, but he did. "Why not? What could be worse?"

"Agnes."

"You're joking."

"Oh no. She's fighting all of us. She says she has a score to settle, and she won't stop until we're all dead."

EIGHT

Tuesday, for all that she was considerably larger than the average duck, was comfortably perched on Vondel's left shoulder. It was, for the most part, a fair arrangement—she was as close as she could reasonably get to the man she'd just fallen in love with, and she served at the same time to keep Vondel's hair from dropping into his eyes. And it would have been a perfect arrangement had the complication of Vondel's brother not arisen as they were climbing the western slope of one of the plain's higher knolls.

Gideon couldn't believe his ears.

"Chute," the redheaded lieutenant said, "you're being a fool."

Vondel's tone indicated an expression not only of smug superiority, but also one that could easily be construed as sibling tough-shittedness. "I am no fool, Morj. I am a man possessed by a very possessing creature."

"It looks silly! And you're the commander!"

"And you are making a fool of yourself in front of the men. Get control, man, get control!"

"Well, it isn't fair. I want to hold the duck."

"You can't."

"But I love her!"

Gideon looked over his shoulder, at Chute and his sister

marching steadily on while a redheaded man just as tall and just as curiously featured as his brother strode backward in front of them. Tuesday was nuzzling Chute's cheek, but she was not in any visible fashion discouraging Morj, either. The other men didn't seem to care one way or the other; they were busily huffing up the rise and blowing hair out of their eyes.

It was midafternoon, and the sun in its westward trek seemed pale and unable to provide the warmth that would stop his breath from pluming over Gideon's shoulder, stop his cheeks from stiffening whenever the wind blew, his hands from reddening whenever he brought them out from the cover of Red's thick hair.

At any moment, probably when they reached the knoll's low summit, he would be able to see Pholler in greater detail. As it was, the Scarred Mountains' circular range was already high enough and close enough to break up the sky, and the forest at the range's foot was already clear enough to distinguish from the plain. He was close, and as long as the Vondels didn't get into a duel over his sister's affections, he knew they would arrive just before sunset.

"You'll pay for this, Chute. Authority can go just so far, you know, before it's challenged."

"You wanna fight?"

"No, I don't want to fight. I'm a civilized man."

"Civilized men don't whine and beg to carry a duck."

"Easy," Tuesday crooned. "Ducks have feelings, too."

"I'm sorry, my love."

"You'll pay," Morj warned. "You won't deny me again."

Gideon supposed he ought to be worrying about his sister, but he was too preoccupied by Chute's comments about Agnes. Agnes Wamchu. The last and the most powerful of the Wamchu's three wives. When Gideon and she had met in Wamchu's former residence—now the home of Whale Pholler, who had done a lot of redecorating, particularly around the dungeons—she had been ordered to fry him. Destroy him. Wither him. Turn him to ash and blow the ashes away. And she had begun just such a sequence when luck had intervened and the session had been interrupted.

But he had never forgotten it.

Nor had he forgotten the agony he had suffered.

Though he had said nothing to Vondel, Gideon knew very well what score it was she had to settle—his victory over the other two wives, a victory that had led to their premature deaths, unless one believed that Fate didn't believe in premature anything. And since she had apparently broken away from her husband, who only wanted to conquer the world, it was logical to assume that the Wamchu was not doubly or, god forbid, triply angry at Gideon as well, and might even be temporarily setting aside his original plans in favor of new ones that put Gideon at the top of the list of things to do before conquering the world.

Agnes, he thought.

And whistled "There's No Place Like Home" all the way to the top of the knoll.

And once there, stopped because the men in front had stopped, and the men beside him had stopped, and Chute had come up to stand beside him with the duck on his shoulder and was shaking his head sadly.

"I think," said Gideon, "I know what your mistake was."

The village of Pholler still lay some distance away, but it was evident even from here that it was deserted. The wooden houses were quiet, the streets were quiet, the fields that surrounded it were stockless and quiet. Gideon braced himself on Red's neck and rose up to look around, scanning the occasional narrow roads that branched off from the main one, and saw no signs of movement. No people. No animals. Not even a decent-sized bird.

He slid down off the lorra's back and began walking. When Vondel tried to keep up, he waved the man back. He didn't want to know what the mistake was. He didn't even want to guess what the mistake was, in case he was right and would then be forced to strangle the man and spend the rest of his life listening to his sister complain about the one that got away. Yet he was also intrigued; he could not imagine what could have caused an entire population to flee their homes if it wasn't the approach of an army that was, at the best of times, unsavory. But there was no smell of burning, no destruction that he could see, no glimpse of an encampment that might have been deserted recently or not.

There was only Pholler, and there was no one home.

"I wanna carry the duck!"

To the northwest, the Scarred Mountains blazed a deep orange in the setting sun's light.

Red began to move more slowly, his claws digging divots in the road, his eyes shading to black. Every few paces he would mutter a low growl. His tail began to switch, and he moved with his head down, his great spiraled horns ready for attack.

The bat was in Gideon's hand by the time they reached the first of the houses, two-storied, wood-and-marble structures, and he noticed that the usual array of family pennants was missing from the lintels and window frames.

"Please let me carry the duck?"

In the village square, a long and low building settled beneath a stand of trees, and when Gideon walked around to the front and tried the double doors, they were locked. He knocked. No one answered. He knocked again, stepped back, and shivered when a breeze kicked dust off the roof into his face.

A look to his right then, to a small building that had once housed Whale's armory shop. He noted it had been rebuilt, and the batwing doors had been replaced with one that had a heavy bar laid across it. He smiled. That was where he'd first met Ivy, and had thought she was going to do him in with a dagger. That was where Whale had made the bat he now held.

A sigh, and Gideon turned around, facing east up the road that ran through the village. Dusk was fast settling across the Sallamin, and it was difficult to see clearly. He had to squint to make out the last of the houses, and squinted harder to make out the line of the horizon. He stopped searching for movement when he started getting a headache; he stopped praying for a miracle when Chute and his company had joined him, and were silent.

"So this is it, huh?" Tuesday said, flapping to the ground and leaning against his leg.

"Yep."

"I think we're too late."

"Yep."

"I was supposed to keep watch," Vondel said morosely. "But Morj said I was wanted at headquarters. The message was a little old. When I got there, it was too late."

A sweep of Gideon's arm indicated the whole village. "You were attacked?"

"You could say that. It was kind of more like an unstoppable wave of horror than an attack, but that's close enough."

Gideon was proud of himself for not asking for details. "And the people?"

"Oh, they got away. You can run pretty fast when there's a wave of unstoppable, not to mention unspeakable, horror behind you."

Morj called to his brother.

"Excuse me," Vondel said. "I think he wants something."

"Wait a minute." Gideon gestured vaguely. "If they ran away, which way did they go?"

Vondel pointed. "There's another village a few days away, on the other side of the Rush. I was there until Ivy found out what had happened. That's when she sent me on my next mission."

"To look for signs."

"Of unstoppable horror, right."

Gideon said nothing more, and the man marched off, so engrossed in his brother's gestures that he didn't notice one of his laces snake off into the grass.

The houses' shadows soon buried the road, brought out the stars, chilled a breeze that hummed mournfully over the rooftops.

"Unstoppable horror," Gideon said at last. "Wonderful."

"He has nice hair, though," she said.

A clash of blade against blade barely disturbed them, only made their heads turn; Chute and Morj were dueling under the trees.

"They want me," she said proudly.

"Yep," he said.

She nudged him sharply with her beak. "Giddy, for heaven's sake, two men, two fine men, are trying to kill each other over your sister! Doesn't that just make your bones quiver?"

He walked up the road out of the square, and stopped when she grabbed a beakful of jeans. Then he looked down and wiped a hand over his face. "What I care about, Sis, is that Ivy's not here. That nobody's here."

Morj cried out in pain; Chute laughed.

"We were supposed to help them," he said. "We were supposed to be here to help them."

Tuesday waddled around until she faced him, stabbed his right knee until he hunkered down to her level.

"Now see here, Gideon Sunday," she said sternly, "you are not Superman, and you're not Batman, and you're not the goddamn Shadow out to purge evil from the hearts of men. You couldn't have gotten here any faster than you did, and you don't even know how long they've been gone. You can't see the future, and you can't change the past, and if you're going to feel sorry for yourself, you might as well go home."

"I don't feel sorry for myself," he said angrily. "I just don't like feeling that I can't do anything to help because I'm always one step behind the rest of this idiot place."

"You really want to catch up to unstoppable horror?"

He conceded the point with a nod, but sighed loudly to tell her he still wasn't happy.

She cocked her head to one side, then the other. "It's not all that bad, you know. You've still got me and that goat, and the boys, right?"

He glanced over his shoulder; Morj was sucking a wound on his wrist, and Chute was trying to prevent his belt from getting away. "They can't even keep their clothes on."

Tuesday gazed at her love, and sighed. "Yeah, I know."

Gideon glared, and she fluffed her feathers.

Chute sheathed his dagger and started to walk toward them.

"Listen, Giddy, you can bitch all you want, but there isn't anything we can do tonight anyway, so why don't we—"

One of Chute's men shouted a warning.

Red's pantherlike bellow echoed off the walls.

Gideon straightened instantly, bat at the ready, and raced toward the square as he saw the company backing toward the longhouse wall, sabers and staffs slashing at large shapes plunging out of the trees in a cleverly staged ambush. The things were too small to be the demonic deshes that generally hunted among the peaks, and too large to be the carnivorous ekklers that seldom left the smooth-pine forests; when one of the men shouted something about aiming for a head, Gideon's vision cleared and he realized that they were being attacked by a scruffy patrol of Moglar, fierce giant dwarves who were the personal guards of Lu Wamchu.

One of the leather-armored creatures saw him as he entered the square, and spun a mace over its head. Gideon swerved and flung the bat at its legs, raced after it, and reached his weapon just as it made contact and brought the Moglar down, and the mace down on its head.

Tuesday honked.

He whirled and faced two more, their black hair greasy on their shoulders, their mottled faces contorted with a rage that was matched only by the distaste in Chute's expression as he plunged his dagger into the left one's back. Gideon dispatched the second by caving in its chest, then turned to swing at another, who deftly leapt into the air, spun around twice, and landed on Gideon's other side.

Gideon turned and swung again.

The Moglar, laughing hoarsely, flipped the two swords it held from hand to hand and tried to pink Gideon's thighs with expert lunges and brilliant backward sidesteps; but Gideon refused to fall for the tactic and waited instead, circling, eyeing the giant dwarf warily until it launched another series of lunges. Then he chopped at a blade and snapped it, carried through and broke the other wrist. The Moglar turned to run; Red rose on his hind legs and clawed off its hair.

The initial shouts and screams settled into a muffled series of grunts and grunted warnings. The Moglar outnumbered them by several to one, but they were hampered by their own eagerness, and by the skills of Vondel's men—the staffs rotated into blurs that pureed fore and aft, the sabers filled

the evening air with blue sparks when they connected with
steel and bone, and the daggers seemed to fly from their
owners' grips, sink into their targets, and fly back without a
sound save the puncture of flesh and the thud of hilt meeting
hand.

Gideon fought with Red at his side, more often than not
deferring to the lorra's horns when a single Moglar was
stupid enough to challenge them on its own. And when there
was more than one, he used his innocuous-looking weapon to
its best advantage, daring the enemy to come closer, then
swinging powerfully from the shoulder. He only missed once,
and found himself tangled in his own legs, falling to the
ground; Tuesday flew into the Moglar's face to distract it
until he could regain his footing.

Though it seemed like days, it was only a half hour later
that a Moglar bleated a retreat from one of the side streets,
and the giant dwarves vanished into the night, dragging their
dead and wounded behind them. Gideon immediately dropped
to his knees, dropped the bat, and leaned over. Despite all his
time here, he was still not used to killing, and the thought of
it filled his throat and stomach with acid.

There were groans.

Morj circulated among the company, dispensing medical
skills and advice.

One man screamed when Chute was forced to cut through
his hair to get at a scalp wound.

And three of those who had not been wounded at all were
dispatched with torches into the streets to bring back the
clothes that had taken the opportunity to flee for their
lives.

By midnight all was calm.

Tuesday, despite Chute's pleading, had stolen Gideon's
cloak again and was sleeping on the peak of the longhouse
roof; Red was curled up against a tree, snoring loudly and
thumping the grass with his tail; and the company at large
was unconscious against the wall.

Gideon couldn't sleep. His hands stung, his arms were
tight, his legs were cramping every five minutes, and he was
so tired he could barely keep his eyes open. But he could not

sleep. He heard only the battle cry of the Moglar, and within that horrid sound the cry of Ivy Pholler pleading for help.

Chute walked over and sat cross-legged beside him, most of his uniform back in place and his face lined with worry. "Are you all right, Gideon?"

"I'll live, I think."

"You were very good."

He grinned, and shrugged. "It isn't my usual line of work, actually. But I suppose it wasn't bad against unstoppable horror."

Chute looked at him oddly. "What? That wasn't unstoppable horror. It was pretty disgusting, but it wasn't all that bad."

Gideon licked his lips, scratched at his beard. "What you're saying is, it gets worse."

"Sure, didn't you know that?"

Gideon lay down, closed his eyes, sat up, and said, "If you wake me before this war is over, Vondel, I'm going to give you a crew cut."

"Is it easy to take care of?"

Gideon went to sleep.

And dreamed of a house in New Jersey, and a pantry in the kitchen, and a telephone call that summoned him to the next Super Bowl.

He also dreamed of a featureless plain, a pale red sky, and a dark figure on the horizon, watching him, and waiting.

When he woke up and saw Tuesday sitting on his chest, he closed his eyes again.

She pecked his nose, his chin, and started on his beard. "C'mon," she said. "You gotta get up."

"I don't gotta do anything."

"You damned well better, if you want to be a hero."

NINE

Gideon didn't want to be a hero. He hadn't asked for the job, and hadn't liked it since the day it was given to him. He didn't even know what a hero was, though he suspected it had something to do with doing things no one else wanted to do, and when he did it he was applauded for doing it while those applauding thought they could have done it themselves if they had really wanted to, and a hell of a lot better besides.

He got to his feet.

He ignored his sister's quacking call to arms.

He looked eastward up Pholler's deserted main street and saw, some distance outside the village, a large cloud of yellowish, reddish dust moving rapidly in his direction. It was difficult to see clearly because the rising sun distorted his vision, but he had no doubt it was a cloud of dust all right, and one that was filled with all sorts of dark shapes indicating that a rather large and determined force was on the road.

Chute and his men were already standing behind him, weapons at the ready and muttering their determination not to be ambushed again; Red was testing the nutritional value of the shrubs around the longhouse, but his tail was twitching; and Tuesday, after delivering her message, had taken to the high ground, precariously balancing on a tree branch and

wondering aloud how the damned robins did it without cramping their toes.

Gideon touched his side to be sure the bat was in its
holster, then began walking up the empty street. His footsteps
echoed against the walls. They made him nervous. He stopped.
The echoes continued. He looked behind him and saw Chute
courageously in his shadow, only once blowing a stubborn
curl out of his eye.

"What do you think?"

Chute shaded his eyes and stared. "I think it isn't the
unstoppable horror."

"That's a relief. Could it be Ivy?"

"I rather doubt it, actually."

Gideon sniffed, took bat in hand, and started forward
again. Of course it wasn't Ivy. Why should it be Ivy? She
was probably busy keeping the Wamchu and his renegade
wife from conquering the world, so why should she bother to
come see him, even though she had sent for him? Personally.
With a plea, no less. To save her life, for crying out loud.

Tuesday flew erratically overhead and landed on the roof
of the last house, gripping the chimney as best she could with
one wing. Her neck extended, her eyes narrowed, and when
her brother came abreast of her she called down to him to put
away the bat, the newcomers looked friendly. Dusty, but
friendly.

"How can you tell?" he called back.

"They have hair like Chute's. I think I'm jealous."

Chute, with a scowl of disbelief, strode toward the cloud,
stopped, strode back and sighed. "Oh, bother, it's York," he
said glumly.

"Who's York?"

"My brother. The other brother. He's probably coming to
tell me I'm in trouble again. How embarrassing. He never did
like me awfully much. The only good thing is that he doesn't
like Morj, either."

Gideon holstered the bat and waited, wondering if York
would fall in love with his sister too, and if there were any
rules for three-way duels. He didn't move when Morj joined
them, heard the news, and tried to kick down the low wall in

front of the last house. He didn't move when Chute's left shoulder pad made a break for it and the soldier stomped a foot on its tail. And he didn't move when the dust cloud stopped moving, settled, and he saw a group of nearly forty men, all dressed in writhing pelts, and all with hair they couldn't keep out of their eyes. The leader was blond, taller than his brothers, and with a slight sneer on his lips, most likely a result of the scar that ran from the corner of his mouth to the corner of his left eye.

Tuesday quacked softly from the roof.

York Vondel put his hands on his hips and glared. "You were supposed to report back this morning."

Morj kicked the wall.

Chute straightened his beret and pointed over his shoulder. "We had a little trouble. Moglar. If you must know."

"And who's this?" the blond said, the sneer shifting to his voice.

"Gideon Sunday," Chute said.

"Oh." No surprise, no disgust, no smile. Nothing. "You're wanted, dear brother. Now."

Chute opened his mouth to protest, shook his head instead, and signaled his men to move up and fall in with the others. Then he took Gideon's arm and pulled him to one side. "He's really not a bad brother," he whispered. "He's just upset."

"Why?"

"He's in love with Ivy."

Gideon's back straightened.

"She tells him to put a desh in it, and he tells her he'll have her before the war is over."

Gideon's chin lifted.

"She tells him it'll be over his dead body, and he tells her he's not afraid to die for the woman he loves."

Gideon's hand tightened around the knob of the bat.

"I just thought you ought to know. When York falls in love, he's awfully impossible. Dreadful. Actually, if he weren't my brother, I'd probably kill him."

York sneered in their general direction, beckoning impatiently until Chute sighed and patted Gideon's arm. "Talk to him," he advised. "Let him get to know you. He needs a friend, actually, because no one else can stand him."

Gideon refused to comment. Instead, he whistled for Red, and made a show of climbing onto the lorra's back when York, like others of his people, professed disbelief that one of the caprines would deign to permit a human to ride it. Then Gideon whistled for his sister, who flew down from the roof, circled Chute's head once, and landed on Red's haunch. Immediately he rode to the head of the column, glanced behind disdainfully, and moved on, leaving the others in his dust.

"Don't you think you ought to wait?" Tuesday said nervously as the troop fell behind.

"For what? Before we've done a mile they'll be fighting each other tooth and nail, and I really don't need that aggravation right now."

She nipped at his back. "Jealous?"

"Of what?"

"The blond with the crooked mouth."

He snorted. "That sort of emotion is beneath me, Sis. I have better things to do than to waste my time wondering how many rivals I have."

"Three so far," she said.

He frowned. "Three?"

"Y'know, Giddy, even for a man you're awfully dense. Why do you think the Vondels hate each other so much? It sure as hell isn't the hair."

He thought about it, thought about it a bit more, and decided that perhaps he could stoop to a twinge of jealousy. But just a twinge. To prove to himself that he still felt strongly about Ivy. After all, he didn't want it to cloud his judgment.

An hour later, he said, "Bastards."

"Who?" she said. "Them or those?"

He reached back and pulled her around to what would have been his lap, were he sitting on the ground with a lap to put her on.

"Who's them?"

"Those guys with the hair."

"And who's those?"

"Those guys over there, the ones with the teeth."

He looked in the direction her beak was pointing. South, as it turned out, toward a narrow, dusty side road along which marched a fair-sized contingent of medium-sized, human-looking creatures whose sunburnt faces seemed to be more fangs than flesh. They were in what appeared to be well-used battle dress—full armor, pikes and swords and maces—and had a look about them of an army hunting for a decent war. Red paid no attention when Gideon tried to turn him around, and Tuesday attempted to burrow into the giant goat's mane, which the giant goat didn't have, which frustrated her into volunteering to fly back to Chute and warn him of the impending conflict.

Gideon agreed, snapped the bat to hand, and turned sideways as best he could when he and the toothsome army reached the junction at the same time. He tensed. He held his breath. He swallowed when the leader, who wore a gaudy red ribbon around his neck, saluted him and snapped orders at his men to fall in behind. Another salute, which Gideon belatedly returned, and the tramping took on a marching cadence.

Tuesday came back and leaned on Red's head. "Chute says they're good guys."

"I gathered."

She craned her neck to look around him. "Ugly little critters, aren't they."

"I don't make judgments on appearance," he said as he waited for his breathing to return to normal. "They are obviously part of Ivy's army."

"I wonder if the guy with the ribbon is in love with her."

He snarled; she laughed and flew off again, returning less than ten minutes later to tell him that at the next intersection there was a group of canaries waiting to join them.

"Canaries?"

"Well, they have yellow feathers, cute little beaks, and a row of spikes down their backs. Except for the spikes, they're canaries. Well, and except for the size."

Gideon wasn't about to ask. He decided he wanted to be surprised. Which he was when he saw the canaries, who had the feathers and the beaks and the spikes, and who were fully twelve feet tall on legs that didn't look strong enough to hold a sickly sparrow on a windless day. The leader, who wore a purple sash across his broad chest, saluted him. Gideon saluted back. The canary saluted the tooth. The tooth saluted back. The canaries fell in between the teeth and the hair, and Gideon rode on refusing to look behind him.

At midday they forded a deep, swift stream, yet no one suggested they stop for refreshment.

An hour later Tuesday landed again on Red's head, and closed one eye. "You're not going to believe this one," she said.

"Try me," he answered.

"Blimps."

She was wrong and, Gideon thought, somewhat uncharitable.

At the next intersection, on a small trail leading into the plain from the left, stretched a column of men whose weight he judged to range between four hundred pounds and out of the question. They carried what appeared to be two-bladed swords, and they wore lederhosen and diaphanous pastel shirts of rainbow profusion, obviously secure in the knowledge that no one would have the temerity to remark on their wardrobe.

Gideon saluted the leader, who was in blue and yellow.

The leader saluted back and suggested, in a rolling deep voice, that he and his men bring up the rear.

Tuesday gagged and flew off somewhere askew.

Gideon merely nodded and looked forward again, seeing in the near distance the sparkling clear water of the Rush, the main river of the land, deep and cool and the cause of his near drowning a hundred lifetimes ago. Again they forded, since he had yet to come across anyone who had ever heard of a bridge over water; such a skill such a structure required was reserved, as far as he knew, for building them only over large holes in the ground.

The afternoon wore on.

The company became an army as several more groups fell in behind him, and when he finally looked over his shoulder he was astounded to realize how many bodies there were back there—if it was less than a thousand, he would turn in his bat. He blinked, looked ahead hurriedly, and tried to forget they were there, and that he, by virtue of a reputation he hadn't known he had, was leading them. Like a parade without music. Like a general before battle. Like an idiot, he thought, who hasn't the faintest idea where he's going, and if someone doesn't tell me soon, somebody back there is going to get awfully mad.

The Scarred Mountains were nearer now, almost fully to his left, and the peaks, though not high, were clouded in mist. He knew they formed a huge bowl on the other side, in which was the village of Kori, from which came the woman Glorian who had gotten him into this mess in the first place. To his right, the plain continued to the forest on the horizon.

The scenery hadn't changed by the time the sun had set, and the air was soon filled with a cacophony of orders in a myriad of languages that sounded more like barnyard bickering than the bark of a prepared military expedition. Campfires were set for those who needed the warmth against the cold of the night, and it wasn't long before Gideon could hear voices raised in song, harmonies alien to the ear but tender to the heart.

He had his own fire. Red was off foraging, and Tuesday was dozing. He ate, added a few more branches to the flames, and wrapped his cloak snugly around his shoulders.

No one came to speak with him.

No one came to pick a fight.

It was very dark, and it was very lonely, and he said nothing when the lorra returned, merely snuggled into the silken hair.

Life at the top, he thought, and fell instantly asleep, and was instantly awake when the sun rose the next day and he could hear the army preparing itself for the march.

"How much longer?" he asked Tuesday once they were on the road again.

"Don't ask me."

"Then ask one of the boys."

"They're not talking to me."

He raised an eyebrows. "Oh?"

"They want me to make a choice."

"So make a choice."

She walked down Red's neck and glared up at him. "A choice? Between them? Have you taken a good look at them lately?"

He smiled. "I thought you were smitten."

"It was the heat of the moment. Besides, they don't even know what steak is."

He petted her, soothed her, and decided that he would know when he got there where he was going. He didn't even mind when she told him, in detail, about the gophers who had joined them sometime during the night, though he was definitely tempted to ask about the kilts they were wearing.

And just before the sun dropped below the theoretical rim of the world, he saw a jumble of boulders, and the flickering lights of a thousand campfires lining the horizon.

A voice called his name.

A look back showed him Chute running toward the front, hair flying, clothes flying, his sword in one hand as if he were expecting one of the canaries to attack him. Red slowed, and Gideon smiled.

"Quite a group back there," he said.

"Easy for you to say," Chute grumbled. "You don't have all that dust and sweat straightening your curls."

Gideon wanted to suggest that the times had produced what he thought were probably more important things to worry about, but refrained when the man pointed toward the boulders.

"Ivy," he said breathlessly.

Ah, Gideon thought; the main camp. The end of the trail. The beginning of the battle. The source of my discontent, and my heart's unrequited aching.

"Boy," Chute continued, "am I in big trouble."

TEN

At a command from Chute, passed along by Morj and elaborated by York, Gideon's troops broke ranks and dispersed over the crowded plain, finding their places among others of their kind. The boulders, Gideon realized, were not rocks at all but massive tents of hide and leather, and the campfires were so numerous that the light was bright enough to remind one of noon. The noise was considerable—singing, laughing, arguing, philosophizing, walking, running, bleating, shouting, snoring, weeping, lamenting, rejoicing, ordering, complying—and the smells of the cooking, the sweating, the animals, the people, the tents, the weapons, and the extraordinary sewage facilities was enough to keep him on the lorra's back where he could hold on with both hands whenever he felt himself growing dizzy. Which happened quite often, and especially when he passed an area devoted to what sounded like hysterical centipedes laden with steel castanets.

Red took it all in long, hasty strides.

Gideon decided he'd best make his way to Ivy's placement, and began a wandering through the deepening twilight that took him past creatures he thought really ought to be in the Wamchu's service, not here. But he was, all in all, proud of himself for not staring too long, neither at the man who looked perfectly normal except for the beards that seemed to

have a life of their own, nor at the men who didn't look
normal at all for reasons he couldn't put his finger on and
wasn't about to just to satisfy his curiosity.

An hour passed. And yet another.

Red began to snort about the condition of his feet.

Gideon wanted to complain about the condition of his
still-healing buttocks, but couldn't find a tasteful way to put it
so that the lorra wouldn't dump him to the ground.

Finally, as he despaired at ever finding her, or knowing the
sweet scent of fresh air again, he spotted a large tent off to
his left. A red tent. A bubble-shaped red tent topped with a
dozen flags, none of whose elaborate designs meant a thing to
him, and around which was stationed a platoon of those
maybe-normal men carrying perhaps-normal swords and standing behind undecorated shields crossed with heavy bands of
what might have been black leather. There was no question
that this was Ivy's headquarters, and as Gideon slid off
Red's back with a groan, his identification was confirmed
when Chute burst from the opening in its center, fell to the
ground, got up, blew a curl from his eye, and let his shoulders sag in humiliation.

"Trouble?" Gideon asked when he reached him.

The man sighed. "You were supposed to come with me
when I reported to her."

"You didn't tell me. Sorry."

"Don't be sorry. York didn't tell me, either."

"Did you tell her that?"

"Of course I did," Chute snapped. "But when you're
groveling it's terribly hard to be sincere. She didn't believe
me."

A woman's voice rose in harsh anger from within, and a
moment afterward, Morj spilled out onto the ground, slapped
a hand on a sleeve that tried to make a break for it under
cover of dark, and swore. When he rose, he saw Gideon and
drew his dagger.

"You were supposed to come with us," he snarled.

"I already told him that," said Chute. "But he wasn't to
know, was he? I mean, York didn't tell me, did he? He didn't
even tell you, did he? So how was Gideon to know?"

Morj created an instant mythology of curses and stomped off, while Chute suggested that Gideon make an appearance without delay, if only to save the nervous hides of two very dismal young soldiers.

Gideon didn't move.

He couldn't move.

After all this time, this was the moment he'd been waiting for, planning for, hoping for—and he had no idea what he was going to say, do, or otherwise comport himself when he first saw the woman who had taken over his dreams when he wasn't dreaming about getting the hell back to New Jersey. Red, sensing his dilemma, purred for a second before placing his forehead against Gideon's back and nudging him gently forward.

"No," he protested. "No, wait a minute, okay? I've got to think first, Red. This isn't—"

The nudge became a push.

Gideon's heels created shallow trenches in the earth. "I really do think we ought to—"

The push became a shove.

A rather decent shove, considering the way Gideon's heels had gone from trenches to ditches, and he stumbled across the threshold, righted himself with as much dignity as he could find, and waited until his eyes adjusted to the dim lantern-light.

And there she was.

Standing in the middle of the hard-packed earthen floor, alone, staring at him with wide eyes and twitching fingers.

Ivy Pholler.

Blonde, a bit shorter than he, emerald eyes dark in the flickering light. She wore her people's traditional leatherlike trousers and a puffy white blouse, neither of which did absolutely anything to conceal the figure he had come so close to examining on a person-to-person basis in the past. So close, and yet so far.

Ivy Pholler.

Queen of his emotions so embroiled in fervent turmoil.

Dear, sweet Ivy, with a dagger in her hand.

* * *

"Well," she said.

He smiled and took a step forward. And stopped when she aimed the dagger somewhere in the vicinity of his midsection. His midsection tightened.

"You've been gone a long time," she told him in a curiously toneless voice, while the dagger beckoned him forward.

He didn't know what to say. This was not exactly the reception he had hoped for, though he understood perfectly how she might be annoyed at his delay in returning to the Upper Ground. After all, their parting had been a poignant one, and his emotions at the time somewhat muddled, since he wasn't sure how he felt about either his position in this strange new world or the people living it. Much, he thought, the same as his confusion now, only more so because, at last seeing her, he wasn't sure that seeing her in his imagination wasn't better; at least there she wasn't poking a really ugly blade toward his vitals, not to mention the general areas of his others.

"It's a long story," he said.

"It better be," she told him. "If you've just been screwing around all this time, you're in big trouble."

He smiled bravely.

She returned the smile, sweetly, and motioned him to a fluffy upholstered camp chair. He sat. She sat opposite him, a firepit between. She put the dagger aside and pulled across her shoulder a long blonde braid intricately entwined with ribbons of such vibrant color that they were difficult to look upon without one's eyes beginning to water.

"You look lovely," he said truthfully, and not a little wistfully.

"The story," she said.

"Tuesday is still a duck."

She blinked only once, slowly. "Whale?"

"Can't find the right touch."

"It's tough being a duck, I guess."

"It's tough being a general too, I'd imagine."

She looked into the fire and nodded solemnly. "It's a bitch, all right. Especially when you keep losing."

Gideon suppressed with some difficulty the urge to leap into her arms and comfort her. Instead, he leaned back, crossed his legs at the ankles, and told her over the period of the next three hours what had passed since they had last saved the world from a fate worse than free enterprise and the occasional band of unsavory raiders. And when he was finished, he waited for her reaction. And waited a while longer while she picked up the dagger, threw it point first into the dirt floor, picked it up and threw it again.

"You didn't write," she said at last.

"Write?" He sat up abruptly. "Write? Jesus, Ivy, didn't you hear me? I was dodging giants, angry Wamchu wives, spider things that dripped disgusting stuff from their mouths, dragons that honest-to-god breathed fire, things in water that had spines like spears . . . write? When the hell did I have time to write, for god's sake!" He stood, sat immediately down when she threw the dagger between his feet, and looked to the ceiling. "I thought about you a lot, though."

She nodded. "Maybe, but you still have your clothes on."

"I what?"

"I said, you still have your clothes on. If you loved me, you'd tear off your clothes, leap across the fire, tear off my clothes, and ravish me on the spot."

"What spot?"

She pointed to a black spot on the ground beside her chair.

Apprehensively, he glanced at the entrance, and saw that someone had closed the flaps in a gesture of genteel military propriety; he glanced around the tent itself and saw no one lurking behind the chests, the chairs, the tables, the piles of weapons and other accoutrements of struggle the leader didn't trust in the hands of the troops.

"Well . . ."

"Quiet," she said. "I'm going to think."

He didn't like the sound of that. The last time he recalled her thinking was just before she defeated a Moglar force virtually single-handed.

She stood, walked slowly around the firepit, and positioned herself just behind him, humming tunelessly. He tensed. Her hands dropped to his shoulders and began massaging them.

He relaxed. The humming stopped. The hands moved to the sides of his neck, and he tensed again.

"Do you remember," she said, "that night just before we fell off the edge of the world? I was going to take my clothes off for you, you know."

He remembered; he knew.

"That was silly of me."

It wasn't; he remembered.

"I'm different now, Gideon. I'm not the same woman you used to know."

Damn, he thought.

"I've learned a lot of things since then. I'm responsible for a lot of people, and not just those who are camped outside, just waiting for the word to march to their possible destruction. Villages and towns all over the world are depending on me to save them once and for all." She sighed, and he squirmed at the hot breath that swept like a moist caress across his nape. "It's a terrible thing, Gideon my dear, having all those people looking up to you, especially when most of them are a good foot taller. It's a bitch."

He patted her hand; she slapped his fingers.

"Gideon . . ." She swung around and dropped adroitly and not very lightly into his lap. "The battle will be joined soon," she said somberly, her eyes examining his face, her right hand tracing the line of his jaw. "And I have to admit that I'm a little frightened."

He did his best not to squirm under her weight, enjoying instead the feel of her, the scent of her, the closeness of her as she laid her head on his shoulder for the briefest of moments. With a tentative hand, he put his hand on her hair and stroked it.

"No need to fear," he whispered. "Gideon's here."

"Ah," she said with a rueful smile, "but so is Agnes."

He grunted. "Yes. I heard."

"She's annoyed."

"I heard that too."

"She wants you, you know. As a present to herself."

His eyes widened briefly. "A present? What is it, her birthday?"

Ivy squirmed to settle a bit more; Gideon squirmed, unsettled. "Not exactly. It's her Day."

"Oh," he said.

"You don't know?" She leaned away from him, the better to look into his face. "You really don't know?"

Patience, he figured, had already made him the most virtuous man on the face of whatever planet he thought he was on. "No," he said. "I do not know. But you're going to tell me, and ruin my homecoming, right?"

"It is," she said seriously, "the celebration of the moment a woman realizes that she is not simply chattel, nor ass, nor slave to the universe. It is," she said more loudly, "that moment when a woman discovers within herself the *power*, the *force*, the invincible and unalterable *magnaenergy* that permits her, above all others except other women, to control, define, and shape her future without the sullying influence of outside distractions."

She paused to catch her breath.

"It happens once every two hundred and twenty-nine years."

Gideon computed rapidly. "But that means—"

"Right. Unless you live to be about three or four hundred, you'd better have a good time when it happens."

And Agnes, he thought then, must be—

"Two hundred and twenty-nine," Ivy said.

"Jesus."

"On that day, Gideon, she will be the most powerful being in the entire cosmos. So you can see why I'm frightened. And who knows?" she added in a husky whisper. "I may never come back."

"No," he protested. "Don't say that, Ivy. You will. We both will."

"Perhaps. Perhaps not." She wriggled a little to make herself more comfortable, and pressed closer, her eyes half-lidded and her mouth not an inch from his. "But I do know that there may not be a tomorrow."

He thought about mortality, and about the impression she was making on his road-dusty jeans. "True. One never knows about these things."

"Tonight may be all that we have left."

Her left hand toyed with the buttons of her blouse.

"True," he said again with a heavy sigh. "No one can predict the future, not in perilous times such as these."

"Then . . ." She backed away, looked away, gave him her profile highlighted and made honey by the dancing flames. "Then we shouldn't waste it, Gideon. We shouldn't throw away these last precious minutes Fate has been kind enough to throw in our direction."

"You're right."

Slowly, her face turned toward him; slowly, she took his hand and brought it close to her breast. "At any moment, the Wamchu's personal nightmares, allied with his personal hideous forces, may come crashing through this very tent and steal whatever future we might have together."

"God, are you right!"

"Yes," she said sadly. "I wish I weren't, but I am."

His palm began to strain toward its destination, though no more so than the fabric of his jeans. "We must—"

"Yes," she whispered. "Yes, I know." Her lower lip trembled; her eyelids closed halfway; her breath caught and held in her lungs.

"Ivy, we've got to do something," he exclaimed.

"And about time, too," she said.

"We have to make plans," he said anxiously. "I still don't know all that's going on around here."

She looked at him for a very long time. "No kidding," she said at last.

He looked at her, looked at his hand that was suddenly flung into his lap, looked at her hand working deftly on the buttons of her blouse, and reeled from the emotional implications that struck him like a brick.

"Jesus," he said.

"Gideon, you are absolutely the most . . ." She flipped the braid back over her shoulder, nearly taking his chin off in the process, and straightened her shoulders, which managed in otherworldly contortions to take swift care of the rest of the buttons. "You are . . ."

"Yes, I know," he said glumly. "I'm a fool, a jerk, a sad sack, a dreamer, a miserable and low-down dirty rat who doesn't deserve to walk in your footsteps or crawl in your wake or touch the hem of your gown or—''

Her exasperated scream was probably not heard beyond the reach of the fire, but it was enough to deafen him, and enough to make him gape when she grabbed his ears and slammed his face into her bosom; a rather nice bosom for all that it was suffocating him, he thought, and one that he supposed he might well be able to get used to if it weren't being used as a most unusual, albeit effective, weapon against his stupidity. Unless, he thought further, it wasn't being used as a weapon at all, but rather as a method of womanly comfort for his troubled soul and his meekness in accepting his destiny. Of course, it might also, when one thought about it long enough and depending on how long one could hold one's breath, be part of a plan she had to seduce him.

He smiled.

He sighed.

He accepted his subordinate position and would have attempted to elaborate on it had he not been unable to get his hands free, and had there not been a knock on the tent's flap.

Ivy froze, scowled over her shoulder and told whoever it was to get the hell out because she was in strategic conference with the man who had traveled the length and height of the world to reach her side in order to assist her in her fight for the freedom of her people.

Whoever it was paused, then knocked again.

"I don't believe it," she said, slipping off his lap and rebuttoning her blouse. "I really don't believe it."

Gideon, deciding it would be better if he remained in his chair, crossed his legs at the knees with some difficulty and envied his cheeks their brush with immortality. Then he stood up anyway when Chute, Morj, and York marched into the tent, saluted Ivy, snarled at him, and announced just this side of primness that there seemed to be something wrong with the sky.

ELEVEN

Ivy found it difficult to keep the scorn and distaste from her voice. "What? You dare interrupt me for a story like that, at a time like this? Are you nuts?"

York stepped forward with a flourish of hair and sword. "We are only doing our duty," he said stiffly. "We saw something we thought you ought to know about, and we could not shirk our responsibility."

Gideon thought it best to stay out of it, especially when the Vondels looked at him as one and as much as told him with their narrow-eyed expressions that they would cut off his head if he so much as opened his mouth.

Ivy did not miss the moment. "York," she said.

York looked back at her. He smiled. The others smiled too, but they kept looking at Gideon.

"So tell me again. What's going on?"

"The sky," he said. "There is something amiss with the sky."

"Where?" she demanded.

"There," Chute said, pointing upward.

At a nod from Ivy, Gideon hurried to the entrance, drew back the flap, and looked up. At first, he saw nothing out of the ordinary; then he took several steps away from headquarters, and noticed that the stars he had seen earlier were not as numerous, nor were they as luminous. At the same time, he was able to detect a faint leathery sound up there, much like the slow flap of many wings that had been somehow muffled.

And as he frowned in puzzlement, he realized that the sky was not the only area that exhibited a certain amount of irregularity more than the usual irregularity which he was, god help him, getting used to.

The encampment, much to his astonishment and unease, had fallen completely silent. The songs had been sung, the chatter silenced, and he knew instinctively that all the men and whatevers around him were not simply asleep.

The feeling he had now was one of an intensive collective listening.

And many of the fires had been extinguished, bringing to bear the full impression of a night soon to be shattered.

Chute came out and stood beside him. "Boy, are you in trouble."

"Not me," he said, still looking up. "Ivy and I got along just fine."

"With York, I mean," the man said. "He thinks you two were having close consultation in there of a kind we never learned in boot camp."

Gideon couldn't help staring at him. "You were in boot camp?"

Chute nodded, and lifted one leg. "Sure. You think you buy these things just anywhere?"

The leathery-winged sounds grew louder, and on the fringes of the camp they could hear animals screaming prescient warnings of doom on the wing.

"So," Chute said, polishing his dagger on his sleeve. "Were you, or what?"

"Was I what?" he answered, squinting at the stars that were fading even more.

"Consulting."

"None of your business," he said absently.

"Morj won't like that."

"I think—" Gideon began, and decided instead to return to the tent, where he found York and Morj dueling silently in the corner. Ivy, ignoring them completely, was strapping on a belt from which dangled various sheaths and scabbards and pouches; when she saw him, she blew him a kiss and said, "The time has come to show me what you can do."

"Here?" he said.

"No, there," she said, pointing to the flaps.

"But there's people out there!"

"So? You think you can shadowbox out of this war, or what?"

Suddenly the leathery sounds increased dramatically, to a great flapping roar that deafened all who heard it; and before anyone could react, the roof of the tent was torn to shreds, and great, leathery bird-things dropped to the ground. There was no time to think, only to react.

Morj yelled a terrified warning; York spun around and pinked one of the attackers on its fleshy, disjointed beak; and Chute blew a curl out of his eye just as another leathery thing landed with a birdlike chortle, swiped him with a wing and sent him pinwheeling through the tent's wall.

Gideon, bat in hand and praying for divine intervention, battered the spine of one creature, dented the kneecap of another too slow to move out of the way, and charged to Ivy's side just as she was snared by a pair of filthy-looking talons that hadn't been trimmed since Wamchu was a baby. He brought the bat down on the thing's wing, and it screamed, released her, and swung its green-feathered, topknotted head like a ram into his chest. He gasped and fell to the ground, scrambled to his feet again and aimed for the other wing as it grabbed Ivy a second time. It screamed and swung its head around, ramming his chest and tumbling him into a chair, which broke when he landed on it and flung him sprawling to the ground. He leapt to his feet, sideswiped with the bat a creature that was snipping the curls from York's brow, and threw himself with a vengeance on the thing that a third time grabbed Ivy in its talons.

The din was horrid.

The smell was overpowering.

When the leathery thing ducked away from Gideon's charge, he dove for Ivy, grabbed her foot, and fell backward when her boot slipped off, leaving him nothing but laces to remember her by. With an animalistic growl he tossed the footgear aside, got to his feet, but was too late to stop the thing that held Ivy from tossing her in a perfect spiral to another thing, which snatched her out of the air with a deftness that belied its clumsy appearance. Gideon swerved to intercept her, but was tripped when Chute climbed back into the tent and was knocked aside by an errant but earnest tailfeather.

He called out.

Ivy swore.

He sprang to his feet and swung the bat wildly over his head. But it missed the leathery flying thing, which launched itself with a harsh, laughing shriek through the tent's rent roof and vanished triumphantly into the night. As if that were a signal, the others left as well, either flying or running, depending upon their condition so long as it wasn't dead, and within moments the four men were left alone amid the devastation.

"Boy," Chute said, "are we in trouble now."

"Speak for yourself," Gideon snapped in disgust, and hurried as best he could into the open. His ribs ached, his left leg felt as if it had been pulled from his hip, and his right eye was watering fiercely. Yet he was still able to spot Ivy, up there, kicking and screaming as she was carried away toward the black of the horizon, and parts unknown.

Helplessly, he waved his impotent bat in the creature's direction, and just as helplessly watched as it outlined itself cleverly against the full of the moon and made sure he was able to see his love's dangling figure—still now, limp, little more than a speck, a mote, a twisted black extension of the thing's black and twisted talons.

Shit, he thought, and slammed the bat at the ground, opening up a hole into which York fell when he raced out, over which Morj leapt agilely, and into which Chute stared.

"Trouble," the man said. "You really love trouble, don't you?"

The camp's stillness erupted into turmoil, concern, and unbridled rage.

Once word had spread of the tragic result of the night

attack on headquarters, it was all the Vondel brothers could do to prevent the entire army from charging out headlong into the darkness to bring Ivy back. It was impossible, they argued; the creatures had flown away, and there was no telling in what direction they had gone or where they had taken Ivy. Still the troops raged and swore and broke into impromptu mournful song as they wandered from place to place in search of something, anything, to do in order not to think that they might already be defeated before the last battle had even begun.

Gideon wandered as well.

With his gaze on the stars in hope of seeing Ivy one more time, he stumbled through the encampment in a doleful daze, ignoring those who called out his name, brushing aside those who would cling to him for comfort.

Ivy was gone.

And it was all his fault.

Not that he would have been able to drive off all the creatures that had so savagely infiltrated the tent, and not that he would have been able to fling himself on the back of one of the flying things and ridden precariously to the enemy camp and there rescue her in a pyrotechnic blaze of surprise and glory, and not that he would have been able to grab her away from the iron grip of those talons.

No; if he had only resisted her seductive urges, if he had not buried himself so willingly in the admittedly delectable pillows of her arbor, he would have noticed the wing sounds sooner, noticed the quiet that had fallen over the camp, and he would have been ready.

Some hero, he thought sourly; some lousy hero.

He had no idea how much time had passed, or how far he had wandered, but when he next took stock of his surroundings he found himself on the eastern edge of the camp, the last tent behind him, the plain stretching ahead toward the dark line of a stand of trees. Perhaps, he thought, he could go there and hang himself with his bat belt; that would teach him a lesson about alertness and temptation. Perhaps he might even find solace in death, and, with luck, a bit of absolution. Of course, if he were dead, it wouldn't do him much good to

know he'd been absolved, but it might count for something if
there was anything on the Other Side.

On the other hand, if there was no Other Side, he'd only be
dead, and that wouldn't solve anything except the misery of
his life.

Slowly, painfully, he lowered himself to the ground, put
his hands to his face and suddenly wanted more than anything
just to rest, to fall asleep and wake up and find everything the
way it once was, the way it should be . . . the way he wanted
it to be, without any of the hassles.

And with his eyes closed, he saw it again—the plain,
unbroken to a bloodred horizon under a pale red sky. And the
figure he had dreamt of before was nearer now, still dark
enough to be featureless, yet close enough for him to know
that it was no man who watched him, no man who waited for
him, out there, in the wilderness.

He could not see the face.

He knew it was Agnes.

Agnes Wamchu, denizen of the dark, empress of psychic
hells, hater of him, and dressed in black silk.

He sensed, suddenly, that she was smiling, a one-sided
smile that told him all he needed to know about his future, if
he was foolhardy enough to carry on with his task, stupid
enough to believe he might actually defeat her.

On her Day, when all who were smart and wise would be
digging their own graves to save her the trouble.

Damn, he thought; nobody's even bothered to tell me when
the hell it is.

His hands dropped quickly, and he blinked to drive the
vision away, blinked again and stood, biting his lip against an
ache that spread across his ribs.

Chute's right, he thought, there ain't nothing but trouble.

He sighed, turned, and saw Red trotting toward him, and
on the lorra's back a young man dressed in rough hides and a
black leather vest. For a brief moment a brief smile twitched
his lips, and he held out his arms as Tag Kori leapt to the
ground and embraced him.

* * *

"I heard you were here," the young man said, almost in tears. "I looked and looked for you; then I saw Red and I asked him to find you."

"I'm glad you did," Gideon said, holding the handsome teenage boy at arm's length and sighing. "I think I was about to talk myself into doing something stupid." They hugged again and patted each other's back in commiseration for their shared sorrow. "I've missed you, lad. I hate to admit it, but I really have missed you."

Tag ducked his head. "Well, I haven't had anyone to save from drowning since you fell into the Rush. It's been kind of boring."

Gideon had to laugh at the memory of their first meeting, and dropped to the ground cross-legged, pulling the boy down beside him. "I guess you've heard."

Tag nodded, his thatch of brown hair spilling over his shoulders, his forehead, his ears, his eyes. He didn't seem to notice. He was more concerned with the dust settling on his vest. "Sure did," he said. "So what are you going to do, and can I come with you? I'm good at this, you know. See, the way I figure it, if we don't take the rest of the army with us, we can get a good sneak up on them, then surround them before they know what's happening, and tear off their wings while we get Ivy back, safe and sound."

"Tag, there are only two of us."

"And Red. Don't forget Red."

"Tag, we—"

"So we surround them on three sides instead of four. We can still dismember a few, then burn their castles to the ground and pillage their crops and—"

"Tag, I don't even know where they've gone."

Tag cut himself off with a gasp, and looked at him strangely. "You don't?"

Gideon shook his head.

"Well, why not?"

"Ivy didn't tell me."

"She didn't?"

"There wasn't much time, Tag. We were discussing the

situation when those . . . those things broke into the tent and took her off.''

"They did?"

He waited.

"Right," Tag said. "They did." Then the boy glanced behind him at the camp, hunched over, and leaned closer. "Well, listen," he whispered. "Don't tell anybody, but I know where they are."

TWELVE

Gideon wasn't sure he had heard the young man correctly, and wasn't at all sure he wanted to. Destiny, however, and the machinations that had contrived his life thus far, prevented him from forgetting what he thought he had heard.

Tag looked at him expectantly.

Gideon struggled with the temptation just to carry on as before and convince himself that Ivy, being no slouch in the killing and battle areas of her life, was probably already on her way home. She was, after all, an independent woman who took what she wanted when she wanted it, and only occasionally did she err on the side of wanting what she couldn't take when she wanted to take it.

In this case, that just might be her freedom.

On the other hand, if she found Agnes, there was no way in hell Agnes was going to let her go, not until she had Gideon firmly in her grasp.

In other circumstances, under other skies, that might not have been so bad a prospect as to cause his flesh to dimple; but this was here, and now was now, and his flesh dimpled, and his throat went dry.

Tag cleared his throat.

Gideon lifted his shoulders in silent resignation and said, "What did you say?"

"I said, I know where they are."

Damn, he thought, I knew this was going to happen.

"You? But how?"

"Ivy told me."

"She did?"

"Sure. First thing yesterday morning. She was planning a major raid there before the big fight so she could knock out some of the bad guys and keep them from coming after us. We were going to kill a few, maim a few, raise a little heck, if you know what I mean."

"You were?"

"Sure we were. We weren't going to tell everybody, because then it wouldn't be a raid, it would be a battle. She didn't want a full-scale battle."

"She didn't?"

Tag managed to look disgusted and sympathetic simultaneously. "Of course not. Not while Agnes is loose. Can you imagine what would happen if she tried a battle now, with Agnes loose, and the Wamchu loose, and . . ." The boy shuddered. "You really shouldn't talk like that, Gideon. You'll scare everyone away, and then there'll be no one left to fight."

Gideon took a deep breath, held it, stared at the sky, stared at the lorra who was curled up beside him, stared at the boy and closed his eyes briefly. This was growing painful, primarily because he was actually beginning to understand what was going on, and that understanding was making him dizzy with the knowledge that he wasn't, he didn't think, going crazy.

"So what you're saying is—and correct me if I'm wrong, for god's sake—what you're saying is that those things tonight took Ivy to Agnes's camp, the location of which you already know, and that if you take more than a few men with you to rescue her, the Wamchu will get mad because he'll think the last battle is starting before you guys agreed it should."

Tag nodded vigorously.

"That," he said with a calmness that amazed himself, "is

the dumbest thing I've ever heard of. How the hell can you agree with the enemy when to start the war?''

Tag was astonished, but when he looked around there was no one to help him. "But the war's already started, Gideon. It's just the fighting we have to agree on.''

Gideon stood, walked away with his hands in his pockets, walked back with his hands out of his pockets, and told himself to be reasonable, that the rules here weren't necessarily the rules back home as he understood them, and he really shouldn't let his blood pressure work its way to the boiling point just because the rules for war here were just as stupid as the rules for war there, only different.

"All right," he said at last. "All right, you win. Let's go and have it done with. Up and at 'em, boy.''

"For what?"

"To get Ivy.''

"Now?''

"Right now.''

"Gideon, we can't!''

"What are you talking about? This was your idea in the first place, wasn't it? Weren't you the one who wanted me and Red to surround them?''

Tag, instantly recognizing the semantic trap he had fallen into, spread his arms helplessly in an attempt to recover; Gideon, seeing the lad's distress, was not moved to help him, and repeated his determination to get on with the timely rescue, though by now it was doubtful that timely had anything to do with it.

"But if we go after Ivy now," Tag protested, "some of the rest of the guys, or maybe even all of the rest of the guys, will know what we're doing and they'll come after us, and if they come after us, then we really will get into a—''

For the first time in a long time, Gideon lost his temper.

He reached down, grabbed Tag by the vest and pulled him roughly to his feet, off his feet, held him face-high and did his best not to shake him until his neck broke. "I don't give a damn about your rules, boy," he said, hoping he sounded meaner than he felt. "Ivy is caught, and I am going to get her back. You can come with me if you want, or you can stay here and explain to all those men back there how the rules have stopped you from rescuing their leader. It's your choice.''

Tag's face grew faintly red.

''All I need from you, in fact, are directions.''

''But—''

Gideon held him a bit higher and smiled without a trace of mirth. ''Directions, boy. Now!''

Tag's legs kicked weakly, his face darkened, his eyes stared wildly over Gideon's shoulder, and his vest began to tear at the seams. He gurgled. Gideon glowered. He sputtered, and Gideon managed to catch a few words, the last of which made him loosen his hold.

Tag dropped, swayed, sprawled on the ground, and readjusted his vest.

''What did you say?''

The boy gurgled.

''No, after that.''

The boy sputtered, and Gideon nodded. ''That's what I thought you said.''

The boy gulped for air, rubbed his face and neck, and pushed himself painfully up to a sitting position. ''True,'' he gasped. ''It's true. Ivy isn't the leader. Not the real leader. She just wanted to impress you.''

''I'm impressed.''

''She knew you would be. She told me so. She said you were a very impressionable person.''

Gideon's nod was brusque, as much to tell himself not to blame the lad for Ivy's deception as to chase off a ringing in his ears. The discordant ringing that began whenever he hesitated to ask the question he knew had to be asked, but didn't want to ask because the answer would only bring him more trouble than he already had. He thought it probably would in this case, since he had a sinking sensation of already knowing the answer.

''So,'' he said. Swallowed. Tried again. ''So, where is the real leader?''

Tag seemed reluctant to say anything, and Gideon immediately looked suspiciously around him, just in case the real leader was standing in the shadows, waiting for a dramatic entrance. She wasn't, not this time. Not that she didn't always make dramatic entrances. The first time he'd met Glorian Kori, she had come out of his pantry, slugged him, got him into a fight with a monster in his kitchen, and brought him back here with her—to search for the white duck.

"So?" he said.

"I don't know where she is," Tag insisted as he staggered to his feet and ruefully examined the damage to his vest. "She never tells me anything. She never tells anyone anything, for that matter, but she specifically doesn't tell me anything because she's afraid I'll tell someone."

Gideon nodded, nudged Red with his boot and stood back as the lorra scrambled to his feet snorting and lashing his tail and generally behaving as if he were ready for a good bloody fight. Then he suggested to both Tag and Red that they get some sleep because, at first light, they were heading out to find Ivy and bring her back.

"Alone?" Tag asked nervously.

"We'll get some people to help us."

"Not a lot, though," the boy cautioned. "We can't have a lot or the Wamchu will get mad."

Gideon frankly didn't give a damn if the Wamchu was mad or not, didn't much care if Tag was worried that the Wamchu would get mad, and muttered that he wished to hell someone would tell him what he was doing here in the first place so that he could tell them what they could do with their explanations so he could go back home and do his crossword puzzles.

"What's a crossword puzzle?" Tag asked.

"None of your business," Gideon snapped, and waited for Red to recurl himself on the ground. He snuggled down beside the lorra and closed his eyes, listened to the hubbub of the camp fade slowly to silence, and wondered why no one else had launched a search party yet. Surely one or more of the Vondels would have done so in their eagerness to prove to Ivy their worth, their love, and their undying loyalty; surely one of the other leaders must be angry enough to want to avenge the humiliating attack in the midst of their own camp; surely Glorian, who didn't really care for Ivy one way or the other but knew what a good fighter she was, would have done something to bring her back.

So many possibilities, and nothing happening at all as far as he could tell.

Unless, he thought so suddenly that his eyes blinked, I'm missing something here.

He sat up and scratched idly at his beard and neck.

None of this makes sense. Ivy is too valuable. They shouldn't be taking it all this calmly.

Unless, he thought suddenly a second time, they know something I don't, like . . . it was planned from the beginning, and this is the way it was supposed to be.

But that was silly. Why would they risk the lives of the Vondels and others just to get Ivy captured?

Unless, he thought suddenly, and winced at the headache he was getting, it was to get someone into the enemy camp so some expert spying could be done.

He smiled at himself. That wasn't much better, but it did make a perverted kind of sense, the only thing missing being a way to get messages out without having the messenger killed in the process.

Unless . . .

He took his time.

Unless they chose Ivy from all the others who could have done it because they knew that Gideon would go after her, which would result not only in her rescue but also in the retrieval of whatever vital information she had, and the only cost would be the possible forfeiture of his life.

He lay down again.

He thought about the dark figure on the red-washed plain, and the smile he was sure had been directed at him; he wondered if the vision was merely symbolic of the Wamchus' hatred of him, or if it was a real place, and the place where Ivy was being held right now.

He wondered, dully, if any of it mattered.

He listened to Red snoring, he listened to Tag snoring, and he listened to his heart thumping miserably away in his chest, too much like a prisoner thumping on the cell door. It meant that he was afraid; it meant he was looking for a way out; it meant he was feeling inadequate again because it meant that he, among all the giant canaries and bubble-eyed centipedes and not quite human men, was expendable.

After all he had done for them since he had arrived, he, Gideon Sunday, was expendable.

Shit, he thought.

And "Shit," he said.

And he sat up again and wondered just what the hell it was he had to do to make them accept him.

And where the hell was Tuesday when he needed her? Why wasn't she here, waddling ridiculously along at his side, needling him, scolding him, showing him the way to save his life and, at the same time, do his duty without shame, without guilt, without the trauma of his past?

Red snored.

Tag snored, and whimpered a little.

Of Tuesday there was no sign, and he knew then that he was truly alone in this dismal predicament.

He stood with a martyred groan that only made Red roll over and snore louder, and walked wearily away from the camp, into the featureless plain, and suggested to his equivocations that perhaps he was only feeling sorry for himself, for the mistakes he had made, and for the mistaken impressions he'd had about what a hero's lot ought to be.

He watched the sun come up and was mildly astonished because he didn't remember falling asleep.

He watched the blue sun come up, and realized it wasn't the sun at all.

After all this time, after all his wishes and hopes, it was a Bridge, an honest-to-god Bridge just like the one he had crossed to come here all those months ago.

"Damn," he whispered.

Because its appearance, here and in this place, made him feel worse than ever, because a Bridge only appeared when there was need, and he understood, fully and for the first time, that his need, whatever it was now, was greater than his desire to save this world, or rescue Ivy. It was even greater than his familial duty to help his beloved Tuesday get back her steak-loving body, god help him.

It was, Gideon thought, a lousy deal, but one that stood shimmering before him, waiting for his decision.

With a glance back at a world that he thought didn't really want him, didn't really care, Gideon felt a sharp pang of regret before he stepped through.

THIRTEEN

"Well, I'll be damned and gone to hell," said Gideon almost reverently, when his vision cleared and his head cleared and he saw where he was.

A miracle, and no question about it; it was a pure and simple miracle of the sort that defies all explanation.

He was in a pantry. His by-god-and-burn-the-lease pantry, if his eyes weren't deceiving him and those ratty, untrustworthy shelves and patina-enhanced jars of his sister's preserves hadn't been cleverly duplicated by someone with an extraordinarily perverse sense of humor. If it was true, and there was no reason to believe it wasn't save for the roaming instability of his mind's present condition, then all he had to do was walk through that door over there and he would be in his kitchen. His very own kitchen. In the splendid Garden State of New Jersey and as far away as he could get from the insanity he'd just left behind.

Which he checked immediately he thought it, and saw that the rear wall still resembled an oversized and slightly tilted window overlooking a dark and featureless plain, and a darker and starless sky. No one seemed to be out there. No one seemed to have followed him.

He took a step back, and the window remained.

There was still no one in apparent pursuit, either to bring him back or to make sure he didn't come back.

He backed all the way to the door and put his hand on the familiar, clammy brass knob, turned it, grinned abruptly at his good fortune—after all, he could have ended up in Fort Worth or Philadelphia—whirled, and stepped boldly into his kitchen.

True, he thought then; it's true!

"Hot damn, it's home!" he shouted, hands raised in victory and feet doing a passable two-step in escapist jubilation. "Hot damn, the boy has finally returned to the land of the living!"

And he didn't even move right away when a woman screamed, and didn't flee when a second and then a third woman screamed shrilly, and something was flung at him from the direction of the sink, which, he noted as he ducked and the plate smashed on the floor behind him, had been replaced with one much larger than the one that had come with the house when he'd bought it.

He straightened cautiously, his hand automatically cupping the knob of his bat, which, when he looked down, suddenly appeared unnervingly ordinary.

Then he looked up again, at the three women huddled together by the sink.

They were, conservatively, old.

They might even have been ancient.

It was difficult to tell, since they were primly swaddled in bulky bathrobes that had long since lost their color and wearing floppy slippers that had the faces of bunny rabbits on them, and their hair, what there was left of it, was netted and haircurled and otherwise unnaturally twisted into shapes they couldn't have managed in their teenage years, which had to have been at least sixty years ago.

One of them, rotund and indignant, advanced on him with an upraised rolling pin. "Who the hell are you?" she demanded, while one of the others scuttled out of the room.

"I live here," he said in amazement. Not only was the sink changed, the whole damned room was changed. Everything, from cupboards to microwave oven, was new, gleaming, and smelled of old ladies, burned toast, and bread that had baked just a fraction too long. "What's going on here?"

"Don't talk to him, Daisy," the second woman said. She was not as heavy as the first, but her jowls were impressive. "Just hold him there while Rose gets the cops."

Daisy, her arm and all that dangled from it quivering under the weight of the rolling pin, nodded and glared at him fiercely. "Who are you?" she asked again, and took a step toward him, intending menace in spite of the bunnies covering her feet.

"I told you," he said. "I live here. So would you mind telling me what's going on?"

Daisy looked to her companion. "He says he lives here."

"He can't live here. Look at him!"

Daisy did, and lowered her weapon with a sigh. "Yes, I am."

The second woman snorted in disgust, marched forward, snatched the rolling pin from Daisy's hand, and shook it under his chin. "Don't you dare try anything, pal. I'm not as fragile as I look."

"Lady—"

"Violet," she corrected huffily. "The name is Violet Dumark, which is none of your business. That's Daisy LaRoy, who is also none of your business."

"Pleased to meet you," he said absently, walked around her and peered down the hall toward the foyer. There was a dim glow from the living room, but otherwise the house was dark. It was not, however, empty. After a moment, he could hear excited high voices coming from upstairs. Obviously, the place had been taken over by an army of bag women, or squatters, and he was going to kill the neighbors for letting this happen without telling him first.

When he looked back, Daisy had stripped her hair of its nighttime security and was trying to coil a strand of it coyly around her little finger.

Violet, however, came after him again. "I want to know why you were in there," she demanded, jowls jumping. "It's a crime, you know, spying on women like this, taking advantage of helpless females in their declining years."

"It's not a crime, it's a miracle," Daisy offered breathlessly, and was hushed by a look that would have sent her instantly to the crematorium had she not taken the moment to pour herself a glass of water to ease the flush that had reddened her rouge-laden cheeks.

Gideon, paying little attention to the strange women in his house, shook his head in wonderment, turned and walked down the hallway, Violet threatening him from behind, the voices louder as he reached the foot of the stairs. Then he looked into the living room and grabbed at the wall for support.

"My god," he said. "My god!"

A lamp was burning in the far corner, and he rubbed a knuckle across his eyes just to be sure he wasn't hallucinating. When Violet jabbed him in the small of the back, he reached around without looking and yanked the rolling pin from her hand.

"Well, I never!" she declared.

"Liar," said Daisy. "Don't you remember that milkman in Omaha? Four times before he could get away, as I recall."

"Three, and don't bring it up again. You know what the warden said—the past is past, and we have to look to the future if we want to contribute our share."

Gideon walked stiff-legged into the room, and gaped. The furniture, his old, comfortable, sagging furniture was gone, as well as his stereo and television and, Jesus Christ, even his crossword puzzle books! All had been replaced with plastic-webbed lawn chairs, fan-backed wicker chairs, an oval braided rug, a bamboo couch, and standing lamps whose shades were tassled and red. The bay window had decorative iron bars on the outside. The fireplace was bricked up.

He whirled, and the two women retreated hastily. "What the bloody hell is going on around here?" he said, fairly shouting. "What do you think you're—" Then he looked at the staircase, and whatever else he was going to say was drowned in his throat when a chorus line of mummified Ziegfeld girls crowded each other to get a good look at him. He pointed a trembling finger. "And who the hell are they?"

Immediately, every woman in the foyer began talking,

questioning, explaining, and paying no heed to Violet, whose jowls were so agitated they were bruising her shoulders. Finally, Rose, the woman who had gone to call the police, stormed out of the dining room, shouted for silence, and stood in the doorway with her arms folded imperiously across the general area of a long-forgotten chest. She and Gideon glared at each other for nearly a full minute before she flung open the door and pointed.

"Go!" she ordered.

"Like hell," he said.

Violet snatched the rolling pin from his hand and stood beside Rose. "Go," she said.

"Like hell," he said.

Daisy joined them, looked up at her friends on the stairs and told them he had just appeared, like a scruffy angel, out of the pantry. There were exclamations of disbelief, of wonder, of yearning, of outright lascivious suggestion, but no one made a move when he unholstered his baseball bat and rested it carefully on his shoulder.

The house quieted.

The bat felt disturbingly more ordinary then he had sensed earlier.

"Now," he said, when Violet reluctantly lowered her own weapon without actually letting go of it, "would someone mind telling me what you ladies are doing in my house?"

"This . . ." Daisy inched forward, her face flushed, her eyes sparkling myopically. "This isn't your house. It's ours." When Rose cleared her throat in obvious reprimand, Daisy hunched her shoulders. "Well, it really isn't ours except in the sense that we all live here from time to time. But it's certainly more ours than yours."

Rose and Violet nodded emphatically.

The women on the staircase nodded as well.

"I'm sorry," he said, "but you're wrong. I don't know what you're doing here or who's been telling you all these lies, but I'm afraid that I am really the owner."

"But you can't be," said Violet, one hand to her face. "The owner's dead."

"I am not," he said angrily.

"But you can't be the owner. It . . ." She frowned, sensing perhaps that this was a classic case of mistaken identity, and only the bat on the man's shoulder gave her pause. "The man who used to own this tatty little place," she said, "is dead. A long time ago. His name—"

"Gideon Sunday," Gideon said.

"Right! A has-been football player. A quarterback, I believe," she added with a moue of distaste. "He disappeared without a trace, and took all the scotch with him. The state bought the place, and now here we are."

Gideon felt his legs giving way, and he leaned against the wall. "Has-been."

"Never was, as far as I'm concerned," Daisy said. "But then, I was always partial to linebackers."

"Partial to postmen, too," said Rose.

Daisy scowled. "That's Violet!"

"Milkmen," Violet corrected. "You're postmen. I'm milkmen. Rose is trees."

"Trees?" Gideon said, then quickly waved the explanation away. He didn't want to know. He wasn't even sure he wanted to know what had happened to his house, which wasn't his house any longer because the state in its totalitarian wisdom had purchased it for some mysterious purpose after he had supposedly died. Mysteriously, no doubt.

But for god's sake, a silent voice argued in lieu of coherent thought, how much time had passed since he'd gone into the pantry? Didn't it take seven years for a missing man to be declared legally dead? Didn't there have to be inquiries, searches, sheriff's auctions, lawyers?

He blinked.

The women waited.

I'm dead, he thought; Jesus H, I'm dead.

Daisy, who had apparently seen how stricken he was, put out her hand and touched his arm. "Was he a friend of yours?" she asked kindly. "Did you know him very well? The man who lived here, I mean."

"In a way," he managed when he'd gotten his breath back.

"I'm sorry."

"Daisy!" Violet hissed.

"Oh, shove it, Vi," she said. "Can't you see the boy's in trouble?" Hesitantly, she approached him, looked at the bat until he lowered it and finally placed it in its holster. Then she led him to the doorway and pointed to the porch. A chilly breeze gusted into the foyer. "Maybe a breath of fresh air."

"Yes," he muttered. "Or a good stiff drink."

"Now that's an idea," Violet said, and Rose silenced her with a firm grip on her arm. "Well, it is a good idea. I always get my best ideas when I've had a bracer."

"Hush, girl," Rose told her in exasperation. "Daisy, don't you think—"

"It'll clear your head," Daisy told him. "Autumn is always the best time to clear your head."

He didn't have the faintest idea what she was talking about, but he stepped out onto the porch anyway and inhaled deeply, slowly, several times, massaging his forehead with a thumb while his other hand rubbed his chest as if fending off a threatened heart attack. Then the door slammed behind him, and as he turned he heard the bolt slam into place.

A fist snapped up to pound on the wood, then lowered when he discovered that somewhere between the bunny slippers and the bamboo couch he had lost much of his strength.

It was, of course, a nightmare.

Just like in those movies he always hated.

He would wake up any moment now and find himself back on the plain—no, back in his bed, up in his room, and the convention of grandmothers would be gone. When he sneezed, he decided that a nightmare might be too obvious; it was probably some sort of alcoholic stupor induced by his polishing off that last bottle of mediocre scotch he kept in the sideboard which, he recalled with a horrified shudder, was also gone. In which case, he was under the influence of one of Whale's spells, except that Whale was in Rayn, which didn't do him any good because none of it existed, right?

He faced the street.

Ivy, he thought; Ivy isn't here, and I am.

The neighborhood was the same, as far as he could tell, even to the burned-out streetlamp on the corner, down by the all-night drugstore that had the largest liquor department in town, and the most extensive display of trusses and wheelchairs in its window.

He staggered down the steps to the sidewalk, looked in both directions, and decided to go left. There was only one person he could call, one person he could depend on to give him the straight answers he required. And once that was accomplished, he would come right back, break down the door, and throw those interlopers out on their collective, padded butts before they had a chance to organize.

There was no question that his desperation had forced him into contacting his agent.

FOURTEEN

Easier thought, he thought, than done.

Ten minutes later, shivering and sneezing, he found a public telephone. With a sigh and a vengeful smile, he lifted the receiver, reached into his pocket, groped and moaned, and replaced the receiver. He had no money. He couldn't call his agent, his accountant, or even the police because he was stranded in the real world without so much as a single dime in his pocket. Then he looked at the telephone and gasped. Christ, even if he had a dime, he wouldn't be able to use it, because now the damned thing required a quarter.

An automobile sped past, and he jumped, startled at the noisy intrusion, realizing that it hadn't taken him very long to get used to the silence of the Plain, the stillness of the villages, the serenity of the forests, the placid acceptance of the quiet that seemed now like a dream that wasn't all that bad, all things considered.

A patrol car drove by, slowed, and backed up. Gideon smiled his most professional greeting and waited for the officers to ask him what he was doing on a street corner in the middle of the night holding a baseball bat. He looked at the bat, and looked at the car, and prayed that they thought he was a baseball fanatic and not a bat-wielding maniac.

No one got out.

111

He could hear the crackle of the radio inside, could see two dark shapes in the front seat, but neither of them made a move to open a door. Instead, the driver rolled down his window, spat onto the street, rolled up the window, rolled it down again and tossed out a cigarette butt, rolled it up again, and released the brake. The car drifted off.

Gideon watched, too confused to call out, or to run after it.

A truck's air horn made him clap a hand to his ear.

A white cat wandered by, hissed at him, and wandered on.

The hell with it, he thought, and started back toward the house. He would do it on his own—rid his land of the squatters, then call his agent to find out what had been going on in his absence. He would make up some excuse about taking a vacation, think of something else if the idea of a vacation didn't fit.

He hadn't gone a block when he saw a quarter glinting in the grass of someone's manicured lawn.

A sign; it was a sign, and he grabbed it up, ran back to the phone booth, and dialed his agent's number. When a man answered, his voice filled with sleep and annoyance, Gideon announced himself as he always did: "Hey, Scottie, when the hell do I get traded to Dallas?"

It took several seconds for the explosion of curses to calm down on the other end, and several seconds more before Giedon realized that his agent thought someone was playing a practical joke on him, at nearly three A.M., in the middle of the week, in the middle of football season. Hastily he tried to reassure the man that this wasn't a joke, the call was legitimate, and if it wasn't an emergency he most assuredly would have waited at least until the sun was up.

"Jeez, pal, who the hell is this?"

Giedon leaned against the booth's wraparound metal hood and grinned into the empty street. "It's Gideon!"

There was a silence.

"Hello? Hey, Scottie, you still there?"

"Who the hell is this?" Scottie was awake, and he still didn't sound happy.

"It's Gideon, damnit. And I need—"

"Pal, I don't know any Gideon, okay? So screw off and let—"

Gideon lost his temper. His agent had always been bad with names, particularly his, but right now he needed clear thinking, and he wasn't going to put up with the man's mental foibles. "Gideon Sunday, you stupid son of a bitch!"

There was a silence.

"Hello?"

"Look, pal, you want me to call the police or what? Just get the hell off the line and—"

Gideon strangled the receiver into submission, brought it back to his ear and said, "Scottie, this isn't funny. Not anymore. I need your help and I need—"

"You're right, pal, it ain't funny. I don't know who you are, but you sure as hell ain't Gideon Sunday."

"The hell I'm not!"

"Then you're a ghost, sucker, because Sunday died eight years ago."

The line went dead.

Gideon stared in disbelief at the receiver, at the cradle, at the dial, at the braided wire, at the receiver again as he slammed it down onto the cradle and caused the dial to spin halfway around.

Eight years?

He stepped away from the booth and shoved his hands into his pockets.

Eight years?

He looked up and down the block, and shrugged. What the hell, he thought; eight years is eight years, except in human terms when it's only a couple of months, and what the hell am I talking about?

He decided to return to the house.

Then he decided to run back to the house, break down the door, roust the old bats out of their beds, and find out just how far his delusion reached before it achieved overkill and sent him screaming into the night.

Eight years. Time can really be a bitch when it's moving on all fours.

* * *

Eight years, he thought as he stood in front of the house and looked at the tasteful black-and-gold sign on the lawn whose letters, even in the dark, well and truly proclaimed his little place the New Jersey Senior Citizen Reclamation Center.

Tuesday, he thought, is gonna lay an egg.

With a sigh at the light in the window that used to be his, he strode up the walk, took the porch steps in a single bound, and knocked on the door. Almost before his hand was back at his side, Rose answered, and he was inside before she could change her mind.

The ladies were gone from the staircase.

Violet was standing in the living room with the rolling pin, and gave him a sad, slow shake of her head. "You lost or something, stranger?"

"I think so," he said calmly.

"Violet," Rose snapped, "smash him one and let's call the police before the parole shits show up."

"Oh, language," Daisy admonished from the dining room entrance. "He may be crazy, but he is a man."

Rose looked disgusted. "Just hit him once, all right? Just once, so I can go to bed happy."

Violet looked at the rolling pin, considered the command, and, judging by her expression, decided she was too old to take on a man whose temper would probably wither her with a glance. Instead, she closed the door over Rose's protest and took Gideon by the arm. He looked down at her, and continued to stare as she brought him back into the kitchen, sat him at the table, and put on the kettle. Rose and Daisy followed.

Dead, he thought; my home is gone, and I am dead.

"The state," he muttered dully.

"That's right," Daisy said, slipping behind Gideon and removing his bat from its holster. "Didn't you know this was the New Jersey Senior Citizen Reclamation Center?"

He shook his head. "Not until I saw the sign out there."

"Well, it is."

He watched without speaking as Violet placed a cup of steaming tea in front of him, then reached into her robe and pulled out a bottle of moderately poor scotch. Ignoring Rose's condemning gaze, she laced, tatted, and quilted the tea until the steam stopped and Gideon was able to drink without gagging.

"My own recipe," the woman said, jowls aquiver with pride.

"Tasty," he said truthfully. "What do you ladies reclaim, if you don't mind me asking?"

I'm dead, he thought; Christ, eight years in the grave.

"Us," Rose said stiffly.

"You?" And then he remembered something, a comment about the warden. "Don't tell me this is a halfway house. For a prison."

"Got it in one," Violet said, grinning to prove that the teeth that were hers and the teeth that weren't were still able to be dazzling when she put her mind and red lips to it. "When we feel as if we're slipping back into our old ways, we come here, rest awhile, and then return to the outside world as productive members of a society that feels guilty as hell about neglecting us."

A longer silence prevailed.

And he didn't move when he heard the others shifting about, didn't look up when he heard someone hushing those who had gathered in the hall. He only sipped, and he only sighed, and when he took in the kitchen again, only Rose was there, sitting opposite him and smiling.

"Gideon Sunday," she said.

He nodded.

"I've heard of you, you know."

He almost smiled.

"Could throw the longest passes in the history of the known world, and once, in the middle of a game, gave twenty bucks to a center so he wouldn't tackle you."

He did smile. "My emergency fund."

Her grey hair was coiled snugly at the back of her head; her eyes were dark blue and starred about with wrinkles that added not age but laughter to her face. "Yes . . . I remember."

"And you're not surprised?"

She leaned back, though her hands stayed folded on the table. "There isn't much left that can surprise me, Gideon. Not much left at all." She looked over her shoulder at the now empty hall, looked up at the ceiling and sighed, deeply. "Actually, I'm only surprised that the things are still working. It's been a long time, and I thought, after a while, I'd only been dreaming."

"Things?"

"The Bridges."

He dropped the cup onto the saucer, fumbled it back into his hands; she laughed.

"Mine," she said without nostalgia, without regret, "was in Utah. In the middle of the Great Salt Lake. I was trying to commit suicide, but that's damned hard when you can't keep your head underwater for very long."

"A Bridge?"

"I don't know how long I spent over there," she continued. "Must have been years. I loved it, make no mistake about it. I really hated to come back."

"You used a Bridge?"

Rose stared at him. "What's the matter with you, boy? You get hit on the head or something?"

He refused to believe it, but there was no alternative. No one else could possibly know about them, no one else save those who had used them.

"Had a trouble?" she asked.

After a moment, he nodded.

"Going back?"

He shrugged. "You didn't."

"I had a man here," she said. "I loved him. When I got myself straightened out, I came back to him, and that put an end to that."

He looked to the ceiling. "He upstairs now?"

"A little farther up than that," she told him. "I shot him just twenty-two years ago today."

He looked surprised.

"You look surprised," she said. "What do you think they're trying to reclaim here, aluminum cans?"

"You shot him?"

"He was messing around with my sister. I would have shot her, too, but she was family. As it was, I broke both her legs and put her jaw in a cast."

Gideon rose, took a step toward the back door, toward the hall, toward the pantry, and stopped. He was confusing himself, and he had to get hold or he was going to scream.

"Go ahead," she said. "Screaming makes you feel good."

The temptation was there, but he resisted. "I . . . I think I don't want to be here anymore."

Rose smiled more broadly, stood and took his arm. "You feel a little disoriented?"

He nodded, and let her lead him to the pantry.

"That always happens when you get away from home for a while. Like a Martian who took the wrong turn at Jupiter. Or so I'm told."

She opened the door, but didn't look in.

He did, and saw the dark plain, the starless sky. Then he turned and put his hands on her shoulders. "You're trying to tell me something, right?"

She winked at him.

"You're trying to tell me that this isn't my home anymore, that it probably never really was, and as long as the world here thinks I'm dead, I should go back to my friends and the people I love, where I'll be happy, if not actually useful."

"Are you kidding?" she said.

"Huh?"

"This is a Reclamation Center, you jerk, haven't you been paying attention? It's a place where we can come when we feel ourselves slipping. Now, considering what most of us were in prison for in the first place, slipping isn't exactly swiping a scarf from the local department store."

There was noise in the hall. A lot of it. And some of it sounded like the sharpening of blades.

"Rose . . ."

She hugged him, reached into her robe and pulled out a small, nickel-plated revolver, which she aimed at his chest without a single waver of her spindly little hand. "He was a football player, too, the son of a bitch. You'd be amazed at how many owners know my name, especially when the other team looks like it's on a long winning streak. As a matter of fact," she added with a smug grin, "they think I killed you, too."

Gideon slugged her.

Armies of kindly grandmothers and obnoxious, wisecracking old maids marched across his vision, but he knew that every football player in the country would build a shrine to him if they knew what he had just done.

Then he slugged her again as she got up and shot him in the left thigh. The bullet burned, but not as badly as his knuckles, and he was just able to slam the pantry door shut before the horde burst into the kitchen. He staggered backward, horrified, as the door bulged, split by ax blades and splintered by feet callused from years of breaking cinder blocks and bricks, and fell in on one hinge as Daisy took the other out with his baseball bat.

He yanked it from her grasp, tripped her, and threw himself through the Bridge just as he heard Rose shrieking something about fetching the goddamned cannon before the bastard got away.

FIFTEEN

There is a message in all this, Gideon thought as he staggered to his feet and wiped blades of loose grass from his jeans; there is a message here about Kansas and Toto and Robert Frost and Thomas Mann, and I don't give a shit because—and he groaned when the trench the bullet had gouged in his leg flared up, and he was forced to drop to one knee. As far as he could tell in the darkness, he wasn't bleeding all that badly, but neither would he be able to do very much until he got himself fixed up.

A message. A theme. Would he ever be the same again, once he learned what it was?

"Damn," he said, "that hurts a lot."

Once, many years ago, his sister had tried to explain why Aesop's fables were so terribly important, why their postscripts had to be engraved on his heart if Gideon expected to make his way successfully in the world.

He'd asked her what grapes and a fox had to do with winning a football game, and she spent an hour drawing so many comparisons that he almost believed her.

But she couldn't explain why the fox just didn't throw a goddamned rock at the grapes. If he could talk, he could throw rocks. And the crow was a jackass.

Tuesday had yelled that he was deliberately being dense.

He had retorted that deliberate had nothing to do with it, and while he was at it, the hare was an idiot and tortoises smell, and if Little Red Riding Hood wasn't too young to get it on with the Hunter, then how the hell did she fall for a wolf in Grandma's clothing?

"That's Grimm," Tuesday'd told him.

"No shit," he had said, and turned on the television to watch the local, not to mention the national, sports news not mention his name again.

A minute passed, and so did some of the burning, and he stood again, wobbled, inhaled slowly and deeply, and began to limp toward the encampment, puzzled as he realized that most of the fires were out and there was so little noise that the place might have been deserted.

He slowed when a stirring of instinct suggested that he not call out to see if anyone was home.

He slowed even further when instinct hinted that making so much noise might bring him answers he wasn't yet equipped to handle, wounded as he was and stumbling around in the dark.

When he reached the first tent, he knew he was alone.

There were no troops, no pack animals, no scavengers, no rear guards, no forward guards. The smoldering fires he saw were not campfires but tents burning to ash, and the blackened earth, visible even in the limited light, told him that either the army had moved out and, as an incentive to continuing, had left nothing behind, or that the Wamchu, or Agnes, or both, had attacked the site in full force while he was gone, leaving no survivors, perhaps even taking no prisoners.

Gone, he thought, and looked up at the sky to see if he could judge how long it had been. But there were no clues to be seen—the stars and the moon were the same, though obviously they shone down on a world that was days, or weeks, or months, older than when he had left it.

Had that dreaded Day come and gone while he was back in New Jersey? No; if that were so, Agnes most assuredly would not only have murdered everyone who opposed her, she also would have done something about the Bridges, so to fend off potential attacks as well.

Unless, of course, she didn't need to because of her newfound power, in which case this was one hell of a mess, one he wasn't going to get out of easily, if at all.

He continued to prowl and, when he was positive he wasn't going to be sneaked up on from behind, or above, or below, or from the road, he whistled for Red and received no response; he called softly to Tag, and heard only the wind; and when he found Chute's beret lying on a pile of ashes near a firepit filled with sooty bones, he stuffed it in his hip pocket and looked at the empty sky again.

This probably means trouble, he thought.

And thought of poor Ivy, once more cruelly separated from him at the junction of their reunion. Gideon also thought of Tuesday, who would probably peck him to death for deserting her.

At that moment a searing wave of guilt dropped him to his knees—guilt for thinking only of himself when he lost the match with temptation and crossed the Bridge, guilt for believing that these people could throw him to the wolves as a sacrificial lamb merely to gain a few miserable bits of military intelligence.

Unless, he thought as he gripped his thigh just above his wound, it wasn't guilt at all but an onset of infection that was going to render him contra-ambulatory, not to mention legless.

He clenched his teeth and waited for the pain to subside.

He rose slowly, and continued his futile search.

An hour later he reached the red tent, and the sight of it, and the memory of his desertion, make him gnaw angrily on his lower lip.

The roof still sagged from the leathery flying things' assault, and the flaps had been viciously torn from their seams. The only sign of life was a flickering within. Stealthily, wincing, he made his way to the opening, whispered a name, and fell inside, his leg giving way with a creak like an old door. He rolled into a sitting position, thanked fortune for the lantern still burning atop one of the posts, and looked at his wound.

"Oh Christ," he said.

The jeans leg was soaked in blood, and the rent in its fabric testified to the size of the bullet Rose had fired at him during his departure.

He needed a tourniquet. He needed a disinfectant. He needed a doctor. He needed stitches. He needed blood.

His eyes closed against the pain; his palms flattened on the earthen floor and pressed down; his jaw tightened and his teeth ground together.

God, that hurts, he thought; sonofabitch, that really hurts.

There was a roiling surge of nausea and a rush of dizziness, and he fell back, groaning, trying to tell himself that the agony was all in his mind, though he knew damned well Rose wasn't that good a shot.

There were visions of Death on a giant goat, Hell yawning a pit constructed just for him, Heaven closing its gates to the tune of silver bells and harps and a tin whistle that persisted even when he reopened his eyes and saw that the sky had turned blue, the stars and moon finally gone.

He was too weak to lift his head, and so groped for his bat as the music drew nearer and there were footsteps outside. He would handle it. He had to handle it. He hadn't been thrown out of his old home and back into his new home for it all to end now, on a dirt floor in a tent that had no roof to speak of, and no comforts at all, and it was going to be hell when the winter rains finally came.

He shifted, and moaned, and the music stopped abruptly.

A shuffling outside, and a shadow filled the entrance.

He tensed, cursing his vulnerability, and his hand's refusal to take a good grip on the bat.

"My lord," a voice said, "you do manage to get into things, don't you, Gideon? Is it part of your football training, or are you that way naturally?"

With superhuman effort Gideon lifted his head and saw a man coming toward him with a ridiculous grin on his face—a thin man who obviously had once been dangerously fat, but whose subsequent weight loss hadn't been accompanied by a cosmetic tightening of his flesh. He wore a tattered purple cloak over a simple gold shirt and black trousers, a pair of dusty red boots, and a sword in a scabbard that thumped against his leg.

"Whale?" Gideon said.

Whale Pholler knelt beside him, plunged a hand into the pouch he wore on his right hip, and took out a vial, which he unstoppered and sniffed. "Jesus," the armorer said, wrinkling his nose and holding the vial at arm's length.

"Whale?"

"I never could pack for myself," the man said, replacing stopper and vial, and pulling out a smaller pouch, from which he scooped a viscous yellow salve. "I don't know what that stuff is for, but I think it would kill you if I made you drink it. This, on the other hand, is just what the doctor ordered."

"Whale?"

Whale spread the salve generously over the wound, holding Gideon down with one hand as the burning doubled, and redoubled, until Gideon lashed out with hands and feet and sent the man sprawling against the sagging tent wall.

"Whale, goddamnit!"

The burning stopped. The leg healed even as he watched. And the denim, for all that it had been through, pulled together in such a way that it left only a faint faded scar.

Gideon was not amazed, save for the fact that the salve had worked at all. Whale was not, even to his closest friends, the most effective of magicians, healers, or fighters. He preferred making armor and weapons, and only practiced the rest when circumstance and plot forced him into it.

Tuesday would vouch for that, though her language might not be quite so diplomatic. He, however, was just happy the man had shown up; the injury was taken care of, and he would worry later about whether or not his leg would turn to wood during the next full moon.

Once the healing process was complete, Whale assisted him to a chair, then fetched him water from a jug and food from another pouch, which Gideon insisted he taste first, in case it was the wrong pouch, or the wrong food, or the wrong century in the making. He was still weak when he finished, but he felt immeasurably better, and was even able to listen to his friend explain how, during every waking hour, he had felt terrible about sending Gideon into a potentially apocalyptic situation without so much as a by-your-leave and good-luck party. It had so weighed upon him that two days ago he had turned the reins of Rayn over to Jimm Horrn and had come up as soon as he could.

"But obviously," Whale said sadly, "not soon enough. What happened here, Gideon? What happened to the good lads who were going to smash the Wamchu?"

Gideon took his time answering. "If . . . if you don't know, then it . . . it wasn't the Day."

Whale frowned, then smiled quickly. "No. Not the Day, as I take you mean it. Not *her* Day, no." He glanced around the deserted tent. "And here? You have no idea what passed in this place?"

"I don't," he admitted glumly. "I was home when it happened."

Whale's greying hair seemed to stir, and his weary watery eyes, the only part of his face that was not vaguely equine, narrowed. "You were home?"

"I found a Bridge."

"You found a Bridge?"

Gideon felt terrible. "I took it, I'm afraid. It was there, and I took it."

"You took it?" Whale's jaw, wattles, and chest sagged. "You took it? You . . . you actually used a Bridge when your people were on the verge of active extinction? You deserted them? You left them in the lurch? You . . . oh my, this is a terrible situation, Gideon. Oh my, yes, this puts a whole new light on things, it really does."

"I don't know what came over me," he said softly. "I guess it was a combination of things, but mostly it was the plan. I felt . . . used. Unwanted. Expendable. Unneeded. Unloved. Like a fifth wheel. A third for tennis. A tenth for baseball. A second for solitaire." He clasped his hands in his lap. "I know, I know. They're pretty rotten excuses for what I did."

"Oh, I don't know," said Whale, pulling up another chair and sitting in front of him. "They sound pretty good to me. I probably would have done the same thing."

"You're just trying to make me feel good."

"No, I'm not," Whale said. "You ought to feel damned

shitty for what you did. All I said was, they were pretty good excuses. Besides, there was no plan."

"You're kidding."

Whale tugged at a wattle. "Did you ever consider that they might have been too afraid to go after those things? After all, we're talking about the Wamchus here, you know."

Jesus, Gideon thought, what an idiot I am. What a fool. What a sucker for ignoring the obvious and homing in on the metaphoric, as well as the nonexistent.

"Oh well," said Whale. "What the hell."

Gideon looked at him, looked back at his lap, and decided that gratitude for his healing overrode the urge to kill. "So now what do we do?"

"Well, if I had a crystal ball, I might be able to find out what happened, and where everyone is. But I don't. So I guess we'll just have to follow them."

Bracing himself against pain that never came, Gideon shifted to sit straighter. "Whale, we can't follow them. How can we? They're gone. Days ago, maybe even weeks. Well, maybe not weeks, because some of the fires are still burning, but they didn't leave last night, you can bet on it."

Whale glanced toward the opening in the wall. "And you truly believe an army this size isn't going to leave a trail?"

Gideon thought for a moment. "Well, it was dark when I got here."

"I see."

"And now that I think of it, I was in a lot of pain."

Whale nodded.

"So I suppose you could say—" Suddenly, his eyes narrowed and his hand reached for his bat. "You *left Rayn and came right up here? Two* days ago? *Two* days?"

The armorer spread his hands. "But of course."

"Two days?"

"Is that significant, Gideon? Is that something important where you come from?"

Gideon pushed himself to his feet, waited to be sure his leg would support him, then took one long stride to place himself in front of the other man. "It didn't take me two days," he said. "It took me a hell of a lot longer than that."

"Yes, I suppose it would, using that escalator and all."

"You . . . you knew about the escalator?"

"Well . . . yes."

Gideon puffed his cheeks, held his breath, blew it out when his eyes started to cross, and walked stiffly out of the tent. Whale followed, muttering and murmuring, and suggested that it didn't matter how they had arrived here, did it, since they were here, and now they had a task to perform.

"Two days." He turned sharply, and Whale staggered back a pace. "If *I* could have gotten here in two days, none of this might have happened! Do you realize that? None of this might have happened!"

Whale tugged at a wattle under his chin, scratched nervously at one beneath his left ear, and shrugged. "I may have made a mistake in sending you off so quickly, Gideon. I guess I did. But all's well that ends well, wouldn't you say?" He brightened. "You discovered your true home, your true love, and your true calling. Now, I wouldn't quibble about a couple of days with results like that, right?"

Gideon thought about it, thought about the fact that he would probably never see a Bridge again and was therefore stuck with these people for the rest of his life, and decided that being charitable in a situation like this was better than losing his temper.

But as soon as the situation changed, he was going to take the old man and pile-drive him straight into the goddamned ground and roll a rock on top of him and plant flowers all around it and make sure that generations to come would believe the adjoining seven hundred acres were irredeemably cursed.

He felt much better.

He smiled, and asked Whale which way they should go.

"I don't know," Whale said. "You're the hero. You figure it out."

SIXTEEN

"East," Gideon declared without much thought. That was the direction the flying creatures had taken Ivy, and that was the direction from which the nightly visitations of the slanted red eyes had come. It would be rather like Daniel and the lions' den, he supposed, but it was either go east, or take the risk of following the army, which might have gone in another direction.

He frowned.

Somewhere there was a flaw, perhaps a serious one, but the day was already nearly half done, and he didn't have the time to figure it out in such a way that he might eventually change his mind and confuse himself to distraction. So, with a nod to Whale and a check to be sure his bat was still in its holster, he moved to the road, trying not to look at the encampment's utter and unpleasant destruction, and started off.

Confidently, with a spring in his step, and a reaffirmation of his commitment to the struggle he was facing.

It was, in fact, a surprise.

The devastation he had suffered upon discovering what had happened to his home in his absence was not, in retrospect, as traumatic as he'd initially believed. Rather, it was a shucking off of moldy husks, a fantastical rite of passage that had ended in a harbor where he could lower his anchor of stability and ride out the storms of Fate's hither and yon, secure in the knowledge that he was stuck, there was nothing he could do about it, so he might as well make the best of it and pray for a miracle that would deliver him from his enemies, if not alive, then at least in one piece; though, he thought on further consideration, alive would be preferable to the alternative.

"Are you finished?" Whale asked a little more than an hour later.

"Finished with what?" he said, smiling.

"Your ruminations."

He thought for a moment. "Yes," he said. "Yes, I'm done."

Whale nodded, his wattles nodding with him, and suggested they follow the road to the Fromdil Forest, which lay just before them. The Scarred Mountains, to the north, would do them no good since there had been no reports of enemy activity within their massive bowl of land. The Forest, on the other hand, was fraught with sightings of strange creatures, strange noises, and even stranger occasions of both.

"You think that's where they took Ivy?"

"I think that's as good a place as any to begin our search," the armorer said. "It's also where Agnes is."

Gideon stumbled, but did not stop, and stared at Whale. "Agnes," he said flatly. "I had almost forgotten about her." He stumbled again, looked down, and saw that the road had lost its smooth surface to a number of cobblestones that had not been set properly. "I understand she's broken with the Wamchu."

Whale shuddered. "Indeed and oh my, she has. It is best, I believe, for you that we confront her first, before we take on the larger task of the Wamchu."

"Do we have to?"

"No, not really. But if my military history is correct, the best enemy to do battle with is the enemy that has divided its forces. With such internal dissension, they cannot help but be in a weakened condition, wouldn't you say?"

He remembered Agnes. He remembered Lu Wamchu. He recalled what he had been told about Agnes, and her approaching moment. "No," he said, "I wouldn't say that at all."

"Neither would I," Whale agreed sadly. "But one does have to look for the silver lining at times like this, doesn't one."

"One has to," Gideon told him firmly, "or one will cut one's throat."

The sun was not as warm as Gideon would have liked, but it sufficed to keep him from unrolling the pacch-hide cloak he had flung over his shoulder. And as the Forest neared, he realized that, just like his old home, the leaves were beginning to lose their green, to transform themselves into the autumn hues that presage the advent of colder weather and snow. The difference was that these hues were far brighter, more intense, and definitely more flamelike in their seasonal immolation in preparation for their seasonal resurrection.

An hour later, he realized he was wrong.

The flamelike colors were not flamelike at all. They were flames.

He stopped, looked back, looked ahead, realized he had been doing a lot of that lately, and waited for Whale to tell him that they were heading into more trouble than he'd originally thought.

"You noticed," the armorer said when he saw the direction of Gideon's dismayed gaze.

"I think so, yes."

"I was hoping you wouldn't."

"How could I miss it?"

Whale shrugged. Such considerations were often beyond him, taking for granted as he did the oddities of his homeland. "It doesn't burn, you know."

"Are you sure about that?"

"Positive. I've been here many times. Many times." His mouth opened to expose a magnificent row of large teeth that had no business not piercing his lips whenever they closed. "In the old days, I came here with my one true love." He sighed. "We would walk the paths, cook our meals under the trees, and pass the time in romantic dalliances the purpose of which I fear I have now forgotten." He grinned. "Well, not exactly forgotten. But I sure ain't the man I used to be."

Gideon touched his arm. "She must have been something."

"Oh my, indeed yes. And it's entirely possible we would have paired for life had not tragedy befallen us."

A flock of high-flying birds soared overhead, their soft whistling cries a tender counterpoint to the melancholy that glazed Whale's eyes.

Gideon, feeling as if he had stumbled upon a shrine, asked if Whale felt up to telling him what that tragedy was.

"Of course," the armorer said, "it was so long ago, I barely remember it. She tried to kill me."

Gideon sniffed.

"She had this remarkable weapon, one of the sort you saw in my shop so long ago. A gun. Silver, it was. She didn't understand that one just doesn't shoot a human being with one of those. She had no concept of the sporting elements inherent in war and personal disagreements."

I'll be damned, Gideon thought.

"It wasn't silver, it was nickel," he said.

Whale looked at him in astonishment.

"Her name is Rose, and she's a lousy shot."

The astonishment grew to something akin to fear mixed with religious awe.

"And she wears her hair in a bun at the back of her head."

"Damn," Whale said.

"She and her cronies have taken over what used to be my house." He looked down at the scar on his jeans. "She missed me, too."

"Damn."

"I wondered how she knew about the Bridges. Incredible, isn't it. What a small world the universe is."

Whale headed down the road again, quickly, and Gideon had to hurry to catch up.

"Did . . . did you see Daisy?"

"The whole damned garden," he said. "Loons, the lot of them. I think they hire out as mercenaries or something."

"I loved Daisy," Whale said.

"I thought you loved Rose."

"I did. But Daisy was, well, different."

"She liked milkmen, for one thing."

"Postmen," Whale corrected. "Violet liked milkmen. It was hell when she had to get her milk at the grocery store. The choice of clerks nearly drove her mad."

"You know what a grocery store is?"

"No, but I've heard of them."

The road forked, and Whale led him to the right, where the cobbles disappeared and were replaced by sullen red bricks no better inserted in the ground than the others. The Fromdil Forest closed in on them, slowly, the nearest trees still a half-hundred yards distant, their leaves burning merrily without, Gideon noticed, giving off much light or heat. Nevertheless, he felt his shoulders tightening, his hands clenching, his very flesh preparing to feel the sting of spark and the dust of ash.

"Are you nervous?" Whale asked.

He admitted he was.

"Not to worry. I told you they don't burn."

A loose brick nearly sprained Gideon's ankle, and with a wary eye on the trees, he elected to walk on the verge; immediately, the armorer warned him that there were dangers in the grass, which, he also pointed out, grew much higher here than back on the Plain itself. Gideon tried to see what there was he ought to be on guard against, and saw nothing; nevertheless, he did not argue, since what he could not see could very likely kill him as dead as what he could see, in the long run.

"Bingoos," Whale said to the unasked questions.

"What are bingoos?" Gideon asked foolishly.

"They are," Whale answered, and hastily drew his sword.

A cloud rose from the high grass, one formed by a swarm of scores of large insects the knowledge of which Gideon wished he had been spared. Each was about the size of a baseball, and nearly as round, except for the five pairs of antennae, the six pairs of serrated legs, the two pairs of gossamer wings, and the single eye that took up most of the bingoo's face. Its coloration consisted of black and red splotches on a field of rippling bronze, and its eye was the dull green usually found on automobiles that have been in the junkyard sun too long.

"Don't move," Whale warned. "If you move, they'll attack."

Gideon froze. "Do they sting, bite, or what?" he said from the corner of his mouth.

The cloud hovered over the grass in perfect silence, then began drifting toward them.

"They suck."

"Vampire beetles?"

"What's a beetle?"

"They are."

"No, they're bingoos, and one false move will have all the vital juices drained from your body within seconds."

Gideon wished he wasn't reminded of a school of piranha as the bingoo cloud neared them, rose, and cast its ominous shadow over his head. He could hear now the thrum of wings, the clack and click of claws, the subtle vibration of antennae testing the air for unwary prey; he could detect the faint odor of vital bodily juices on their foetid breath and could only hope that they had already eaten their midday meal and were simply checking out the new boys on the block; and he could sense a probing in his mind, a tentative touch of psychic infiltration that told him more clearly than the unwinking Cyclopean eyes that these creatures were not being driven by their own natural instincts, but rather by the unholy and unhealthy malevolence of a power far greater than theirs.

The cloud descended.

Whale stiffened, his hands gripping his sword tightly.

Gideon speculated on the time it would take to bring his bat to bear should the cloud break up and the attack begin, and realized that he would be a prune before he could get in the first blow.

The cloud resumed hovering less than a foot over his head, and his hair wafted side to side in the gentle breeze of their wings. He could see Whale watching him fearfully from the corner of his eye, and he tried to signal the old man not to make a move in his defense—his lower lip twitched, and the cloud dropped an inch; his right eye winked slowly, and the cloud dropped again; his cheek developed a tic which drove the cloud back up to a height of three meters, and when his left nostril flared, the cloud lowered again, this time to less than a hand's breadth from the crown of his skull.

Shit, he thought.

Someone called his name from the depths of the Fromdil Forest.

Oh, shit, he thought.

A bingoo detached itself from the cloud and flew around him several times, finally stopping less than a foot from the tip of his nose, its antennae snapping back and forth, its eye trying to focus on his mouth. It was all he could do not to smile at the thing, and in thinking that he'd better not do it, he did.

The bingoo darted back a yard.

Someone called his name again, and there was at the edge of his vision a sign of movement under the flaming trees.

Oh shit, oh shit, he thought as the bingoo returned, and the eye winked at him.

"Damnit, Gideon," a woman yelled, "are you going to stand there all day or what?"

He couldn't help it; he turned his head and saw, just under the nearest tree, a woman with long black hair, a gold-trimmed white gown, and high-heeled white boots. Her hands were on her hips and she was looking at him as if he had just made a public nuisance of himself.

Glorian! he thought. Oh shit; oh shit; oh shit.

The bingoo whirled at the intrusion, its claws clacking in fury, its eye racing through the rainbow of its insectoid spectrum; then it rejoined the cloud, which instantly rose like a meteor above the trees, the backwash staggering him to one side. He looked up, bat in hand, as the swarm performed an intricate dance of frustration and vowed vengeance, then vanished once again into the high grass.

"Jesus," he said, and dropped weak-kneed and mouth-dry to the road, wiped the sweat from his brow, and glared back at the woman who had started it all. "You could have killed us both, you idiot!" he shouted. "Are you crazy, or what?"

Whale joined him on the ground, panting and trying unsuccessfully to sheathe his sword. "My word," he gasped. "My word, indeed."

Glorian strode unconcernedly through the grass to stand before them, and Gideon smiled in spite of his reaction—she was still regally lovely, still had those uncanny violet eyes, and still roused in him the feeling of wanting to put a fist to her chin just to see if she wouldn't mind landing on her ass for a change.

"My dear," Whale said, "you really ought to be more careful with other people's lives. Those bingoos—"

"Bingelas," she said scornfully. "God, don't you even read your own books?"

Whale sputtered, then laughed, slapping Gideon on the shoulder as he accepted her hand in assisting him to his feet. "Bingelas! My heavens, what a silly mistake."

Glorian gave him a brief, friendly smile. "It's the eyes, Whale. You never remember about the eyes."

"What about the eyes?" Gideon said.

Whale waved the question away impatiently. "No time for lessons now, my boy. We have to be on our way."

"In there," Glorian said, pointing to the Forest. "We've been waiting for you."

"We?"

"A few close friends," she explained as she started off. "We thought you'd been killed, but of course you weren't, so as soon as Gideon gets up, would you mind bringing him along so he can help us figure out how we're going to take care of Agnes?"

Gideon didn't move.

Bingelas. Bingoos. It's all in the eyes; what a hell of a way to run a war.

On the other hand, he decided as he got up and followed them into the shadows of the trees, it beats getting killed.

Then he heard Glorian say, "Jeepers, really? The bingoos have green eyes? Damn, I thought it was the bingelas."

SEVENTEEN

Gideon was worried that his neck was going to atrophy. Walking as he was under the burning leaves, with shoulders hunched and breath held most of the time, his neck seemed permanently thrust into his chest cavity. It bothered him when he swallowed; and once he noticed that, he couldn't stop swallowing, and decided to get hold of himself, be a man, and walk tall. But first he made sure that Whale was right, that the leaves wouldn't scorch or sear or otherwise turn his skin black.

The Fromdil Forest was, he was forced to admit, an incredible sight. The leaves really were burning. When he stretched up a finger toward one of them, he nodded—there was little heat, and certainly little light; the shadows beneath the high foliage were as dark as if there was no fire at all, and they moved as if the leaves were being gently rustled by a breeze which had somehow lost its way from spring. Nevertheless, it was a while before he was able to extend his neck to its proper length, and a while after that before he could stop flinching whenever a burning leaf spiraled in a brilliant flare to the ground and hissed as though it had been plunged into water.

Not bad, he told himself as his stride lengthened; one of these days you might even get used to this place.

Whale was directly ahead, and Glorian had already disappeared around a bend in the narrow path they were following. She had mentioned a few friends, and he wondered who they could be. He knew several people, but half of them were on the other side, and he had no illusions about Agnes joining up with the good guys just to get back at her husband. Especially when she wasn't getting back at her husband but, rather, was getting back at him for knocking off her co-wives.

Of course, he could be wrong about that. He had no proof, yet, that Agnes Wamchu even remembered him, much less enough to want to jeopardize a conquering of a world just to wreak a little murderous vengeance.

Except for the visions, of course, which were, he supposed, proof enough.

"Whale?"

The armorer looked over his shoulder and with a jerk of his head urged him to hurry.

"Whale, who—"

"Hush," Whale said, a cautionary finger to his lips. "There are ears in this forest, Gideon. We don't want anyone to know what we're planning."

"No problem. I don't know what we're planning."

They walked for nearly an hour, perhaps more, before the trees fell back to surround a small meadow in the center of which a group of people sat around a campfire. There was singing. Beautiful singing, in a harmony he hadn't heard since . . .

"I'll be," he said in delight.

And broke into a trot when a portly, green-clad figure with a longbow slung across his back rose and waved to him. Beside him, another, younger man rose, spindly and green-clad as well. A wave, and twelve more equally green men rose to their feet, singing their hearts out as Gideon reached Vorden Lain and shook his hand, embraced him, shook Croker Boole's hand, and gave a large grin to the rest of the merry band who had fought side by side with him so long ago.

Then he looked across the campfire and saw Jimm Horrn, looked to his right and saw a white bundle huddled on a pile of what looked like sheepskin, though it was hard to tell since the pile was still moving. He grinned again and pushed his way through the welcoming throng to sit beside his sister.

She glared at him. "What the hell took you so long?"

"Nice to see you, too," he said.

Her feathers fluffed. Her voice lowered. "Do you have any idea what it's like having to sit here day after day, listening to the Robin Hood Boys' Choir sing every verse of every song in the known universe? Where the hell have you been?"

He cleared his throat, wondering if he should tell her. "Home," he said softly. "I've been home."

Her duck eyes widened. "Home? You mean . . . as in home, New Jersey? Tatty ranch house in the middle of the block? Home? As in that home?" She stood, her beak fairly quivering. "Home? Without me you went home?"

He tried to explain the turmoil he'd been through, the soul-searching he'd undergone, which had prompted the appearance of the Bridge; then he tried to explain why he had used the magical conveyance to return to the pantry, and to a life that, for him, no longer existed; he tried to explain that beating his head in with her wings wasn't going to accomplish much more than give him a monumental headache, but she refused to listen.

"Home? You sonofabitch, you went home without me?"

He crossed his arms over his head and waited until she was too wing-weary to continue, then told her what he had found. She didn't believe him. He told her again. She snapped her beak less than an inch from his nose, his chin, his right ear, until he clamped a hand around it and held it until her feathers took on a distinctive blue tint. When she slumped in defeat, he told her a third time, and slowly, finger by finger, released her.

She looked at him mournfully, and waddled off into the gathering twilight, while Lain and his men hummed a tune of heartache and sorrow.

Glorian and Whale came over to sit on either side of him, Whale shaking his head, Glorian staring off into the invisible distance.

"Will she be all right?" Glorian finally asked.

"I think so," he said. "It's a shock, coming home one day to find out you don't have a home anymore."

She nodded, and he knew that for a change she understood exactly what he meant. The village of Kori had been virtually wiped off the face of the Upper Ground in one night, the result of an attack by the burrowing horrors these people called pacchs. Only she and Tag had survived. And no one, now, believed that it was merely a whim on the beasts' part; it could only have been part of the Wamchu's vicious, long-term plan.

They listened for a while to the band of thieves run through their repertoire; then Glorian gently suggested that they all put a cork in it while she and her companions decided what to do next. Vorden Lain agreed and ordered Boole, his right-hand man, to send the boys out to hunt something for dinner; then he joined the others, not sitting but leaning on his longbow, his green hat pushed back rakishly on his head.

"It's been some time, lad," he said to Gideon.

"I know. How've you been?"

"Oh, a bit of this, a bit of that, you know how it goes. Poor old Croker tried to take over again, but he still hasn't got the hang of it." Lain laughed heartily, but quietly. "I expect that one of these days he'll either do it or strike out on his own, form his own band and give me quite a run for my money. A good lad. A little slow, is all."

Glorian adjusted her legs until she was sitting Indian fashion, demurely spreading her gown until it covered those parts of her that she didn't deem necessary for exposure at the moment. "We have to talk," she said.

"Aye, that we do," agreed Lain.

"Indeed," said Whale.

Jimm Horrn wandered over and flopped onto the grass behind them, and fell asleep.

"I want to know what happened to the camp," Gideon said. "And I want to know where Ivy is."

Glorian rolled her eyes in exasperation. "Typical hero," she muttered to the others. "Doesn't see the big picture, only the centerfold."

Gideon smiled at her as sweetly as he could. "I found your

duck, I saved your ass, if you don't tell me I'll pound you into the grass.''

"Burma Shave," Whale said.

Glorian fluffed her raven hair about her shoulders and smiled just as sweetly back. "I wish you had the power to see yourself as others see you, you worm."

"Burns," Whale said. "Sort of."

Gideon, in order not to grab the bat, clasped his hands in his lap and said, "You're disspicable."

Whale frowned. "Daffy Duck?"

"I heard that!" a voice quacked from the other side of the meadow.

Glorian shrugged. "I care not what you think of me, so long as you think of me when you think. Which, considering the state of your mind these days, I doubt."

Whale looked at Lain, who said, "Browning."

Gideon sighed. Every moment they sat here was one more moment Ivy spent in the claws of her abductors, though he had a strong suspicion that she was perfectly safe, that her abduction was, despite Whale's earlier disclaimer, merely a ruse to lure him into a trap of either Lu's or Agnes's devising; but if that was so, he was fully prepared to walk in.

Brother, he thought then; you are out of your goddamned mind.

"Well?" she said. "Are you ready to listen?"

He spread his arms wide. "Though I hear the sound of midnight in your voice, I will ignore the last call of mourning and follow you to the grave, even though it means facing the bloodwind of our enemies, listening to the soft whisper of the dead, heeding the dark cry of the moon, enduring the long night of the grave, and living a life of nightmare seasons until the day I perish."

He grinned.

Lain looked puzzled; Whale scratched his head; Glorian stared at the sky until, at last, she turned to him, slowly.

"That was Grant, and it's very, very tacky."

"Yeah, but it was pretty neat, huh?"

Her anger couldn't resist the grin, the wink, the raised

eyebrow, and she leaned over to kiss his cheek. "You're a pain in the ass, Gideon Sunday."

He nodded, and leaned back as she, with Whale's and Lain's help, explained how, shortly after Gideon's no longer unexplained though still inexplicable disappearance, a great army of walking and flying things had swept down the slopes of the Scarred Mountains during the night. The battle had been fierce, and many lives had been lost on both sides. The fighting had raged for more than a week, with no quarter asked and no quarter given. The sky was dark the entire time, and a pair of slanted red eyes watched the conflict constantly, winking now and then, frowning here and there, finally vanishing when the Vondel brothers rallied a company of long-haired men and men who weren't really human, and charged the slopes recklessly. The enemy hadn't expected such idiocy and fell back before the onslaught. The camp, what was left of it, cheered; Glorian had gathered the rest of the army and ordered them to follow the Vondels into the Scarred Mountains' bowl, where to this day the fighting continues, at such a fierce rate that no one now expects it to last more than a year or two at the most.

"A year?" Gideon said.

"Of course, a year," Whale said. "Do you think we can wipe out this menace with one magnificent battle?"

"Or one ingenious swoop into the enemy's stronghold?" said Lain.

"Or one clever sortie behind the lines which results in the capture of the leader of their forces?" said Glorian.

"Well, sure," he said. "Why not?"

"Gideon," she said, as a mother speaks to a child who has gotten into the cookies, not knowing they are laced with strychnine for the neighbors' pesky dog, "the only way this can end as quickly as you seem to want it to end is if both the Wamchus are killed before they kill us."

"And if they're killed," he said, with an apprehension he was becoming familiar with, and thoroughly sick of, "their troops will throw down their arms and return to the Lower Ground forever, or at least until another leader arises to lead them out of their self-imposed bondage in another—"

"Right, right," she said hastily. "You've got it."

He thought he had; he just wanted to be sure.

"And I suppose," he said when no one else seemed inclined to talk, "that you're all here instead of there because you feel that you're going to lose if that isn't done, and done soon."

"Lose?" Whale yelped. "Who said anything about losing?"

"I didn't," Lain said. "What I said was, we have rather a sticky situation on our hands, and if I weren't so busy training the lads, I'd be the first one to go to Thazbinn and do my duty."

"Thazbinn?" Gideon said.

"Well, I'm just too damned old," Whale said. "Oh yes, there's no question about my age. I'd drop from exhaustion before I even got to Shashhag."

"Shashhag?" Gideon said, weakly.

"I said lose," came a voice from the dark.

They turned, and watched silently as Tuesday waddled into the campfire's light, sneered at them as best she could considering the rigid lips she had to work with, and plopped herself uninvited onto Gideon's lap.

"Right, I remember that," Whale said.

"Leave it to a duck to see the future," Lain agreed.

Glorian folded her arms across her chest and watched the low flames for a while. Then: "She's right, you know."

"Of course, I'm right," Tuesday snapped. "You think I got to be a duck because I was a movie star? I got to be a duck because some bastard in a fluffy black suit knew I was special. And why am I special? Because I don't blind myself with fantasies, dreams, and pretty pictures of pastoral coexistence."

Gideon leaned over. "You got to be a duck, Sis, because the Wamchu needed a duck and you were in the wrong place at the wrong time."

"Yeah, well . . ." She shifted, wriggled, pecked his left kneecap for good measure. "You're still going to lose unless you off the Wamchus."

Glorian sighed. "There's no other way," she said, a hand up to quiet Whale's protest. "We can fight to the last man, and they'll still be able to send more against us. We have no choice.''

"And that," said Gideon, "is why you're here."

They nodded.

"To pick a sucker."

They nodded.

"Whom you have already picked, and would have sent out long ago if he hadn't gotten sidetracked by going home and being an idiot and not staying there."

They didn't need to nod; the chuckles were enough.

He shook his head. "No."

They dropped twigs into the fire, rearranged themselves, tilted their heads when they heard the strains of the hunting party returning with their dinner.

"You realize that this is not going to be one of those deals where I keep saying no and you keep ignoring me until I finally see the inevitability of it all and agree."

They ignored him.

"It isn't," he insisted.

"Ivy," Tuesday whispered.

"Ivy," Lain echoed.

"Ivy," Whale said.

"Tramp," Glorian sneered.

"Shit," Gideon said, and picked up his bat.

EIGHTEEN

With a great deal of restraint, which even he in all modesty recognized as admirable, Gideon did not inflict a single injury on the woman who had slurred the woman he had decided he might as well be in love with since she was causing him all this trouble anyway, and it might as well be for someone he cared about as someone he only met on Wednesdays in the supermarket.

He put the bat away.

And he smiled at the greenmen who settled down around the fire with tales, and song, of their exploits in the Forest.

The evening repast, as prepared by a relieved Croker Boole who had learned he wasn't the one who had to beard the Wamchu in his den, was a veritable feast of culinary ingenuity, with a smattering of virtually every edible creature in the Fromdil Forest, and a few who usually considered themselves immune to the carnivores that preyed on their cousins. Whale, with a dexterity that astonished even him, conjured a smooth and silky mead to go with the meat, and it wasn't long before the Lain band had discovered the delights of barbershop quartets.

The night was cool but not cold, the Forest glowed with pastel fire, and the nightsky was momentarily alight with a meteor shower whose greens and pale yellows reminded Gideon of a spring many years ago, when he and his girlfriend had gone on a picnic at a secluded spot on the Delaware River. He didn't remember anything else about it, but he was positive he'd had a good time, and the memory settled him into a mellow mood.

Tuesday was nestled against Jimm, grumbling herself to sleep about living on bread alone being a bitch when all she wanted was a halfway decent steak.

"A penny for your thoughts," Glorian said as she wiped a smear of cooked juices from her chin.

Gideon stared into the campfire. "I suppose, to put it simply, I don't want to die."

"Ah," she said, chewing thoughtfully. "Ah."

"Not a large request, right?"

"Depends."

"On what?"

"On whether you don't want to die because you're afraid of what the Other Side might be like, or you don't want to die because you know what the Other Side is like and you don't want to go there."

He nodded, sipped mead from a shallow wooden cup Lain had given him, and lay back. "Well, I don't know what the Other Side is like, and I don't care. I would prefer not to find out, except maybe secondhand, and even then I'll reserve judgment because I haven't seen it myself."

She wiped her mouth on a sleeve that refused to hold the stain, and took another bite from the well-done leg she was holding. "Ah."

"And it also seems to me that you people have put up with an awful lot from Wamchu, and I wonder why you haven't gotten rid of him already."

"A good question." She chewed, spat, chewed, wiped. "I don't want to give you the wrong impression, Gideon, but the reason is that we haven't had a hero before."

"You don't have much of one now."

"Not much of one is better than none at all."

He sat up quickly, cursed the mead that didn't move his head as fast as the rest of him, and looked at her. Was that a crack about his abilities? Was it a compliment? Or was it that his ears had a strange buzzing in them and he had misunderstood her intention?

"So when are you going?" she said.

"How about next week?"

She laughed, touched his shoulder, and tossed the half-eaten leg into the fire, where it burned as well as any rotted log. "At dawn, I suppose."

"I need my rest, how about noon?"

She laughed, touched his shoulder, and drained her cup of mead as if it were water. "Naturally, I won't be going with you."

Of course not, he thought; leaders don't go with the troops to fight the battles; that's why they're leaders—they're not dumb enough to expose themselves to possible death.

"As a matter of fact, it might be better if you went alone," she continued. "That way—"

"I'll die sooner, if I don't get lost first."

"Oh, I'll draw you a map."

He pointed at Lain and his men. "What about them? Why can't they go with me?"

"Well, I'm certainly not going to stay here unprotected, Gideon. My god, why don't you think!"

I am, he thought.

"Then what about Whale?"

"He thinks he ought to stay here in case we're attacked and need his medical services."

"Right."

"Besides, he's old."

Right; and everyone else is off fighting in the mountains, which leaves me with Jimm.

"And Jimm," she said, with an affectionate look back at the sleeping thief, "is my personal bodyguard."

Any number of snide, rude, crude, and telling off-color remarks came to mind, but they were crowded out by the realization that he was really going to have to do this on his own. All by himself. Without a single hand to hold when he got scared, without a single shoulder to cry on when he was terrified, without a single body to watch his back when he got into trouble. And he was going to get into trouble; he knew that, even without Chute telling him he would, and he didn't much like it.

"So," Glorian said with a smile that would have melted his heart had it not been moving around so much, from throat to knee and back again, "let me tell you what you'll need to know so you don't screw it up."

There is a lot to be said, Gideon decided sometime between dawn and noon of the following day, for living under the heel of a tyrant. In the first place, you never have to worry about security, because there isn't any; in the second place, you never have to worry about where your next meal is coming from, because there probably won't be one; and in the third place, you never have to go looking for trouble, because trouble will come looking for you, sure as hell.

He stopped, pulled off a boot, shook out a pebble, put the boot back on, and stared up the road. The very same road he and Whale had taken the day before. Only this time he was alone. The others, true to Glorian's word, were back in the meadow, sleeping off the effects of the armorer's mead.

There hadn't even been a farewell breakfast.

Glorian had shaken him awake, showed him the map she'd scratched in the ground, given him a pouch stuffed with what she said were necessities from Whale, a kiss on the cheek for good luck, and gone back to sleep.

Tuesday was gone, probably looking for something to eat.

He rubbed one shoulder, his chest, the small of his back, and started off again. At least, thus far, the walk wasn't dreary. The Forest, even in daylight, gave off its peculiar glow in a most gentle and pleasing fashion, and several times over the next couple of hours he had to remind himself that he was, in fact, heading deeper and deeper into enemy territory, and at any minute he could be attacked by one of the Wamchu's minions.

Ten days.

That's what she said, he told himself.

Ten days, before the Day.

After that, it was oblivion and nasty doings.

The bat remained ready in his hand.

The sky remained blue overhead.

And though he occasionally heard something moving in the trees off to his right, there was no sign that he was in immediate danger of getting hurt. He supposed he was merely being tracked, followed, and reports on his movements sent back to Shashhag where his ultimate enemy was most likely preparing a most diabolical trap for him, not to mention an excruciating demise.

Shashhag.

He wanted to shudder at the very sound of the name, but he couldn't bring himself to speak it aloud. Neither could he bring himself to forgive Glorian for telling him about it; there are some things that man is meant to find out on his own, or he'll think about them too much and decide not to go.

Shashhag.

He shuddered anyway.

Beyond the eastern rim of the Scarred Mountains, he'd been told, there was a desolate plain unlike any other on any level of this world, and it was there that he could expect to meet either Agnes or Lu Wamchu. It was likely, Glorian said, to be Agnes because she had a particular fondness for desolation, whereas Lu had a yen for opulence and creature comforts. And Glorian's spies had told her that many of the creatures now in mortal combat with the forces of the ordinary people of this world made their original home in Shashhag. Which meant that either Agnes or Lu had control of them. Which meant that Gideon would have to be alert for leathery flying things and other disgusting beings that would not look kindly on him trespassing since no one, ever, visited Shashhag unless there was a war on.

"And how often is that?" he had asked.

"This is the first one," she had said.

Shashhag.

The desolation was evidently enhanced by the fact that no living thing ever grew there, except maybe the leathery flying things, which were, after all, pretty big when you thought about it. But there were no plants of any size, and the one river that flowed through it did so at an extremely rapid pace so not to have to touch its banks any more than it had to.

"Slow down!"

Good idea, he thought.

"Hey, idiot, wait up!"

He looked over his shoulder, but he didn't slow down. Tuesday, burdened with a lumpy pack on her back, was flying not more than four or five inches above the road, panting heavily as she worked on her speed, her altitude, and keeping her orange feet from scraping over the rocks. Only when he nearly tripped himself, so fascinated was he that he'd forgotten to look forward again, did he shorten his stride until she landed beside him and begged him with a look to relieve her of her burden.

"Nice of you to join me," he said.

"That bitch wouldn't tell me the direction," she complained bitterly. "I've been flying all morning and my wings are ready to fall off."

"I thought ducks could fly all day."

"I am not a duck," she said, her beak cracking shut with each word. "I am a woman in a duck's body."

"You look like a duck to me, Sis, and what the hell's in here anyway? It weighs a ton." He shook the pack. It wobbled.

Tuesday bobbed her head. "Mead," she said. "I got it to keep us going when the sun gets too warm."

She was right; it was heavy, and he only barely managed to get the makeshift straps over his shoulders. Wonderful, he thought; here is the great hero of Chey, sloshing along the road with his faithful companion, duck, at his side.

"I heard what she told you," Tuesday said, walking as fast as she could to keep up with him. "You're really going there?"

"Yes. It's probably the place Tag knew about, and that's where Ivy probably is."

Tuesday snorted, flew to his shoulder, and perched without asking permission. "You really believe that kid knew where she was taken?"

He explained what Tag had told him about the planned raid on Agnes's headquarters, and as he spoke speculated on the boy's odd absence from the meadow. Not to mention the fact that Glorian had not mentioned him at all, and he was her brother.

"Damn," he said. "Do you suppose the dope has gone off to rescue her himself?"

"I wouldn't know."

It would be just like him, Gideon thought; the bloodlust ran deep in his veins, and it would be no surprise at all to come across him once they reached . . . that place.

"He probably thinks he's going to surround them," he muttered, without an ounce of admiration for the boy's stupidity and courage. "He'll probably get to Ivy before I do."

Tuesday, as only ducks can, groaned. "Good god, you really have it bad, don't you?"

"I don't know. Do I?"

"You're asking me? I'm only a duck."

"But you just told me you're not a duck, just a woman in a duck's body."

"Jesus, Giddy, are you going to believe everything a duck tells you?"

He did not give her an answer. On the one hand, what answers he had were decidedly ungentlemanly, and on the other, he had spotted a pile of bones at the side of the road. They were very large bones, and there wasn't a speck of meat left on them. As he passed them, swerving away in case it was a trap, he thought he recognized the general shape and size—a pacch, which meant that whatever had killed and eaten it was either a damned lucky fool or had damned big teeth.

And the bones reminded him of Jeko Junffer.

And Jeko reminded him of how much he had gone through just to get to this point in his travels, his travails, and his uncertain lust for a certain young woman.

And the certain young woman reminded him of Shashhag.

And Shashhag made him shudder.

At which point Tuesday fell off his shoulder, flew back, and told him to be more careful with the only sister he had left in the world and would he like to hear a few songs she'd learned from Lain's band of merry men.

"No."

"It's going to be a long trip," she muttered.

They passed another pile of bones, this one not picked quite as clean as the first, and a cloud of bingelas hummed over the feast, ignoring the two travelers completely, though Tuesday's fowl genes soon had her mouth watering in a most unseemly manner.

The third and fourth piles, within two hundred yards of each other, were more meat than bones.

"Oh boy," Gideon said, and put the bat on his shoulder. "I sure do wish Red was here."

"Well, he's not."

"Why not?" he said.

"How should I know," she said testily.

"That was a rhetorical question, Sis. I only asked, as if praying to the gods for Red to come springing out of the trees over there and save my feet from wearing down to the bone."

"Well," she said, suddenly lifting into the air, "that isn't Red over there, that's for damned sure."

NINETEEN

Tuesday's talent for spotting the enemy in the open served them in good stead. The thing she had mentioned, and was now flying rapidly away from with a prudence she had not normally shown in her human form, bounded out of the burning trees with a garbled roar and landed four-square in the center of the road. It was shoulder-tall, muddy brown, and canine, though it had no tail, no ears, and no fur to speak of except for a dangling brown beard under its elongated jaw, which was, Gideon noted dispassionately, a good eighty to ninety percent of its face, having as it did more teeth than he had ever seen in his life.

It slavered, spat, and salivated, and the disgusting strands and coils and strings of its saliva instantly burned hideous holes in the earth.

Gideon swallowed to keep his gorge from rising, swallowed again to keep his bile from roiling, and swallowed a third time when gorge and bile paid him no heed. Nevertheless, he stiffened his chin, sniffed once, and kicked a stone out of the way, the movement shifting the creature's attention away from its salivating and slavering and back to him.

It took one look and threw back its head to howl at the sun. There was no mistaking the sound—it was bellowing its triumph, and its thanks for finding a snack so early in the day.

Gideon also noted, as he ran his hand along the bat to be sure it was indeed still in his hand and indeed the weapon it was supposed to be, that the creature had an odor about it akin to a pile of rotting meat that not even a hyena would touch on a particularly bad day. And when the gentle wind changed direction and he dropped to his knees at the power of the stench, he knew how it was that the massive pacchs had been trapped long enough to be buzz-sawed by those teeth.

He turned his head, took a deep breath through his mouth, held it, and rose. Faced the creature, and waited for the charge.

Tuesday called hysterically to him.

Gideon shook his head, felt his lungs already protesting their inactivity, and turned his head away, exhaled, inhaled, held his breath, and looked back.

The creature ambled toward him, snorting and growling and tossing its head side to side, its acid saliva scorching the grass on the verge and drilling smoky holes in the boles.

This would have to be a head-on confrontation, he decided; to attempt to sneak around its side would only result in an agonizing shower that would immobilize him just long enough for the thing to grab him—if he didn't have to take a breath again and wasn't immobilized by the stench of its bodily and oral emanations.

It was less than ten feet from him when it stopped, puzzled why its snack was still on its feet. The head lowered, and two small eyes examined him carefully.

Gideon smiled at it, showing his own teeth, and lunged forward, the bat swinging through the dental minefield like a cold knife through solid butter. But though he might not have broken anything, he certainly made an impression—when the bat rebounded off a fang, he spun and ran back a few steps, gasped another breath and turned, watching as the tooth-thing fell back on its haunches in astonishment, shook its head in pain and scattered bilious chunks of plaque and untasted food morsels into the burning trees, which flared at the contact.

C'mon, Gideon thought; c'mon, c'mon, let's get this over with.

But the tooth-thing was in no hurry. It scratched behind its head with a blunted hind paw, trembled as if dissipating the last of its hurt, and rose again, leg by trunklike leg. Then it exposed its eyes once more, judged the distance between itself and Gideon, and without so much as a single pawing of the ground or threatening roar, it charged.

Gideon waited, swung the bat and flung himself to his right and as far backward as he could. It wasn't very far. Droplets of acid landed around him, and one caught him on the forearm, tearing open the sleeve of his shirt and raising a blister on the skin so painful that he considered himself lucky getting away with just a scream.

The tooth-thing, however, was down as well. Writhing on the grass, setting itself afire here and there, and generally making a hell of a noise as it scrambled with its clumsy forepaws for the three teeth that had been slammed out by the roots.

Gideon staggered to his feet, staggered over as close as he could get, and used a particularly effective backhand, one-handed blow to loosen four more canines before he was forced away by the blast furnace of its mouth. Again he approached, more cautiously now since the creature was writhing even more spastically, its roars of anger and pain subsiding every few seconds to whimpers of defeat and what the hell happened? And a second time the backhand, one-handed blow sheared through the dental forest, and once again he was breath-bludgeoned until he could stand the torture no longer and stumbled away, up the road now and not looking back.

He was, for the time being, safe. There was no doubt that the tooth-thing would be out of action for quite a while, and with luck he would be far enough down the road for it not to want to bother to follow.

He breathed deeply, wiped a hand over his face, and breathed again until a vague swell of dizziness vanished in the fresh air. He examined the blistering skin on his arm and saw that there were no signs of deeper infection, rampaging poisons, or spreading in the manner of some monstrous disease. He checked the bat before holstering it, and was amazed again that its properties were such that not even the acid had marred its smooth and sensuous surface.

Tuesday rejoined him a few minutes later, apologized for her desertion, and wanted to know if he was going to smell like that all the way to wherever they were going.

"Smell like what?"

"Like a mouth that hasn't been washed in six or seven years."

"It was that thing," he explained, while surreptitiously sniffing at whatever parts of him he could reach without actually squashing his nose against them.

"Oh," she said, fluttered up over his head and looked back. "You did a number on it, I see."

"It'll think twice about coming back," he agreed, at the same time quickening his pace when he saw the sun now at its zenith. A sense of newborn urgency sparked the muscles of his legs, and he cursed the creature for stalling him. Even if they weren't waylaid by anything or anyone else now, he would have to develop an arduous and boring routine of run-and-walk if he wanted to get to Ivy before it was too late. Which, when he thought about it, was probably not the smartest way to get where he was going since, when he got there, wherever the hell that was, he would be too exhausted to do anything about why he had gotten there in the first place.

Jesus, he thought, what I wouldn't give for a bicycle right now, or a car, even if it had only three wheels.

The duck landed lightly on his shoulder. "Maybe it's about time to break out a little liquid refreshment."

"No," he said. "I need a clear head for this, Sis."

"Well, maybe you ought to think about it, okay?"

"What's to think about? Mead plus I'm tired equals drunk, and there's no way I can do anything to help anyone if I'm drunk."

She was silent for several yards.

"Funny, that's not what Whale said."

After a dozen yards, he stopped and tried to look her in the eye, even though she was on his shoulder. "What are you talking about?"

"Whale. What he said to me. When he gave me the mead."

He reached up, took her gently in his hand, and gently swung her down until she was pressed gently against his chest. His smile was gentle as well, and Tuesday looked a little nervous.

"You didn't tell me he talked to you. You just said you had mead for the trip. Why didn't you tell me he talked to you? I thought you'd just taken the stuff, for god's sake; I didn't know he'd given it to you."

"There's a difference?"

Gently, he placed her on the ground, unslung the pack and hunkered down beside it. A close examination of the cool leather soon showed him a stiff bone spout tucked into a depression on its bulging side. With a steady finger, and one eye on his sister, he worked it out, making sure the opening pointed upward so not to spill one precious drop.

"What did he say?" he asked as he ran a finger over the spout, caught a precious drop and touched his tongue to it. It didn't taste any different than what he'd had the night before.

Tuesday didn't answer.

He looked at her. "Sis, stop pouting."

"You think I'm a thief," she said with a catch in her voice.

"You said you took it."

"I said I got it. That's not the same." She waddled to the verge and looked up at the trees. "It's a pretty mess we've come to, Gideon Sunday, a pretty mess indeed. You, of all people, think your own sister is a thief, and one who would steal from dear and loving friends! What the hell kind of a duck do you think I am, anyway?"

"It's pass," he said. "A pretty pass."

"Something," she snarled, "you wouldn't know anything about, since all yours were ugly."

He didn't answer. Instead, he cupped a hand and lowered the spout slowly, letting his palm fill with the golden liquid before stopping it. Then he sniffed it, could find nothing out of the ordinary about its aroma, licked it gingerly and could find nothing unusual about its taste. So he drank it, refilled his palm and drank again. It was warm, but not unpleasantly so, and a third palmful, he decided, should be his limit, lest he be tempted to partake from the spout itself and thus lessen the weight on his spine when he started off again.

Tuesday, hearing his tentative slurping, came over and waited her turn, took her ration from his hand and tilted her head back, closed her eyes, and sighed. "He was right, I feel better already."

"He was right?" Gideon said, reslinging the pack.

"Sure. He said he knew that time was vital and strength was limited, and this would take care of the strength part so we can get where we're going as if we had wings." She giggled. "I forgave him the slip."

Gideon looked down at his feet, flexed and stretched his arms, massaged his neck and shoulders, and was almost convinced that the mead did indeed have some of Whale's erratic magical properties. He was absolutely convinced when he glanced at his forearm and saw that the acid blister had healed.

"Damn," he said. "If he can do this, why the hell can't he turn you back into a woman?"

"An unknowable mystery," she said.

He frowned. "Isn't that something like a double negative."

"You mean like, no, no, here it comes again?"

He didn't ask.

He whirled, pushed Tuesday out of the way, and whipped out the bat just in time to catch the tooth-thing across its grinning, slavering, salivating, foetid mouth. It screamed, dropped a pair of really wretched molars, and charged into the trees without breaking stride.

"Nice," she said. "Want to try it again?"

He whirled to face front, just in time to bring the rounded end of the bat raking across the gleaming fangs of another tooth-thing whose breath was not nearly as lethal, though it too could have used a floss now and then. It screamed at the touch of the mystical wood, spat out a fang and bicuspid, turned in midair and tried a backslash that Gideon, with a forehand, interrupted behind its ear. Another scream, and it leapt into the trees.

"You're on a roll," his sister said from above him.

He jumped to one side and brought the bat down on the ribs of a third creature, which had been slinking up on him, belly to the ground and teeth clenched until the last moment; the clenching, however, undid it as the bat slid off the ribs, up the side of the head, and down on its muzzle. The teeth cracked and shattered, and the beast crawled into the trees, howling.

"Yo, Giddy!" The duck beckoned from several yards away, and he broke into a slow trot, eyeing the pastel flames for signs of another attack, scanning the rough bark of the trees beneath for hints that something else was lying in wait to prevent him from reaching his destination.

For that was what all this was, and he knew it.

The tooth-things, like the leathery flying things, were too ugly and too vile and too foul on the face of it to appear naturally, not without some sort of diabolical assistance from equally diabolical creators who needed either to prove their power to themselves and thus bolster their evil self-esteem, or perhaps to build allies of their own nightmares because no one else in his right mind would have anything to do with them.

It was not, he thought, unlike a school bully who gathered to his side all the dregs and slime of the schoolyard because the dregs and the slime couldn't get friends otherwise. Until, of course, some kindly person showed them the evil of their ways and set them on the straight and narrow. Or fried them in the electric chair.

Eastward, then, and farther eastward.

The sun set.

They slept uneasily beneath a burning tree, which offered them no light beyond the light it had, which didn't reach them so they weren't disturbed save for the husking of the leaves and the creak of the bark.

At dawn Tuesday roused him, waited impatiently for him to eat a morsel from the pouch Glorian had given him, then flapped off to scout the road ahead.

Which curved, and straightened, and curved, and dipped, and rose, and Gideon availed himself sparingly of the sustaining mead so that his legs would continue to metaphorically devour the distance and shorten the time to that time when it would be time for him to take arms against the sea of troubles, and by opposing, and with a hell of a lot of luck, end them.

It wasn't going to be easy.

In spite of the mead, his legs were killing him.

The entire day passed without incident, since he wouldn't count the four attacks by the tooth-things; they had become almost commonplace, like ingrown nails and swatting flies.

Then, without warning, Tuesday called from around the next bend.

"Yo, Giddy!"

The bat popped into his hand.

As he slowed to a brisk walk, he looked at the Fromdil Forest and wondered how something so ethereally beautiful could harbor such horrid things as the tooth-creatures, such deadly forces to the prolongation of his already precarious existence. It was, he imagined, a system of checks and balances that he was not capable of understanding. A Mystery. As all life is a Mystery, until you lose it and discover that life is life, and death is death, and when you put the two together in the same room, all hell is going to break loose.

He rounded the bend.

Tag was standing in the middle of the road. Red was grazing on the verge. And Vorden Lain and his merry men were just completing the arrow-puncture of a tooth-thing that had been lured to its demise by a camp song.

TWENTY

I will think good thoughts, Gideon decided some time later, when he had gotten over the shock of seeing the greenmen, the lorra, and Tag grinning stupidly at him as if they expected yet another overwhelming display of his affection when, in fact, what he really wanted to do was rescue the tooth-thing and sic it on them, one at a time, while they were tied to a tree, with their boots off.

I will think good thoughts, even though Vorden had explained in a truly apologetic yet jovial manner that he and his lads had been unable to remain behind in the meadow because to a man they couldn't help thinking of him, all alone on the road, facing danger at every step, without some meaningful gesture of support from those who were experienced in this sort of thing—as though his time here hadn't given him anything but an ulcer and a desire to retire to the mountains and live the good life with his duck. They had, they explained, taken the short way through the Forest, a route Glorian had somehow, in her haste to see him on his way, neglected to mention, or to draw on the map, unless it was that squiggly line at the top which he had seen but thought was a result of her nervousness at having the gall to ship him out without clueing him in.

When he asked about Glorian and her protection, he was

told that Jimm was still there, and Gideon assumed, without much hope, that the rest of the world knew something he didn't.

For Tag and Red, it wasn't necessary to compose himself. He had been right—after the airborne assault on headquarters and Gideon's mysterious disappearance, the boy had persuaded the lorra that Ivy needed rescuing, and they had gone off on their own to hunt down the miscreants and give them their due. Fortunately for Tag's future, they had failed; they had gotten lost somewhere in the Forest when Red wanted to try out a particularly edible-looking green-flame leaf. When they'd finally rediscovered the road, they'd come upon Lain skewering what Gideon was informed was a magrow.

And I will think always good thoughts, he concluded with a certain flair of magnanimous élan, because he was now comfortably astride the lorra, his feet no longer hurt, his legs were grateful for the respite, and his sister was off his back, in a sense, hanging out with the greenmen and teaching them the words to a ballad that featured a Cornish fisherman, his wife, a whale, and the kings of five countries who, for some obscure reason, wanted to hang Joan d'Arc for talking to herself.

Tag strolled beside him.

"Are you sure you want to do this?" the young man asked.

"What choice do I have?" he said.

"You could walk and I could ride."

Gideon changed his mind, and composed himself.

And it wasn't long, and too quickly for Gideon's peace of mind, before the Forest began to alter its appearance: the leaves burned with less abandon, and the colors that had defied the brilliance of the sun were fading rapidly to a simple, unexciting glow; the trees themselves grew farther apart, their trunks exchanging their rustic bark for dribs, then streaks, then large patches of moss that looked disturbingly like the unwashed hair of an anthropomorphic toad.

The air too had lost that brisk comforting chill, became damp and clinging, as if they were riding through an invisible fog. The sky's sharp-edged blue had dulled sometime during

the last hour or so, and the sun itself had become a pale
imitation of its usual, robust yellow.

No, Gideon thought, the Forestland just didn't seem to
have its old oomph anymore.

"You know," said Tag, "we really ought to have a plan."

He nodded; the boy was right.

"We just can't go in there and tear them up unless we have
some kind of plan."

"What do you have in mind?" he said, slipping his hands
into Red's silken, and warm, hair.

"Nothing right at the moment. I just thought I should
mention it."

He nodded a second time. "I thought perhaps you and Ivy
might have concocted something when she told you she was
going to raid the place."

Tag's brow furrowed in an attempt to remember. "Well,
maybe she did."

Gideon allowed time to pass before he prompted the lad to
remember harder, and preferably aloud.

The muted bellow of a magrow broke the silence, but it
was a fair distance behind them, and none even bothered to
look over a shoulder.

"Well," said Tag, "she did say something about not being
taken in by that goddamned bitch with her funny-looking eyes
and shit for brains." He blushed. "That was a quote. I
wouldn't say anything like that. Especially about Agnes.
Boy, especially not about Agnes."

The feeling, though restrained, was mutual.

"Then," Tag continued, "she said something about chang-
ing her mind because there was no way in hell we could do it
without the rest of the army."

Red swung his head around and poked the point of a horn
at Tag's shoulder.

"Thank you," Gideon said. "I was thinking along the
same lines myself."

"But it's not my fault," the boy protested.

"What fault?" said Lain, who had come up on the left side
and was swishing his rapier about to test the air's mettle. "Do
we have a problem, Gideon?"

Tag, pulling nervously at his vest, repeated the entire conversation, blushed twice, and dodged Red's horn, which this time was aimed more in a thrust than a poke.

"Well," Lain said, and walked on in silence.

"I suppose," Gideon said, "it's too late to turn around and get the rest of the army."

"Oh, I would think so," the greenman told him.

"No chance?"

"Why bother? We're here."

Red protested with a threatening growl as Gideon's fingers took hold of the russet hair and twisted it, knotted it, pulled it, and otherwise made the lorra exceedingly uncomfortable until he had bucked Gideon onto the ground.

He didn't notice the impact.

All he saw was the plain.

Shashhag.

He nodded knowingly.

All this time his nightmare visions had not been visions of the mystical sort at all, but visions that mirrored an essential reality on the far side of the Fromdil Forest. Not that he had been aware of it at the time, but he was definitely aware of it now, and that awareness didn't make him feel any better about having had what he could well label premonitions—unless, he thought as he pushed himself to his feet, the visions of this reality had been deliberately and callously sent to him telepathically by the woman who sought to have his heart for lunch.

Shashhag: miles of utterly flat, utterly unbroken, utterly depressing plain. Generally brown, though streaked here and there with muddy yellows, blotched once in a while with shadowy greys, and marked on occasion with dots of moldy green. Not a plant broke the surface, not a rock interrupted the flow to the far horizon. The only features out there that caught the eye were the cracks in the surface—sometimes short, sometimes long, sometimes of middling length, none of them straight, none of them very wide except where they were wide enough for a man to crawl into if he were suicidal.

And the sky.

Gideon looked over his shoulder, and saw the bleached blue that only turned its proper shade when it touched the far horizon.

Then he looked overhead, and straight ahead, and saw that the blue had been replaced with shades of red, from rose to blood to almost black at the far horizon.

It was a desert without sand, a sea without water.

It was illuminated by a sun that was but a reflection of the true star, which shone only on places with more promise than this.

"Jesus H Christ," he whispered.

Red, his eyes an uncertain grey, pawed at the earth and kicked the divots to one side; his long tail twitched, his hair rippled, and his great spiraled horns seemed anxious to find something to pierce, if not mangle.

Lain, watching the lorra's behavior, sheathed his rapier and turned to his merry men, who had congregated rather solidly behind the thin Croker Boole.

"Gentlemen," he said, "I see you have made a decision before I have been given an opportunity to offer you that choice on the basis of my experience and rather extensive wisdom."

"We like to think ahead," Croker said with an apologetic smile.

"I see."

"You're not holding it against us, I hope."

Lain shook his head, and smiled. "Not as long as you're not trying some devious method of taking over, Mr. Boole."

"God forbid," Croker gasped, and looked to the others, who corroborated his sincerity with muttered protestations of their own. "We took up a collection, too," Boole continued, and held out a quiver packed with arrows. "In case you need them."

Lain nodded. "Very thoughtful of you, I'm sure."

Gideon had turned to listen, and was surprised to see a tear shimmering in the younger greenman's eye.

"It's not that we don't care about you, you understand," Croker explained.

"Quite," said Lain.

"It's just that it's so . . . brown out there."

"Indeed. The nature of the beast, as it were."

"What beast? There's nothing out there but brown!"

"Well, lad, it is the Shashhag, you know. That's what the Shashhag's all about these days. Brown. A bit of color for relief of the eyes. But, essentially, brown."

The greenmen mumbled.

Croker hushed them with a look. "What they mean to say is, sir, that we'll stand out. Like sore thumbs. We won't be able to blend in, as it were, the way we're used to. No sneaking about, and things like that."

"I see."

"We'll be exposed, sir."

"I suppose we will, yes."

Croker drew himself up. "So we're not going."

"I didn't think so." Lain looked at Gideon and said, "This is a habit of theirs, you know."

Gideon remembered. "I remember."

"They mean well."

"Of course they do."

"Not bad lads, not all of them."

"Of course not."

"Good." Lain smiled, and turned back to Boole. "Well, boys, then you'd best be on with it. No scenes, if you don't mind. I appreciate the gift. I'm sure it will come in handy."

Then they shook hands all around, and the greenmen formed up and ran back down the road, not singing, just a little three-part puffing from those who were out of shape. Lain watched until they vanished around the bend, shrugged, and slipped the quiver over his shoulder.

"A shame," he said.

Gideon didn't know what to say.

"They mean well, but I wish it had been a watch." The greenman looked up at the red sky. "Never could tell time by the sun. Not part of my training."

Gideon decided to leave him alone with his thoughts, and slipped an arm around Red's neck. "Well," he said softly, "are you going to head back to the green pastures of home, or are you going to stick it out?"

Red examined the wasteland ahead, checked the Forest behind, and suggested with a grunt and some nudging and a pawing of his clawed hooves that if Gideon really expected him to take one step out on that oversized dried mudbed, then he'd better lay in a supply of grass, easy on the weeds. Gideon agreed, and Tag, without prompting, took off to find what he knew the lorra needed for sustenance.

"What about me?" Tuesday said in her best petulant voice. "Aren't you going to have a touching scene with me about filial loyalty, my present condition as a duck, and your hots for the broad with the blonde hair?"

"You wanna go?" he asked.

"Shit, no."

Gideon crouched down to look her in the eye. "You don't have a choice, you know. I came here in the first place to find you, even if I didn't know it was you I was looking for, and now that you're here and I'm here, I'm not letting you go, so stop complaining and go help Tag."

"Very touching," she said.

"I love you too, Sis."

He rose, stepped onto the plain and put his hands on his hips. Though there was nothing obstructing his vision no matter what direction his gaze took, he knew he was missing something. Something was out there he could not see, and he knew he ought to be able to see it.

Agnes!

He snapped his fingers.

He couldn't see Agnes. She wasn't on the Shashhag the way she had been in his dreams.

As a matter of fact, there wasn't anything on the Shashhag, so where was Ivy?

Then Tag and the duck returned; Red was loaded down with bundles of long grass, hold the weeds; and there was nothing left to do but stall for the night, explaining that it was vital that they be at full strength for the journey.

No one argued.

And the following morning, Gideon was at the edge of the plain again, thinking that seven days was not a really reasonable time in which to expect him to sweep the world clean of most of its troubles and come out of it unscathed.

Seven years, maybe, he thought, and blew out a breath that told his companions he was ready to start.

He took out the bat and examined it for flaws, though he knew there wouldn't be any; he checked his boots to be sure they weren't wearing out in strategic places so as to hobble him at inopportune moments; he made sure there was enough life-giving mead in the pack in case they were faced with circumstances that required strength and endurance above and beyond their own fragile capabilities to provide; and he snapped at Tuesday when she told him to quit his damned stalling and get on with it or get off the pot.

"All right," he said decisively. "All right." He looked ahead, left, and right. "Which direction?"

"I doubt that it matters much," Lain said.

"No," he said.

And no, he thought; no, damnit, it really didn't matter at all.

TWENTY-ONE

"You know," Tuesday said from her perch on Red's back, "this isn't exactly my idea of a lot of fun. In fact, I had more fun at my last audition, when that slimy little director tried to plank me on the couch."

"It's still not too late to fly back," Gideon told her. "And watch your language."

"What language?" she said indignantly. "I was merely trying to emphasize my feelings toward the subject in question."

"We don't have a question, and you're making my ears ache."

"Your ears, my—"

"Tuesday!"

Tag giggled.

Lain averted his head.

The duck grumped a little, groused a little more, and when Gideon suggested a second time that if she felt so strongly about it, she ought to just take wing and bug off, she clapped her bill several times and said, "What, and leave you alone here? All by yourself?"

"You insult Vorden."

Tuesday allowed as how Lain might well be insulted by her exclusion of him in her description of her brother's company should she return to the relative safety of the Fromdil Forest, but she also allowed as how Vorden might be too polite to say what she had just said, and would relish the chance to return to an environment where he didn't stick out quite so much, thus making him a ready target for whoever might attack them.

"Red's red," Gideon reminded her.

Tuesday allowed as how Red's color could easily make him an inviting target as well, though she doubted it since his size was something all potential predators would have to take into consideration before executing an assault, especially when they got close enough to take a gander at his horns.

"Well, damnit!" she said.

"Not to mention Tag."

"Oh, shut up."

Tag laughed nervously, and moved a step closer to the lorra, who didn't mind the company at all.

They were walking abreast across the Shashhag, not bothering to look behind because the Fromdil Forest had long since dropped below the horizon, and there were no footprints to use as a guide for their return. In fact, it was debatable whether they were moving in a straight line at all. There was nothing to use as a goal, a destination, a guide, save for the cracks they generally ignored because they were too erratic and too numerous.

It was, Gideon had noted at one point, like crossing a cracked and disgustingly filthy mirror.

There weren't even any shadows to keep them company.

Desolation, he thought, has found a home here, and make no mistake about it.

Nevertheless, and no matter how hard he struggled to avoid thinking about it, he knew they were not unnoticed. He could feel it in the oppressive atmosphere of the place, in the spectral touch of the dry-cold air, in the hollow sound of their heels on the hard, dustless ground—no, they were not alone, and probably hadn't been since they'd begun their uneasy journey.

Someone was following their progress, but though he frequently checked the skies and the land around, he was unable to fathom how it was accomplished. Neither was he reassured when he saw the expression on Lain's face, and the way Red continually tested the air for scents, and the way Tag lashed out with his dagger at shadows that weren't there.

It was nerve-wracking, and several times he came close to wishing that whoever was doing it would stop it and become visible, if only to ease his mind about which way he was going to die.

And the moment that thought crossed his mind, he slapped himself, hard, and ignored the others' stares.

Then he pointed with his bat: onward, don't look back.

"Giddy?"

"What."

"You really must love her."

"I hadn't thought about it. I'll tell you when I see her."

"Still, you've gone through a lot for a woman who's been around."

"What the hell are you talking about? What do you mean, been around?"

"You think she's still a virgin?"

"Shut up, Tuesday, and ride the goat."

"Men," she muttered.

"Ducks," he snarled.

"Gideon?"

"What."

"Do you think my sister sent us out here to die so she could use us as martyrs to rouse the troops so they'll defeat the Wamchu in the Scarred Mountains?"

"Jesus, Tag, what the hell made you think of that?"

"I don't know. I'm just trying to figure out what we're doing here, that's all."

"Well, think about something else. Think about how good it'll feel not to have the Wamchu threatening you the rest of your life when we get him off our backs and put him where he belongs, permanently."

"You think we'll win?"

"Beats me."

"What about Agnes?"

"A piece of cake."

"What's cake?"

"It's an expression, that's all. It means we won't have any trouble taking care of her."

"You really believe that? Really?"

"Would I lie to you, son?"

"We're gonna die, right?"

"Shit."

"Jesus, Gideon, what a hell of a thing for a young kid like me to think about at a time like this."

"Gideon?"

"What."

"The lads took all the tips from these arrows."

"Thanks."

"Just thought I'd tell you. I knew I should have held out for a watch."

Some time later they came to one of the more ambitious fissures, one that ran more or less diagonally to their left and was a good ten feet across at its center. Cautiously, Lain walked along the rim, peering down, once whistling a sonar note to check on the depth, which he announced to be slightly less than fifteen feet. Large enough to hide a small raiding party, but not large to permanently damage them if they fell in, unless they landed on their heads.

Gideon looked down and saw darkness; the Shashhag's celestial illumination was not strong enough to reach more than a few inches below the surface, though it was reasonably adequate in keepinig the ever-retreating horizon in sight. Neither was a comfort, and he stopped looking down.

A second such depression they discovered just as the sky began to shade toward night, and they debated using the hole as their encampment until dawn.

"I can't sleep down there," Tuesday said. "Do you have any idea what it's like for a duck to be underground?"

"We'll have to keep watch all night," said Tag. "One up above, and one down there. If anyone comes, the one up here can throw the attacker down, and the one down there can bash out his brains." He smiled. "Can I stay down there?"

Lain and Gideon unloaded the gear from Red's back, and dropped it at the fissure's midpoint.

"I think," the greenman said, "it would be best to remain aboveground."

"Hear, hear," the duck agreed.

"Down there we could be trapped. Up here, we can use down there as a last ditch for a stand, should we need it."

"Sounds good to me," Gideon said.

Tag sighed.

"Now all we have to do is decide precisely what constitutes a threat to our well-being," Lain added as he sprawled on the ground and rubbed his thighs and calves.

"Out here, I think that would be anything that moves, or looks like it's moving, or even thinks about moving," Gideon said.

"Hear, hear," Tuesday agreed.

Tag fed the lorra, and sighed.

"Not necessarily," the greenman said. "For example, is that person a threat, or merely a spectator?"

Gideon ordered himself in no uncertain and probably obscene terms not to look in the direction Lain was pointing. He didn't have to. He knew what he would see—a dark figure standing against the blood-red sky, menacing and patient, with an invisible smile on its invisible face.

He looked.

The dark figure was outlined against the blood-red sky, and he could sense the smile on its invisible face.

"I am not optimistic about our chances for a good night's rest," Lain said glumly.

"No kidding," said Tuesday, who had ducked under Red's belly and was watching the dark figure from the protection of the lorra's chin.

Tag had his dagger out and was walking carefully around the rim of the fissure. Once, he spun around and shook his buttocks at it, once leapt into the air and slashed the blade in the direction of the dark figure's throat. Gideon watched the performance without comment; he had seen it before and knew it to be a Kori war dance of provocation, which hadn't worked the first time, and he doubted very much it would work this time, even if he wanted the figure provoked.

"How far away would you say it is?" he asked Lain.

Vorden rose up on an elbow, squinted, sighted along the shaft of an arrow he pulled from his quiver, and closed his eyes in calculation. "Two hundred and thirty yards, give or take. Do you have something in mind?"

But Gideon was rummaging through the pouch Glorian had given him on his departure. She had mentioned something about Whale, and he was hoping that somewhere among all the things he didn't recognize in there was something he had used before.

It was there.

He pulled it out.

"It looks like a round rock," the greenman said, interested enough to get to his feet.

"To me, it looks like a baseball," Gideon said.

"Really? It doesn't look like horsehide to me, though it could be the light, you understand."

Gideon looked at him in astonishment. "Horsehide? You know baseball?"

Lain shook his head.

"Then how did you know about horsehide?"

"Lucky guess. I'm rather good at that, you know."

Gideon didn't doubt that he was, and he didn't doubt that the baseball-like sphere he held was one of Whale's better devices, a sideline of his armory business. It was a bomb. Small, to be sure, but meant to be thrown great distances in order to disrupt the swarming hordes that might be bearing down on one during a day's fighting. Gideon had used one before, throwing it as he did his specialty when he was a professional quarterback—long and hard and with no clear idea where it was going to land.

Close enough, in this case, would be close enough.

"Gideon, please," Tuesday said from under the lorra.

"Think of it as a sign," he told her with a grin.

"It isn't a sign, it's a bomb."

"Think of it as a sign that if it's a bomb, then it might

blow up where it's supposed to and give us some peace, at least for the night.''

The duck stuck its head out, exchanged glances with the giant goat, and lifted a wing in capitulation. "All right, then, go ahead. You want me to call signals?"

The dark figure hadn't moved.

Gideon tossed the bomb up a few times to check its heft, then in one single and marvelously smooth motion drew back his hand, hesitated, and threw.

"Lord," said Lain.

"Wow," said Tag, who was under the lorra with the duck.

And in the Shashhag there was complete silence.

Complete, that is, except for the humming of the sphere as it soared in an incredibly high arc over the ground, leaving behind what appeared to be a faint trail, like a comet. It quickly became lost in the darkened red of the sky, appeared again as it began its descent, and vanished just before it struck the earth.

Gideon waited.

The dark figure hadn't moved.

The bomb landed, and exploded, and the concussion on the otherwise noiseless plain was deafening. Gouts, divots, and spumes of earth fanned into the air; dust formed a cloud that hovered because there was no wind to take it. Red bleated, and Tuesday quacked, and Tag came out to stand beside Lain while Gideon watched patiently for bits and/or pieces of the dark figure to litter the landscape.

For he had hit it.

He had no idea how he'd managed to get it that far, nor how he had been so miraculously accurate.

But he had hit it.

And he waited.

Until the dark figure emerged from the cloud and began walking toward them. Slowly. As if in a solemn processional. A dark hand up to brush debris from its shoulders, the cowl that covered its head, the puffed and hanging black silk of its sleeves.

"Oh hell," Gideon said, and rummaged frantically for another bomb.

Tag drew his dagger, and Lain drew his rapier, and together they formed a wall in front of Tuesday, who was running for the fissure and getting nowhere because Red was standing on her tail.

"Oh hell!"

"I believe," said Vorden Lain, "we have made an error."

Gideon agreed.

"I wonder if it would be fruitful to arrange a retreat at this point."

Gideon doubted it.

There was no sense in running. Not now. Not when their mistake was striding confidently toward them, strawberry-blond hair blowing in a nonexistent breeze, elegant clothes reassembling themselves after their disarray, boots thudding in echoes, spurs chink-chinking, and the red lining of its cloak perfectly matching the bloodtint of the sky.

"Got it!" he cried, holding up another bomb.

"Too late," said Lain.

"Too late indeed, you miserable little worm," came the voice from the dark figure, the voice of the Wamchu.

TWENTY-TWO

It had been some time since Gideon had seen Lu Wamchu, and he didn't regret a single moment of its passing. The Wamchu, however, evidently felt quite the opposite emotion since, as he positioned himself in front of the band, his expression was one that could only belong to a man starved for the company of those he was about to crush beneath his heel.

He was exceedingly tall, his silken ebony ensemble giving him an aura of insubstantiality, and highlighting his fair complexion and Orientally aslant eyes—the product, perhaps, of an errant cheerleader on a tramp steamer bound for Shanghai. Or so Gideon thought as he waited for the man to step away from his sister so he could throw the damned bomb and be done with it.

Despite certain unpleasant displays of magical tendencies, which the man overdid on occasion, the Wamchu was no immortal, nor was he immune to the ills of hand-to-hand combat. Gideon had proven that at their last meeting. And since he knew that the others knew the Wamchu's essential if not demonstrable humanity—in at least the physical sense—he wondered why they didn't take action. They were two able men, a reasonably enthusiastic boy, a lorra, and a duck—certainly that should have been enough to overpower the man, despite his size.

But no one moved.

And he would have been hard-pressed to prove that any of the others were even breathing.

Cautiously, while the Wamchu hooked his thumbs into a belt wide enough to strangle a society matron, he edged over to Lain and whispered, "If I distract him, you can nail him."

Lain adjusted his green cap without making a single sign that he had heard.

Gideon covered his puzzlement with a brief spasm of coughing while he sidled over to Red and suggested, sotto voce, that the lorra be prepared to charge as soon as Gideon made his move.

Red's eyes remained distressingly white.

Tag was doing a magnificent job of cowering while standing up, and the duck was under the lorra's belly again.

I'm missing something, Gideon thought; something's going on that's escaped me.

"Well, hero," Lu said, his silent gloating done for the moment. "I imagine you are thinking that it would be a wise thing on your part to attack me, since it would appear that you have me outnumbered."

Gideon, in spite of himself, nodded.

"I think not," the man said, leaned back, and laughed.

"Where's Ivy?" Gideon asked, and twitched the bat in front of him, slowly. "Five seconds, Lu, to tell me where Ivy is."

"Oh! And then you will kill me, is that it?"

"Four."

The Wamchu turned his back on them, spread his hands as if appealing to the horizon, and said over his shoulder, "Idiot! What kind of an idiot do you think I am?"

Gideon considered the choices, weighed them, and was about to spit out a list that would have had the man reeling in his tracks, when he heard scuffling off to his right. He whirled, just in time to see a company of Moglar leap from the fissure, weapons brandished, grimly leather armor creaking like saddles that have been in the sun too long. Then, to his astonishment, another fissure not ten feet from where he stood peeled back, and another company of Moglar leapt to the surface.

"Son of a bitch," he said.

Lain sheathed his rapier and readjusted his cap.

Tuesday and Tag made for Red's back, and were aboard just as several more ostensible fissures were revealed to be little more than clever camouflage covers for untold hundreds of giant dwarves, who swiftly gathered in a large circle around them, mumbling ominously to themselves while the Wamchu leaned back and laughed again.

By the time Gideon was able to recover from the shock of seeing both his plan—whatever that was—and his future slip away from him, he realized that the Shashhag was no longer a plain of uninterrupted monotony broken only by the infrequent fissures, but now only a plain of uninterrupted monotony.

He was surrounded by an army.

He was surrounded by an army of greasy-haired, uncouth and unpopular warriors whose only lot in life was to do the Wamchu's evil bidding, for good or ill, and think nothing of their own lives unless they were threatened by superior forces or people who could hit a lot.

It was humiliating.

It was also, he thought while the Wamchu laughed on, awfully puzzling, since an army here meant one army less fighting in the bowl of the Scarred Mountains; he was positive that this wasn't right. There just weren't that many giant dwarves to go around. And there weren't, so far as he knew, any other warrior clans, castes, or social classes.

Which meant that the Vondel brothers were fighting someone else.

Or, that the fighting wasn't as far away as he had thought.

Or, that the Wamchu had been defeated and was using the remnants of his army to capture him, and only him, for the sole purpose of delivering his oft-promised revenge.

And that didn't make sense.

Why use a whole army?

Unless Lu was more afraid of Gideon than his present attitude let on.

Wamchu wiped tears from his eyes and put his hands on his hips. "So, hero, you were counting?"

"Three," Gideon said.

It was a long shot, but it was just possible, as Glorian had speculated, that the Moglar would not fight if their leader was incapacitated, or dead; it was conceivable that the muttering louts would turn tail and run as soon as they realized that there was no one left to tell them what to do.

Lu was puzzled, and hooked his thumbs even more snugly behind his belt.

"Two."

Of course, Gideon reminded himself, it was also possible that they could get so pissed off that they would trample him into the ground, cut him to pieces, and feed what was left of him to whatever disgusting creatures made their home on this dread-inducing plain.

He paused.

The Wamchu watched him warily.

The Moglar shifted side to side with impatience, their stringy black hair whipping their shoulders unmercifully.

"For god's sake, Giddy, do something!"

Lu turned his attention to the lorra, and to the white duck on its back. "Well, well," he said. "Whale's little starlet is still a bird, I see."

Tuesday strode up Red's neck and stood defiantly between the rise of his deadly horns. "Bird enough to know you're a chicken, blondie."

"Hey, Tuesday," Gideon said softly.

Wamchu took a step forward, and the Moglar stopped muttering. "Blondie?" He brushed a hand through his long, thick locks and smiled mirthlessly. "Jealous? Is the little duckie jealous of the big man's hair, which the little duckie hasn't got any more of since she has turned into a little duckie by the big man with the pretty hair?"

Tuesday's tail rose, her feet dug in, and her eyes narrowed to an impossible squint. "Step over here and say that, you wimp."

"Wimp?"

Jesus, Gideon thought, and tried to pick out which would be the first hundred Moglar he would have to fight.

"Wimp, you say?"

The warriors edged in, edged back at a brusque gesture

from their leader, and edged away yet again when the Wamchu did indeed take that step toward the duck, who was hissing, beak-snapping, and flapping her wings in such a vile manner that even Lain, wise to the ways of the forest and the world, felt constrained to throw caution aside and nock a tipless arrow in his bow.

Tag was too busy getting off the lorra and behind Gideon to do much else but drop his dagger, pick it up, drop it, pick it up, drop it, and throw his hands up in confusion.

"Wimp?" the Wamchu shouted.

Gideon hurried to Red's side, reached up, and tapped his sister on what passed for a shoulder. She glared at him, hissed at the Wamchu, who was taking a third step toward her, and looked back to her brother.

"Well, what do you want?"

"To stay alive," he suggested.

"Better red than dead, is that it?"

The lorra snorted in digust, bucked, and Tuesday agilely landed on her feet, which she instantly used to scurry over to her brother.

"No," he said. "Caution. We are, as the man says, rather outnumbered."

"Well, I'd rather be dead than be a duck any longer."

"But you'd be dead," he pointed out.

"Yes, well, there is that," she conceded. "But Jesus!"

"Enough," ordered the Wamchu imperiously. "You will follow me, now, and make no attempt to escape."

Gideon checked the hundreds of giant dwarves surrounding them and wondered if Lu thought he was alone.

"Where are we going?" he asked with no great enthusiasm.

"Just follow me, and watch yourselves at all times," was the answer. At which point, the Wamchu turned smartly, smoothed his shirt down over his chest, and began walking. Away. In a straight line toward the horizon.

Gideon looked at each of his companions in turn, saw no desire there to attempt either an escape or a clever ruse that would fool the Moglar into believing they were involved in a lost cause, and gestured them forward.

Minutes passed.

The sky deepened to a hue close to crimson.

Hours passed, full night descended upon the plain, and the Wamchu ordered them to sit down, sleep as best they could, and keep their weapons about them because one never knew about a restless Moglar who was faced with the temptation of a good fight.

"You think one of us is going to challenge all of them?" Gideon said incredulously.

"I know heroes," the man said pointedly. "You are a foolish lot, and a bunch of damned fools. You'd try anything to prove yourselves."

"I wouldn't attack an army," Gideon said, and concentrated on letting his feet and legs understand that all was not lost, that they were not, as far as he knew, destined to be worn down to the kneecaps, though he felt oddly guilty when, at the same time, he crossed his fingers.

Incredibly, they did sleep.

Incredibly, when they awakened to the Wamchu's booted prodding, they felt as though they hadn't slept at all.

Fifteen minutes later, they were moving again, under a sullen sky that had turned the color of sluggish blood, over a plain that reflected that color without much spirit but with a fair amount of grimness, and through the day and into the next night, which boasted no stars, no moon, no wind.

Walk. Rest. Walk.

An interminable march of hellish proportions.

Walk. Stumble. Rest. Walk.

Tuesday was so disheartened she didn't even try to sing.

One foot in front of the other, mindlessly, soullessly, numbing the brain to all but the most primitive of thoughts.

Tag's face was taut with the effort not to cry, to prove that he too was a man and could take all the punishment the Wamchu could hand out.

The Wamchu seemed indefatigable, and the Moglar who dropped from exhaustion were ignored by their brothers after they had been relieved of their boots, their armor, their weapons, and what little food they carried in tiny pouches slung under their chins.

Tag and the duck slept on the lorra's back; Lain managed

an hour's dozing when Tag fell off and was dragged along by Gideon, who refused to give in to his body's demands for renewal and rehabilitation, because he did not want Lu to think less of him than he already did.

Dumb, he thought when he stumbled over his shadow.

Dumb, dumb, he thought when he bumped into Red's tail, and the tail lashed at him wearily.

This is stupid, he thought, and pulled Tag off the lorra, climbed on with Red's sleepy permission, and buried his head in the animal's hair.

He had no idea how long he slept.

But when he woke up, they were still tramping across the Sashhag, Wamchu striding briskly as though he were heading down to the corner store for a box of ammunition, and the Moglar strung out on all sides, not terribly alert but still on their feet.

Groggy from sleep, Gideon slid to the ground and did a few walking exercises to loosen his tightened leg muscles, his aching back muscles, and the rest of the muscles that ached just to blend in so unnecessary demands wouldn't be made upon them. Then he saw how weakly Tuesday clung to Red's hair, how wobbly were Tag and Lain on their feet, and he began to lose his temper.

He snapped the bat into his hand and lengthened his stride until he was only a few feet behind the Wamchu, who heard him coming and looked disdainfully over his shoulder until he saw the expression on Gideon's face, then quickly slipped a hand into his shirt and brought out a gleaming, nine-pointed silver throwing star whose edges were so sharp that not even he was able to handle it without the cost of a few drops of blood.

Gideon had seen the weapon before; he was not afraid.

"Enough," and he set the bat on his shoulder in an attitude of casual but hair-trigger menace. "We have to rest, or we'll all be dead before we get to wherever it is you're taking us."

"Out of the question," said Lu, tossing the star up, catching it, wincing, and tossing it up again.

"I'm no good to you dead," he said.

"You shall be dead anyway, hero. I will not grieve at your passing, whether it be here or there."

Gideon glanced around, and realized that the nearest Moglar was only a few inches shy of a hundred yards away. "Where is there?"

"Shashhag, of course."

One eye closed. "But this is Shashhag."

"And so is there Shashhag. It is," the Wamchu said with a wave of the starless hand, "all Shashhag. And it is all mine."

Gideon felt reckless, and was glad that Tuesday couldn't hear him. "Really? Does Agnes know that?"

The effect was precisely what he had predicted in that last moment before he called himself a shithead—Lu stopped, turned, and gripped the star in its close-quarters throwing position. His eyes were hooded, his lips bloodless, his chest rising and falling in graphic demonstration of his extreme agitation.

The main body of the Moglar army, receiving no orders to the contrary, marched on.

Red and Lain took the opportunity to fall down.

"You will die for that," Wamchu said, as close to hissing as he could get in a sentence without sibilants. "This all would have been over if it wasn't for her. And you are the reason it isn't over, hero."

"You just said it was Agnes," he said, flexing his fingers around the bat's handle.

"Agnes. You. One and the same."

Gideon turned sideways toward him. "It isn't my fault your wives aren't happy at home. It isn't my fault you can't provide them with enough diversion to keep them out of trouble."

"You are a murderer," Lu said heatedly. "You have killed two of the only things I have ever loved!"

Then Wamchu drew back his hand; Gideon tightened his grip on the bat.

A tense moment.

"If we weren't so close," Wamchu said, "I would kill you here and now."

"Close? Close to what?"

Ask a stupid question, he thought then, as the Wamchu whirled and threw the star.

It whirred, hummed, soared, spiraled, arced, and Gideon was just about to wonder aloud what the purpose of that demonstration was when, suddenly, the star seemed to explode, and the air shattered like glass before it.

TWENTY-THREE

"In my dressing room," Tuesday said, "I had a mirror that had six panes, so you could see yourself from the back when you had to. Do you have any idea what it's like sneaking up on yourself when you're sitting down?"

Gideon grunted.

"I mean, it's really spooky. Especially if you're wearing makeup and you don't recognize yourself. I was dressed like a guy for one part and almost proposed to myself. God, was I fresh. What a mouth."

He grunted again.

"Nice pecs, though."

"Tuesday, be quiet," he said gently.

Chatting with an hysterical duck was not at the top of his list of priorities just at the moment, though he had to admit that she had a point, since it seemed as if all this time they had been walking toward the biggest mirror he had ever seen in his life. And an odd mirror at that, since it had reflected only the plain and not those traversing it.

Wamchu was silent as well, except for an occasional spate of curses the general drift of which damned himself for knocking down a perfectly good illusion instead of opening the damned door.

And a door there must have been, for beyond the large

opening the nine-star had created was another plain. This one, however, was green, and treed, and the sky was blue, the breeze refreshing, the flowers brilliant, and the noise Gideon had been subliminally hearing since Lu had confronted him more distinct.

It was the sound of fighting.

Lots of it.

Luckily, not within easy walking distance.

"Well?" the Wamchu said, and stepped through.

The others, too stunned to argue, too pleased by the change in venue, followed; and as soon as they did, and looked behind them, Shashhag was gone.

"Fascinating," Lain said, and pointed to the west. "My word, Gideon, those are the Scarred Mountains, eastern slope, if I'm not mistaken."

"Very clever, woodsman," Lu said with a harsh cackle. "Very clever, for all the good it will do you."

The Scarred Mountains rose immediately to their left in a forested wall toward towering clouds scudding across the sky. Streaks of red gave the range its name, and though they were not terribly high as mountains go, they were still daunting. And it was from there that the wind carried the symphony of battle.

Gideon stood with his hands on his hips. "Do you mean to tell me," he said to no one in particular, though he wished mightily that Glorian were here, "that all we had to do was walk around the goddamned things instead of—" He sputtered.

"Right," said Tag.

Gideon noted with some astonishment that most of the Moglar army had disappeared. Nine Moglar lined up behind the Wamchu, looking as if they'd be hard pressed to lift a leg, much less their weapons, but they were fierce enough to settle the tiny band into an uneasy silence while Lu scanned the plain for several minutes before nodding to himself.

"Still four days to go," he muttered.

"Aha!" Gideon said, feeling a sudden surge of hope. "You, too, huh?"

Wamchu turned, slowly. "If you have the nerve to suggest that I am concerned about the upcoming Event . . ."

Gideon grinned, and leaned casually against Red, who was so busy grazing on fresh, moist, tender grass that he didn't object because permission hadn't been asked. "Damn right I am."

The wind shifted; the battle sounds faded.

Wamchu hooked his thumbs into his belt and studied the former quarterback sullenly. "She could do us all great harm," he said.

"Slice us," Tuesday explained.

"She could," the Wamchu continued, "insure our subjugation to her will."

"A little seasoning, maybe some mushrooms."

The Wamchu looked thoughtful. "She could make sure, if she wanted, that we would never walk the earth again."

"Well done," Tuesday said, and fell off Red in a swoon.

Tag hurried to her side, fanned her with his vest, and held her close.

"Don't worry about it," her brother told him. "She's thinking about steaks again." He looked to his archenemy. "And I suppose you're wondering how to stop her, before the Day makes her too powerful? No. Don't answer. I can see it in your eyes. Lu, you are as afraid of her as we are. Which makes me wonder why you're bothering with us instead of her."

The Moglar sat down, sensing a long bout of exposition scarcely a word of which they would understand since it didn't have anything directly to do with killing things.

The Wamchu toyed with his ringlets, his strands, his curls, his locks, and shook his head. "Bait," he said at last.

"Ah," said Lain. "A ploy."

Gideon nodded.

The Moglar, confused, stood up.

"A trade," Lu continued. "You for my life. If I don't succeed in taking care of her first."

Gideon looked at Lain, looked at Tag and his sister, looked across the rolling, idyllic plain, and sighed. It was, he thought, ever thus. A pawn in the great chess game of power.

The Moglar, seeing his expression, sat down.

Wamchu, he went on in silence, will hold me until he

strikes a bargain with his wife. Then he will release me, and I
will die. Or Agnes won't bother, but simply wait until the
Day and just take me because no one will be able to stop her.
Or Wamchu, knowing that he doesn't really have anything to
bargain with unless she is set on a lot of torture before the
Event, will pretend to use me as a hostage while, all the time,
attempting to find out the disposition of Glorian's armies.

Unfortunately, the wind shifted, and they all knew the
disposition of Glorian's armies. The fighting was fierce, by
the sound of it, and he hoped, suddenly, that the Vondels
weren't getting scalped.

Lu cleared his throat, and the Moglar stood up.

Gideon shrugged. "You're not that stupid," he said. "You
know it won't work. There's an ulterior motive."

"Ivy," Tuesday said from her position in Tag's arms.

Gideon gaped.

Wamchu might or might not have blushed.

Lain rubbed his chin thoughtfully, and nodded. "But yes,
that's it, and that's been it all along, hasn't it, you sneaky
little devil? God, you're diabolical when you want to be. You
want Ivy, and Agnes has her, and you think that trading
Gideon for her will make Ivy so grateful to you that she will,
perforce, ally her many warrior skills with yours, so that, on
the Day, your losses will be kept to a minimum."

"Something like that," Wamchu said brusquely, and gestured to his men, who drew their weapons and sneered,
growled, and trembled their heads in a threatening manner.

"No," Gideon said.

"You have no choice."

"I do so. I can say no, I won't be a part of it. I'd rather
take my chances with Agnes, without putting myself in a
position of vulnerability."

"Christ," Tuesday said, "you're sounding like him now."

Gideon didn't care. The Wamchu didn't have his army,
didn't have him over a barrel, didn't have him anything
except maybe furious for not having done something about it
sooner. Though, he recalled, there were all those Moglar,
which would have made doing something a bit on the dicey

side. As it was, nine of them plus the Wamchu still was not in the best interests of his continuing health.

Lu drew himself up, and his hands disappeared into the folds of his cloak, reappeared with two highly polished daggers which he pointed at Gideon. "You will come with me to Thazbinn, now, hero, or you will die, now, hero."

"No," Gideon said.

"Then I will kill your friends, one by one, until you submit to my will."

"No."

Lu drew back his left arm. "I'm very good, you know."

Lain and Tag leapt to flank Red, sword and dagger at the ready; Tuesday fluttered to the lorra's back and bared her beak; and Red, looking up from his grazing and noting the situation, stopped chewing long enough to turn his eyes black.

"Honest," said the Wamchu. "I haven't missed in ages."

Gideon, getting tired of quandaries, predicaments, and no-win situations, realized in a blinding flash of belated insight that the main reason for the Wamchu's ascendancy to the throne of chief unmitigated bastard and general all-around pain in the ass was his three wives. They were the ones with the magical and psychic powers; they were the ones whose ambitions had loosed the canines of conflict; they were the ones who were two down and one to go, and the Wamchu was suffering a severe case of mortality.

The Moglar grumbled impatiently.

The Wamchu also wanted Ivy, and Gideon would be damned if he was going to give her up that easily.

"Take a long walk on a short pier," he said angrily, whipped out his bat, turned, and headed northward, with the abrupt slopes on his left. Tag, not wishing to be left behind to partake in the slaughter the giant dwarves were preparing, ran after him; Lain swatted the lorra's haunch and ran as well.

For his part, the Wamchu could only gape at the astounding and unprecedented bravado of the hero with the unsightly beard and really filthy jeans. "Hey!" he bellowed. "Hey, you can't do that!"

Gideon ignored him. Somewhere along the trail he had spotted at the base of the slopes was Thazbinn, and in Thazbinn, whatever that was, was Ivy. And Agnes. And he was going to have it out with all of them, once and for all, so he could get on with figuring out what the hell he was going to do with his life.

It occurred to him that getting rid of the Wamchus would effectively put him out of business.

It also occurred to him that he just might be able to get enough villages interested in football to start his own league, which wasn't all that bad a prospect unless the coaches he picked didn't want him on their teams.

A dagger slammed into the ground not five feet in front of him, and he whirled, colliding with Red, who was moving rather more quickly than the suddenly shrieking Moglar who were chasing him, and Tag, and Lain, who stopped every few feet, spun, fired a tipless arrow, and sent one of the warriors spinning to the ground.

The Wamchu did not run; he strode, spurs chinking loudly, and threw another knife.

Gideon sidestepped it, and tried to decide whether or not to wait. When the first Moglar caught up with him and narrowly missed taking off his left shoulder with a studded mace, he said, "Son of a bitch," and let his temper go.

The resulting melee was chaotic: Gideon was swinging at anything that moved. Lain was pinking anything that came within the thrust of his rapier, Tag was viciously bruising shins and slicing leather, Red was running back and forth between bites of a succulent blue shrub and butting Moglar from the back, and Tuesday was flying overhead, shouting the positions of the enemy, which eventually no one paid heed to since no one knew who she was talking to.

The Wamchu stood in the middle of the road and threw knives. Lots of knives, four of which landed in the skulls of his own men, two of which creased the thighs of the greenman and the lad, and one of which glanced off the bat and buried itself in a nearby tree, which instantly shriveled like a pricked balloon.

The clash of steel, the groans of injury, the shrieks of the dying, all were absent from this skirmish, since those who were wounded died without a sound, and those who were not wounded were wounded so slightly that in the heat of the moment they were able to clench their teeth against the pain and fight on.

At the death of the seventh Moglar, from a well-aimed rock dropped from Tuesday's beak from a height guaranteed to exhaust her before she could make it to the Wamchu, who was her primary target, the two remaining giant dwarves recalculated their positions vis-à-vis old age, and ran up the slope, thinking they had a better chance in the main war on the other side.

Gideon lowered his bat and gulped for air.

Red found another blue shrub, much larger than the first one.

Tag and Lain bound each other's thighs while Tuesday crooned soothingly to take their minds off their agony.

"Well?" Gideon said.

The Wamchu fussed with his hair, searched his cloak and blouse for more weapons, and smiled. "You think you have defeated me, hero?"

"No."

"You think you have me now, at your mercy?"

"No."

Lu glanced at the slope, then looked across the plain and laughed—loudly, and long, and shook a fist at his adversary. "You are a fool, Gideon! This is only a temporary setback, and I shall return with enough stout men to crush you into the ground!"

Gideon imagined he could do just that. "What about Agnes?"

"Agnes," the man sneered, "can take her Day, and shove it where it'll—"

He never finished.

One moment the Wamchu was standing in the middle of the road, and the next the road had opened a perfectly circular hole beneath him. He had only time enough to yelp before he dropped, straight down, and the hole closed over him.

It was as if, Gideon thought, he had never been.

"Wow," he said.

"Agnes," said Lain.

"Trouble," said Tag.

"Now what?" asked Tuesday.

"There," said Gideon, and pointed his bat to the northeast.

Tuesday stared in the direction he indicated, stared at her brother, then took wing and flew as high as she could without getting dizzy. When she returned, she waddled up to him and slapped him a good one on the calf.

"How did you do that?" she said.

He pointed again.

She slapped him again. "No. I mean, how did you know there was a city over there?"

Gideon knelt beside her and put a brotherly hand on her neck. "Because," he said, "Lu didn't bring us out of the Shashhag at any old place along the line. He said there was a door, remember? And on the other side of that door was this trail, this road, and that was no accident.

"He also said that he was taking us to Thazbinn, and it had to be along here somewhere."

"You figured that out all by yourself?" she said.

He smiled and kissed her pate. "I am the hero, after all," he told her.

"So, hero," she said, "how do you know Agnes won't open a hole under us, too?"

He stood angrily and marched off, wondering why it was that whenever he came up with a decent idea, coupled none too closely with a bit of luck, someone always had to come up with a question he couldn't answer. Why the hell couldn't they just let it be, just once, and let him revel for a few minutes in his own internal glow of satisfaction.

"Well, Giddy?" she shouted after him.

"I don't know, okay?" he called back. And stopped, turned, and said, "And for the last time, would you please stop calling me—"

All right, he thought; all right, who's the wise guy?

The road was empty.

Everyone was gone.

And so, when he looked down, was the ground beneath him.

TWENTY-FOUR

It wasn't the first time Gideon had noticed the Wamchu family's penchant for using chutes when a simple "come with me, please" would have done. As it was, this was better than most—the slope was gentle enough to prevent him from feeling as if he were falling, the metal of which it was constructed was friction-free enough to keep his jeans from burning through at the seat, and though the tunnel through which he passed wasn't much more than an elongated blur, he also caught glimpses of some rather impressive murals the subjects of which seemed to concentrate on various degrees of disorder and disruption among civilian populations of cities burning down around their heads.

At one point there was an intersection with a route to his left, but it came upon him too rapidly for him to do anything but make a futile grab for the edge of the wall, yanking his hand back just in time when he realized that grabbing the edge would have neatly amputated his fingers, and a good portion of his palm if the grip had been a strong one.

He felt himself in no immediate danger.

The ride was almost completely silent.

And for the time being, he was at least free of those horrid battle sounds, which, muffled though they were by the Scarred

Mountains being between him and the action, were haunting enough when he considered the lives being lost.

Another intersection, just as the chute banked to the right, and as he passed it he heard Tuesday singing.

Making the best of it, he supposed, and pulled in his arms as the tunnel began to narrow, the chute's angle decreased and rose, and he found himself sweeping upward and to the left.

Another twist and turn, and another intersecting tunnel gave him a winking glimpse of Red on his back, legs in the air, and Tag sitting astride his belly, holding onto his forepaws and using them to steer.

If I see a white rabbit, he thought, I will give myself a medal for not screaming.

Down again.

Up again.

The friction-free surface showed signs of wearing out, as did the seams and cheeks of his jeans.

He attempted to dig in the heels of his boots, but nothing happened; he tried the baseball bat, but all that did was make the metal walls resound like an off-key gong; and finally he tried leaning back and enjoying the trip, except that he had a terrible suspicion of what lay at its end, and he wasn't exactly sure he knew how to get out of it.

Suddenly, as he was thinking that there might be something in Whale's pouch to aid him, the chute straightened, the tunnel ceiling vanishing upward, and he saw some yards away a large room approaching at a speed deceptive by its slow progress toward him, or he toward it.

After the relative darkness of the tunnel, the light in the room was blinding, and he covered his eyes, braced himself, and managed only a few mild obscenities and a groan before he was shot out of the tunnel mouth, into the air, across the room, and onto a tall pile of multicolored, thick cushions, another one of the Wamchus' odd little touches for their prisoners.

He bounced, slid, scrambled, and managed to reach the floor on his feet—a little wobbly, but ready for anything.

And ready he was to get out of the way when Red and Tag

flew over his head, followed swiftly by Tuesday, who was frantically trying to conquer the unusual skill of flying backward, and Lain in a shower of tipless arrows that had come loose from their quiver.

He made no move to untangle them from the pillows. Once he was assured they were uninjured—mainly by listening for signs of pain amid their varying exclamations and curses—he examined the room more closely.

Fifty feet on a side, he estimated, its floor covered by a massive, thick, shaggy carpet a uniform and comfortable brown, its walls save where the chute ended unbroken by openings of any sort, and unrelieved by tapestries or paintings or the pathetic scrawls of previous incarcerants. In fact, aside from the pillows and the carpet, there was nothing in the room at all. And though there was plenty of light, he could find no source.

He wondered, then, where the Wamchu was, if he had been here and had been taken away, or if he'd been routed to yet another place.

Then Red, needing a good long brushing to get the chute-blown tangles out of his hair, came up to him and lowered his head so that they exchanged meaningful glances. The lorra was panting, and his eyes, though no longer black, were a definite temperamental grey. Gideon stroked his neck, tugged playfully at the beard, and patted the animal's muzzle until the lorra had calmed. Once done, they began a systematic search of the walls, which, Gideon noted, were made of an odd sort of brown-gold wood that did not seem to have any grain at all.

Tuesday flew to the ceiling, hovered, darted, hovered again, and returned to report failure. "This place is like a damned prison, Gideon," she complained.

"Well, what the hell did you expect?"

"A steak. The condemned duck is supposed to get a steak before it's executed."

Lain, trailing behind them and double-checking the solid virtue of the walls, raised an eyebrow. "My dear, what makes you think we're going to be executed?"

"Stands to reason," she said.

"Oh."

"We could always get out," Tag called to them from just to the right of the pillows.

"Of course we could," Gideon said, laying on the sarcasm to be sure the boy wasn't disillusioned. "If you find the door, open it, and we'll just walk out, okay?"

"Sure," said Tag, and opened the door.

Gideon was in an alley narrow and choked with piles of neatly stacked garbage crawling with the largest and most well-fed calico rats Gideon had ever seen in his life. The feeding rodents had ignored him when he slipped out of the room, froze when Red appeared, and ran like hell when Tuesday flapped out to land on the lorra's shoulder.

"Incredible," Gideon said.

"Thazbinn," said Lain, looking up at the sky. "Also, close to sunset."

The buildings were of stone carved into the size and shape of irregular bricks, and the few windows overlooking the alley were too high for them to see into, even if they could have seen through the shutters that were closed and locked over them. In the distance they could hear the unmistakable clamor of pedestrian traffic, market sellers, gongs, whistles, horns, and the infrequent crack of an impatient whip.

For a moment they were undecided about the direction. Whatever was to their left was hidden because of a sharp turn the alley took, and what they could see to their right was little more than a glimpse of passing movement through the intricate network of garbage mounds. Lain and Tag professed never to have been here in their lives, Red was no help, and Tuesday refused to fly in any direction to scout for possible escape.

"Damn," Gideon said. "We can't stay here all night, you know. She's bound to find out we're gone, and I am not waiting around to see what she'll do when she does."

"I have a fairly decent idea," Lain said.

Gideon, in order not to hear it, struck out to his right, weaving through the intricacies of garbage-maze suballeys until he crouched behind an imposing cone of orange peels and peeked around it.

"Looks to be a main street," he said to Lain, who was rummaging through the mounds for discarded arrow tips. "We could lose ourselves in that mess and she'd never find us."

The greenman looked doubtful, both at the idea and the V-shaped walnut he'd found in a discarded pair of socks. "We are not citizens," he reminded him. "We may be spotted all too easily."

"But if we hurry," Gideon said, "we might be able to find out where the palace or mayor's house is, and that's probably where Agnes is, and that's probably where Ivy is."

Lain considered it, but gave no encouragement. "She might be in the prison, have you thought of that?"

"But that's where we just were, weren't we?"

Lain shrugged.

Jesus, Gideon thought, and broached the suggestion to Tag, who was pawing through the garbage for something to eat since, he reminded them all, they hadn't had a bite since they'd started out that morning.

"Forget your stomach for a minute!" he snapped. "Just tell me whether or not you're going with me, for god's sake."

"I think it would be better if we stormed them, you know? Really scare them to death and panic them, and that way we wouldn't be any different from anyone else."

"Tag, you can't storm a city once you're inside it. The idea of storming is to get inside. We don't have to get inside. We're already inside. Storming—" He heard thunder, closed his eyes, opened them, and saw Red quickly devouring the main source of his cover.

"We go," he decided. And straightened. And began to walk toward the street. "Move it, children, before the bad guys come."

"Wouldn't it be quicker if we went over the rooftops?" Tag asked hopefully.

Gideon glared over his shoulder. "Sure. You find the stairs in these solid walls, and I'll follow you on my knees."

"Sure," said Tag, and pointed to the stairs.

* * *

Incredible, Gideon thought as he rushed up after the others and found himself on a wide rooftop that gave him a panoramic view of the entire city, or that part of it that wasn't hidden by a series of glittering white towers clustered in the city's center.

"What are they?" he asked the greenman.

Lain took off his cap, scratched his head, replaced the cap, and said, "They are the fabled towers of Thazbinn, if I have it right."

"No kidding. What do they do?"

"I wouldn't know. They're only fabled, not terribly useful. Look nice, don't you think?"

The wall around the roof was only waist-high, certainly low enough for him to shove the man over and later claim it was an accident. But he only smiled, and walked to the building's front, skirting a round stone structure that he assumed was the entrance to a stairwell leading down to the street, though a quick examination failed to uncover an entrance.

He leaned over, Tuesday poked her head over, and Red sat and refused to look.

The street two long stories below was wide and, now, massed with thousands of people moving purposefully in all directions. He could see shops, stalls, riders on things that looked like giraffes with their necks cut off, wagons, carts, riders on things that looked like lorras shaved to the bone, the rich, the poor, the hearty middle class, riders on things that looked like nothing he'd ever seen before and was sorry he was looking at now.

And every one of the people he saw—young, old, ugly, beautiful, fat, thin, well-nourished, starving—was carrying a weapon of some kind. A new weapon, or at least a weapon that was in remarkably good condition if it was an old one dug out of the attic for the occasion. They looked, in fact, as if they were preparing for an invasion, and the invaders were going to have a hell of a shock when they showed up.

He pulled away from the wall and looked around him. Most of the neighboring buildings were no taller than this, but they were separated by gaps that ranged from ten to twenty-five feet. Behind them was a street much like the one he'd just seen.

"I don't know," he said, dropping down to sit with his back against the wall. "I don't know. We're here, and it's where we've been trying to get all this time, and I don't know what to do next."

Ivy, he thought.

"We could wait," Lain said.

"For what?"

"For Agnes to make her next move."

"Oh sure." Then: "Oh shit."

He was dumb. He was stupid. How could he have thought that their escape from the chute room was a matter of extreme good fortune? Agnes was not, by any account, a dense and dim woman. She was up to something, and they had been permitted to go free. Permitted, and she was probably watching them right now, and laughing.

Tuesday made a swift waddle around the wall, and returned with her beak snapping. "Well, let's go, let's go, boys. If we stay here we'll never get this thing done. Four days, my dears, in case you've lost count. Tomorrow's three, and we can't afford to sit around feeling sorry for ourselves."

Lain frowned.

Gideon told him to pay her no mind, because she always got hyperactive just before a crisis crashed down on her head. It was, he explained, an instinct she had. A little uneven in its control, but useful on double dates.

Tag, meanwhile, had been examining the circular structure closely, hunting, Gideon imagined, for another one of his tricks—like an elevator or something.

"Hey," Tag said, waving at them frantically. "Hey, c'mon, I've found an elevator."

Gideon stood and grabbed Lain's arm desperately before the man could run off. "How does he do it, huh? I mean . . . how does he do it?"

"I don't know him well," the greenman said, "but I would suggest that he simply looks for the obvious. We, being sophisticated beings, tend to obscure things with the complex. Which may be a trifle facile, perhaps, but not terribly far off the mark, I shouldn't doubt.''

Right, Gideon thought, and ran over to collar the boy before he disappeared down the hole he'd uncovered in the curving wall.

Gideon closed the door carefully.

"No," he said. "Not now."

"But why?" Tag protested. "This is our chance!"

"And that," Gideon said, pointing up, "is night. Night is dark. At night it's hard enough finding your way around the places you do know when there isn't any light."

And there was no light.

None from the shops, none from the empty streets, and barely enough from the moon and stars to let them see the ends of their respective noses and muzzle and beak.

"Tag," he said, "you don't know this place, I don't know this place, Lain doesn't know this place. Assuming there isn't anyone in this building who will kill us on sight because we are who we are, what happens if we get lost? If we get lost, we'll never find her, don't you understand?"

"Well . . ." The boy hit the wall with his palm. "Yeah, but we're already lost, so how can we get any loster?"

"Oh god, lobster," Tuesday wailed quietly. "Jesus, kill the little brat before I starve to death."

The argument continued until it was too dark to see, and though Gideon felt guilty about not immediately charging off to save Ivy, or fight Agnes, or discover the whereabouts of the Wamchu, he also knew that for a change he was right. They needed rest, and they needed food, and they needed a plan. To do anything else would be stupid, irresponsible, and a sure sign he was beginning to believe he really was a hero.

Tag sat by the elevator door and grumbled until he fell asleep with his arms folded over his chest. Lain proposed a series of watches, said that he was still wide awake and would take the first one if it was all right with the assembled company. The assembled company curled up against Red, and watched the night sky grow more stars, another moon, and a crop of bitterly cold gusts that swept across the rooftops every hour on the hour.

I think, Gideon thought, maybe we should go inside before we freeze to death.

I think, he thought an hour later, my ass is frozen to the roof.

TWENTY-FIVE

Gideon sat by the elevator door and watched the sun rise over Thazbinn. The temperature had risen considerably, but he was still shivering in spite of Red's protection, and was still annoyed that it had taken him nearly twenty minutes to get himself unstuck from the roof. Tuesday had suggested he just slip out of his jeans, but the thought of exposing a fair portion of himself to a female duck, in a strange city, even if one was his sister and the other didn't know he was there, stalled him until the denim pulled loose.

"Oh, honestly," she'd said with a look to the sky. "I'm family, for crying out loud."

"You're a duck," he'd answered flatly, looking at the sky because he couldn't look anywhere else, being on his back the way he was and some of his hair being also frozen to the roof.

"You're embarrassed to show your shorts to a duck?"

"What are shorts?" Tag asked.

"I am not embarrassed," he'd said sharply. "But I can't very well get caught with my pants literally down, now can I? You'd never let me live it down. If I lived."

"So you can fight better that way?"

"What are shorts?" asked Tag.

Gideon drew his bat and swished it around a few times.

201

"Wonderful," she'd said to Lain. "He can cut them off at the kneecaps."

"What are shorts?" Tag begged, and blushed when Tuesday blew him a kiss and suggested they meet after this was over, and she'd tell him all about them.

Then he had sent Vorden and the boy down the steps to get some food from the alley while Tuesday, on her own, took off on a planned brief flight over the immediate neighborhood.

That had been an hour ago.

No one had yet returned.

"Red," he said, "am I too far off in left field in thinking that all is not right here?"

The lorra bobbed his head.

The immediate reference was to the empty streets. After the mass crowding the day before, he fully expected the same now, on what was probably a business day in spite of the fighting; but no one was there. The stalls were closed, the shops locked, the windows without light or movement, and the street itself was filled with nothing but dust devils, with only other dust devils for company.

The greenman hadn't known what it meant, since, as he explained apologetically, he was more in tune with the trees than the workings of a community that lived behind stone. "I might say, however, that it is not beyond the realm of the impossible to imagine that some sort of national emergency arose whilst we slept, and the good townsfolk went out to aid their leader."

"But who's their leader?" Gideon had said. "Agnes, or Lu?"

"Who fell in the hole?" Lain countered.

Tag, after examining the streets carefully and testing the direction of the wind, had guessed it was some sort of natural disaster that had passed them by since they were on the roof and couldn't know about it to be done in by it.

"That doesn't make sense," Gideon said.

"Take it or leave it," the boy said. "I found the elevator."

Gideon had left it, had sent them off on their errands; and asked the lorra now if there wasn't something he had missed.

When he received nothing but a stare in return, he pushed himself to his feet, walked to the front and looked down.

Nothing.

Left and right, and there was nothing.

The rooftops were empty as well, and the only animation was the drifting formations of clouds, high and ridged and tipped with dark grey, which came out of the east, threatening a monstrous storm.

"I have a feeling," he said then, "that our answer lies yonder." And he nodded toward the towers not all that far away.

In full light they were not quite as daunting as they had been the night before, but they were still four times larger than any other building he'd been able to spot. They had no windows that he could see, and their tops were split into five separate sections that reached for the clouds like twisted bone. Though he stared until his eyes watered, he was unable to spot any guards, or anything that might conceivably be a guard, which would indicate that someone distrustful resided or worked within.

He sighed.

He walked to the alley and looked down, and saw no one. "Damn."

He checked the skies and saw nary a feather. "Damn."

He looked at the elevator door and saw Agnes. "Oh . . . nuts."

Though the bat was in his hand, he knew it was useless. This, of all the Wamchu wives of which only she remained, was the most dangerous, the most immune to physical threat, the most cunning, and the most vicious. If she were a jungle animal, she would be a panther; if she were of the forest, she'd be a lynx; if she were a bird, she'd be a hawk; and if she were of the sea, she'd be a manta ray.

He had never much liked zoos anyway, and so was not surprised when he shook his head at her beckoning finger.

Agnes stepped into the light.

Red, who had backed hastily to the wall, pawed at the

stone and scampered down the steps into the alley, a look over his shoulder telling Gideon not to worry, he wasn't running away but only going after help, hold the fort, he'd be back in a few minutes.

Gideon waved to him; it was the only polite thing he could do when he considered the alternatives that sprang instantly and bitterly to mind. Then, hating himself for not trusting the beast, he walked over to the wall, leaned out, and looked down.

Red was already halfway to the bend, and the way he bulled through the mounds and piles and stacks and pillars, it was obvious he wasn't looking very hard for the greenman and the boy.

I live, he thought, for the day when that son of a bitch does what he says he will.

A noise behind him—the scraping of a soft leather slipper over stone that wanted no part of it.

Two stories, he noted when he looked again, was a long way down when you're two stories up. And the confluence of orange peels and cardboard boxes directly below didn't look as if it would enjoy trying to keep him from smashing himself, should he decide to test their give-and-hold attributes.

Jumping is out, boy, he told himself. Turn around and face her like a man.

He turned, paled, and told himself he'd do better the next time.

"You," she said.

He nodded, knowing full well she wasn't attempting to establish his identity.

And for a brief moment, one he would have gladly traded in for a fall from a two-story building, he was transported back to the day they had first confronted each other—in the dungeon holding room of the Hold, the mayor's citadel in Rayn, when the Wamchu had ordered her to fry his brain and several other parts of his body for refusing to reveal the whereabouts of a certain white duck.

She would have done it, had indeed started to do it, when Whale had intervened with one of his little bitty bombs.

Now she was ready to do it again.

"You," she said.

He shrugged, and was suddenly heartily ashamed that, after all she had done to him, all that she stood for, she was still able to cast over him an intangible spell of masculine weakness simply by her presence. It was galling. He shook himself, steeled himself, gripped the bat more tightly and silently dared her to take another step closer. It would do his heart good to test Whale's magic against hers; and as soon as he thought it, he changed his mind.

The bat was Whale's, but the strength behind it had to be his. And as long as she looked the way she did, he would find it awkward having to bash in her head.

For she was, despite her sensational aura of palpable evil, despite the vile vibrations that rippled obscenely, a marvelously lovely woman, if you liked the type, which he knew he did when he wasn't thinking about peace of mind afterward. Her features were decidedly Oriental in their cast, her unblemished skin so pale it appeared translucent, her abundant hair an amazing fall of unreflecting black that bobbed on her shoulders in waves a sailor would kill for.

But it was her eyes, not the snug fit of her black-and-gold satin dress; it was her eyes, not the legs so trim and the ankles so well-turned; it was her eyes, not the way her hips volleyed and thundered as she walked; it was her eyes that fascinated him the most—they were blue one moment, green the next. They were brown and black and not always at the same time. They were large, they were enticing, they were focused on his face, and they were telling him they didn't like a single thing they saw.

"You," she said, her voice the sliding skin of a molting rattlesnake.

He nodded.

"You know who I am," she said, stopping in the center of the roof.

"The resemblance to your husband is remarkable," he told her, bringing the bat close to his chest.

She spat. "I spit on him," she sneered. "I have no use for him anymore."

He shrugged, and decided it wasn't meant for him to know

where the Wamchu's chute had taken him. He also felt a little queasy when several possibilities came to mind and he couldn't banish their images.

"Well," he said, "I'm here."

"And you have come to stop me before my Day."

"It had crossed my mind," he said.

She laughed, a trilling, delightful laugh that peeled stripes off the walls, and knocked the elevator door off its hinge.

Oh well, he thought.

Suddenly, she raised an arm to the sky, and he looked involuntarily, taking a step back when he saw the drifting clouds begin to speed up, to turn black, to boil and collide and disgorge vast amounts of black lightning, which struck the roof all around him in blinding explosions that sent him reeling to his knees, leaping to his feet, sprawling on his face, staggering to his knees, popping up to his feet where he gripped the edge of the encircling wall and waited for her to complete her demonstration.

And when she did, the sky, and the clouds, returned to normal.

"You have no chance, hero," she said, slinking closer, but stopping just out of the bat's effective arc-range.

"It ain't over until it's over," he quoted stoutly.

"Yogi Berra," she said, "and he got fired. It's over."

"I want Ivy," he said hastily. "The least you can do is take me to Ivy."

Agnes, for the first time, seemed to lose her control—her eyes flashed through their colors, her lower lip trembled with contained agitation, and her right hip jounced as though bouncing a rubber ball against a wall and back.

"Well?" he said, as close to demanding a verbal response as he dared. "I want to see her."

"You can't," she said.

"I can if you let me."

"I couldn't if I wanted to."

"You could if you did."

Her lower lip protruded in a pout. "No, I can't."

"Well, why the hell not?"

"Because . . ." She grimaced, groaned, tightened her jaw, and said, "Because she has escaped me."

Gideon couldn't help grinning, not even when she filled the air with a strange language evidently based on the baser messages of several countries he'd not yet seen. And though he was pleased that Ivy had slipped out of her clutches, he was on the one hand annoyed that she hadn't waited for him, and on the other suddenly understanding why Agnes was threatening him with death now, and not on her Day, which everyone had agreed was her original plan.

She was, finally, and after all, only human.

"Agnes," he said, "why don't we—"

Her arm came up again, her fingers closed into a delicately large pointing machine, and he tensed, waiting for the bolt of energy that would strike him full in the chest and send him tumbling to his death if he wasn't dead already.

Ivy, he thought, forgive me for not being your hero.

Then: Jesus H Christ, Sunday, what the hell was that supposed to mean?

Poised there, she smiled.

Poised here, he thrust out his chin. "I'm not afraid of you, Agnes," he said. "As long as Ivy is away and safe, I am ready to take anything you think you can throw at me. Besides, I'm sorry to have to tell you this isn't your day."

"I know that," she said smugly. "Three days from now is my Day."

"I doubt you'll last that long."

Her arm began to quiver. "Is this your last request—to be able to taunt me, knowing you will not be around for the end of the world as you came to know it?"

"Oh no," he said. "But if you don't watch out, a very big and pissed off lorra is going to either dump you over the edge, or tear out your heart from around your spine."

She laughed, a waterfall of innocence with just a hint of depravity. "Gideon, Gideon," she said. "How can I consider you a worthy opponent when you try an old horse like that?"

"Not horse. Goat."

Her laughter grew, her arm lowered to her side, and her

hair flew in many directions when she shook her head in an effort to return calm to her system. "Gideon, how silly, how wonderfully and naively silly you are."

"Suit yourself," he said, and nodded.

She whirled, and blasted the elevator housing with a bolt of pink lightning.

Gideon realized that he had begun taunting her too soon, that she was still too far away for him to be able to reach her before she could turn around and blast him as well. Which left him with only two options, the second of which would mean he'd never have another option again.

So he jumped off the roof.

TWENTY-SIX

If it was not the worst of times, he thought on the way down, it was close enough for jazz; and since he had no great affection for oranges in any form whatsoever, the moment he hit the mound he was scrambling to get off, which motion did him little good since his downward velocity, coupled with his momentum produced by that velocity, carried him through the peels, the boxes, and a few other things he was moving too fast to identify until, as a car puts on the brakes just before it pitches over the edge of the cliff, he stopped.

It hurt a lot, and he was stunned for several seconds, knees and ankles and one elbow letting him know that he should leave the flying to his sister the duck.

Agnes.

Suddenly, he remembered Agnes, and instantly grasped the idea that a garbage pile was not going to offer him much protection against one of her lightning bolts. He scrambled again, arms and bat thrashing, until he fell into the open, jumped to his feet, looked up, and saw Agnes looking down at him.

He ran.

The lightning ran after him.

Pink bolts shattered bricks on his left, green bolts disintegrated a stack of old newspapers on his right. Thick smoke filled the alley as the garbage began to burn, and heat-seeking bolts more often than not only redoubled the fires; when they didn't, they struck the ground or the walls only inches from his body.

He had run to his right, and thanked all the gods when he darted around the bend and realized he was temporarily out of her range. At which point she began a random blasting of the rooftops, hoping to bury him beneath the rubble that exploded and showered and rocketed all around him. He was struck several times on the back and on the backs of his legs, but he didn't fall; he weaved in and out of the piles of garbage as if he were racing for a touchdown, dodging linemen, listening to the crowd, knowing in his heart of hearts that it was only an illusion but a fairly nice one considering the fact that he was only a bolt's breadth from death.

When, at last, he burst into the street, he wasted no time looking for a direction—he ran straight ahead, into another alley, and into another after that.

There was no more lightning.

That did not mean she wasn't following.

At one point, he forced himself to set aside his fear long enough to lean against a wall and rest, ease his lungs, give his legs the opportunity to let him know that any thought of moving again was going to be met with considerable protest.

He checked behind him, and saw only curls of smoke where the bolts had struck the buildings and the ground, and a larger stream of smoke where the garbage burned. There was no sign of Agnes yet, and neither was there any sign of anyone in the city having heard, seen, or been disturbed by the explosions.

It was as if the entire place had emptied out during the night.

Blowing hard, gulping harder, he pushed off the wall and moved down the alley, a clean one this time with no windows overlooking it and no doors interrupting the surfaces of the walls. He was tempted to call out for his friends, but resisted; he spent as much time checking the line of rooftops as he did the ground beneath him, but still there was no indication that Agnes, having lost him, was attempting to find him.

All right, then, he thought.

At the next street he turned left, passed several alleys, and turned left again. Slower now, listening more carefully, walking more lightly, more apt to jump at shadows and swing his bat at ghosts.

An hour later he reached an avenue that was paved in gold brick, the shops sparkling with diamonds in their walls, and the tower directly across the way waiting for him with a door that stood fully open.

This is a trap, he warned himself.

You will go in there, and the door will close, and you will be trapped until the Day, and then she will do bad things to you that you won't like a bit.

Then he felt the blade of a knife poke him gently in the small of his back.

If he had learned nothing else during his sojourn in this world, he had learned that there are traps and there are traps: there is the kind like the open door over there, which tempts you because you know damned well it's a trap and is therefore appealing to your innate sense of accepting a challenge that could very well mean your death; and there is the trap like the open door over there, which, because you know it's a trap, makes you pause while you try to figure out if you're going to accept the challenge, which gives the person who set the trap time enough to sneak around behind you and poke a hole in your back.

It wasn't easy to fall into two traps at the same time.

He looked over his shoulder.

Ivy winked at him.

He turned.

Ivy sheathed her dagger and put her hands on her hips.

He held out his arms.

She stared at them, stared at him, and pointed to the open door across the way. "She's in there, Gideon."

"I figured that," he said. "But you're here, and for the moment, that's all that matters."

"What?"

"You heard me."

"I know I heard you, but I don't know what you're talking about."

He sighed gratefully, his arms lowered, and he leaned back against the alley wall, content for the time being just to know she was still alive, and in one rather decent piece.

"Gideon?"

"What I'm talking about," he said, "is coming all this way to get you free after those flying things took you away, that's what I'm talking about."

"But I got out," she said.

"I know you got out."

"So what are you doing here?"

He touched the bat in its holster, told it to stay where it was, he was in control no matter what it looked like, and smiled at her. "I came here to rescue you. You didn't need it, but I came anyway."

"Oh, I needed it," she said. "You just weren't here to do anything about it."

"But I was coming," he said, his voice rising.

"So's the Day, but that didn't help me." Then, before he could speak again, her eyes widened. "Oh! You mean, you came to rescue me, but I already got out so you don't have to rescue me after all, but it was the thought that mattered because you were on the way and couldn't know that I'd gotten out."

"Yeah," he said. "I guess."

"Y'know, that's really sweet."

"Sure," he said glumly, and turned his attention back to the open door.

"I mean, you did all that for me."

"Right," he muttered, standing when he thought he saw movement in the dark room beyond the open door.

"I suppose you want me to take my clothes off then, so you can get your reward."

He looked at her, at the blouse whose buttons she was toying with, and shook his head. "No."

"What?" Her eyes narrowed and her voice deepened. "What do you mean, no?"

"No," and he nodded his head toward the door.

"Well, Jesus, you sure are hard to please, Gideon Sunday. Do you have any idea how many times I've almost taken off my clothes for you? Do you have any idea what all that does to my self-respect, not to mention my self-esteem?"

"No," he said, and tried to wave her silent when he saw something white flash past the door.

"Well, it doesn't do it any good, I can tell you that," she grumbled. "And what's going on over there?"

"I don't know. What is that place?"

Ivy stood openly beside him. There was no sense attempting to hide because there was nothing to hide behind, and it was broad daylight so there was no sense trying to pretend they were part of the wall or something sneaky like that.

"It's the Thazbinn Monetary Disposal Center," she whispered, tickling his ear with the breath of her words. "It's where the people bring their taxes."

"Bring them? They bring them?"

"Of course. You think someone comes along and takes them from people?"

"I've heard of it, yes."

"What a quaint idea."

They waited, and a few seconds later they saw the white flash again, like a ghost pacing the room.

"Why is Agnes there?" he asked.

"Because she wants to be."

"No," he said, turning to look at her and blinking when he saw her eyes not more than two inches from his own. "I mean, what's so special about that place? Why didn't she choose one of the other towers?"

"There's nothing really special about it at all," she said, frowning. "Gideon, why are you wasting time asking me all these questions?"

Patience, he cautioned.

"Because I need to know before I go in there. If there's something special about it, I don't want to be surprised. I am not a great fan of surprises, especially in this place."

"Well, that makes sense."

"Thank you."

"But there's nothing special."

"Then why did she choose it?"

She took a disconcertingly deep breath. "Because, when you're Agnes Wamchu, you can pick any goddamned place you want, that's why. Jesus."

He nodded, and inched forward until he could check up and down the street. Which was empty. After which checking, he looked up at the fingerlike projections at the tower's top. Which were clear of guards. After which checking, he looked behind him down the alley. Which was clear except for Red, Tag, and the duck. Who were trying to move quietly so not to alert anyone who didn't need alerting at this time, and at the same time trying not to startle either Gideon or Ivy into attacking them before they knew who it was who was moving up the alley toward them.

To accomplish this, Tuesday was whistling the theme from her last movie, very quietly.

Gideon held Ivy's arm and drew her back toward the group, waved them all hurriedly back to the next street, and pushed them around the corner. He did not scold them for leaving him on the rooftop to face Agnes on his own, and he did not ask them where they had been all this time while he was risking life and limb trying to find them, and Ivy, who didn't need finding, and only peripherally the Wamchu, who seemed to have temporarily dropped out of the picture.

What he said was, "We are going to rush the tower." And wondered where the hell he had gotten such a stupid idea, though it might not have been so stupid had he given it some thought.

"Why?" asked Tag, who was trying to explain to Ivy that he and the goat had been trying to rescue her when they got lost in the Fromdil Forest, but it was the thought that counted, and didn't she think she owed him something for that?

She didn't.

Tag was depressed, and the giant goat didn't give a damn.

"Because Agnes is there."

"Is there a back door?" a voice asked over his head.

Leaping back to avoid an ambush, he spotted Lain's face poking over the lip of the roof. "No," he said when he got his breathing back in order.

"Did you check?"

He looked at Ivy. She shook her head. He nodded. "I checked."

Lain, using a skill Gideon didn't know the portly man had, agilely climbed down the face of the wall and landed neatly on his feet. When he subsequently fell over, Tag put him on his feet and dusted him off.

"Then I expect we shall have to rush the door," said Lain, "though you understand, don't you, that if anyone in there wants to stop us, they'll be able to pick us off one by one."

It was a consideration. They discussed it. They also discussed the sky, which was filling with those massive, high, terraced clouds, sending messages in lightning between them, the resulting thunder beginning to echo endlessly down the empty streets.

The wind picked up, and blew clouds of dust off the rooftops, out of the alleys, into their eyes.

"Gideon," Tuesday said, and with a puzzled shrug he followed her down the street, until she stopped and bobbed her head to get him to kneel at her level.

"Are you really going to go in there?" she said.

"She's in there," he said. "As long as she's in there and we're out here, she can sit there until the Day, and then come out to where we are and skin us alive. If we're lucky."

Her beak opened in a silent hiss, closed, and she moved until her head was pushed lightly against his stomach. "This isn't kidding around anymore, is it?"

"Was it ever? Really?"

She didn't answer. She didn't have to.

"Gideon?"

He laid a hand on her neck, stroked her feathers.

"You weren't such a bad player, you know," she said so softly he could barely hear the words.

"Thanks."

"You just never got the breaks."

He smiled, though she couldn't see it. "Thanks, but it's not true. I was at the top of my form when I was mediocre, and you know it as well as I do."

"Well, I'm your sister and I can't say things like that."

"You used to."

"I'm a duck now. Ducks have a code."

"You said them when you were a duck."

"That's the code," she said.

He laughed, and pushed her away gently so he could look at her face. "Are you going to come with me?"

"Are they?"

"I don't know. Ivy probably will. Lain, maybe. I don't know about Tag, he's awfully young, and you never can tell about the goat."

And finally: "I don't know either."

"That's okay. You're a duck. It's the code."

"I'm also your sister, you sonofabitch."

He stood, looking down at her, and walked slowly back to the others, took a breath and asked them to stay where they were while he made his way back up the alley. No one argued, and when he reached the other end he stood square on the street, arms folded across his chest, and watched the tower, the open door, and the storm building above him. His hair blew into his eyes, but he did not blink; his bat felt light in his hand, but he did not heft it; the voice of self-preservation was screaming in one ear, and the voice of what-the-hell was whispering in the other.

He listened to neither of them.

So, he said to himself. You can either stand here all day and look heroic, or you can get your ass in gear and see what happens.

And decided that as long as they were going to keep calling him "hero," he might as well stop feeling sorry for himself and do something about it.

Damn, he thought then: that's what I was afraid you'd say.

TWENTY-SEVEN

The clouds continued to mass, here and there merging in cacophonous collision, all of them turning black and bulging with unreleased rain. Glimpses of blue sky were few and far between, and the heavy twilight that covered the city was tinted faintly with green.

The lightning, its colors gone, reached for the city now, and more often than not struck at the crooked fingers of the five towers. The explosions were deafening, but the stone remained unmarred.

And in the mouth of the alley, Ivy stood with a dagger in one hand, a rather ordinary club in the other; her hair had been rebraided more thickly so that, if she wanted, she could clobber a Moglar simply by shaking her head.

Lain had begged for time, then run off without explanation, returning an hour later with fragments of stone in his hand. With Tag's help, he fashioned arrowheads from them, and with Red's help and some of his hair, he affixed them to the shafts his boys had given him as their going-away present.

Tag waited beside Ivy, dagger in one hand and Lain's rapier in the other, licking his lips and shifting his weight from foot to foot. He had suggested they scale the walls and come down from the top, but was at a loss to find convenient ladders with which to do so, and could think of no other way to get there unless Tuesday carried them. When she refused, adamantly, he chided her until she belted him with a wing.

The duck and the goat stood together, or rather one atop the other, and turned their heads away from the wind that screamed down the streets and shrieked along the alleys. Red's eyes were dead black; Tuesday's eyes were closed.

Gideon had his bat, and decided that sneaking up on the open door would be not only a farce in terms of having nothing to use to sneak with, but also a farce in terms of trying to maintain anonymity, since it was evident that the door was open as an invitation to a specific person or group of people and animals, and he was it, and so were they.

When he started across the street, walking, he heard someone mutter what sounded like a prayer behind him.

When he reached the door and hadn't been bolted, zapped, electrocuted, fried, bombed, stabbed, punctured, or trampled, he wondered what the hell he was doing wrong.

At the threshold he waved to the others.

They waved back.

He waved again.

They smiled and waved back.

He raised a fist, shook it, turned his back and went in, came right back out and stood there until they joined him in varying states of eagerness, none of which offered much promise for the future. As a measure of confidence in their abilities, then, he motioned them in ahead of him, pushing a little, smiling a lot, and twitching his bat at the backs of their knees until there was only Tuesday left, defiantly on her feet.

She looked at the door, at the tower, at the lightning, at the city, and said, "Fuck the code," and bit him on the leg.

The room was surprisingly circular, a good and brisk forty paces side to side, and the only one on this floor as far as any of them could tell. It was also completely barren of furnishings or wall hangings, and only Tag muttered an oath when the door slammed behind them.

There were no windows, or torches, but the walls themselves seemed to glow from within, providing them with enough light to see that they ought not to be here.

In the center was a spiral staircase carved from crimson stone that took a hell of a lot of turns to reach the ceiling, a not so good fifty or sixty feet away.

Two weeks, he thought glumly; it's going to take us two goddamn weeks to do one floor at a time, and when we get there we'll be so damned dizzy we won't know our own names.

With a sigh born of the knowledge of the inevitability of a rotten time ahead, he approached the staircase warily, took hold of the iron banister and looked up. The gap in the ceiling that led to the second story was filled with light, but he could hear no voices nor sounds of things or people moving around.

So far so good, he thought, and started up, turned around and asked Red if he thought he could make it. The lorra checked his footing on the stone steps, nodded, and backed away, snorting almost a laugh at the dismay on Gideon's face.

Oh, well, he thought, and started up again. One step at a time, listening at every step, keeping his gaze on the opening until it was level with the top of his head. The staircase, he noted, continued on, so far up he couldn't see its end; and what he could see of the room told him it was as empty as the one he was leaving behind. That didn't bother him. Not as much as the shadow he saw on the wall.

Regripping the bat and taking a breath for courage, he charged up and away from the staircase, spinning for a sign of what caused the shadow—the shadow of a very tall man with long hair and a cloak.

He saw it just as the others crowded up behind him.

It was the Wamchu.

"Oh," said Ivy quietly.

"That's one way to put it," Gideon said.

The Wamchu had been shackled to the wall, his arms stretched over his head, his legs spread, his feet just barely touching the bare floor. His head was lowered so that his hair covered his face, and he was wearing his red-lined cloak, and not a stitch more.

"My," said Tuesday. "There sure was a lot of him under all those clothes."

There were no other instruments of torture or confinement in the room, and Gideon walked cautiously over to see if the man was still alive. The chest, full-muscled and tanned like fried chicken, stirred, but barely. And though Gideon could see no indication of external injury, he had no doubt that Agnes was the one who had done this, and that the Wamchu was never going to be a threat to anyone again.

"Gideon!" Tag whispered sharply from the staircase.

He turned, and the boy pointed up, made signs of people walking around, made another sign that they ought to adjust the Wamchu's cloak a little, for decency if nothing else.

Gideon didn't care. He was disappointed that a confrontation with the man had been taken from him, but he was also wise enough to understand that a man who looks for a confrontation with someone like Lu Wamchu ought to be damned grateful that it was taken away from him. Unless, of course, that confrontation was going to be replaced by another one.

"Well," Ivy said to the duck, "I can see why he had three wives."

Gideon motioned to Lain, who walked with him up the steps. It was a little crowded, but he figured that having two fighters explode into the room together was better than being picked off one at a time. When they reached the top, however, he realized that the greenman's portliness was going to prevent anything but getting stuck if they tried it, so he charged up himself, Lain right behind, and the five Moglar guards seated at their luncheon table had only enough time to wipe their mouths and grab their weapons before Gideon was upon them. And Lain. And the lorra. And when Tag came puffing into the room behind Ivy, it was all over.

"You know," the lad said, "if all I'm going to do is climb stairs, I might as well go all the way up and wait."

"Patience," Gideon told him with a clap on his shoulder. "See if they have something longer to use than your knife."

They did—a pike with a pitchfork on one end and a chain mace on the other. A few practice swings that demolished the table and one of the corpses, and Tag pronounced himself ready, though the weapon was a good four feet taller than he and had a tendency to drag on the floor with the most appalling noise. Ivy solved the latter problem by loosely wrapping both ends with bits of leather she cut from the Moglar's armor. Tag protested. Ivy explained that a good thrust or whack would easily shear the leather off. He muttered, but accepted the solution with reasonable grace, then took up his position at the staircase.

Gideon began climbing.

Lain and Red followed.

Ivy came next and told Tag to watch where he was pointing the thing, while Tuesday told him to watch where he was pointing that thing in the other direction.

The fourth room was as empty as the first.

In the fifth they found several ancient chests filled with jewels of all descriptions, bound stacks of paper money, leather sacks of gold coins, silver candelabra and table settings, a solid gold suit of armor, eight watercolor portraits of the Wamchu, seventeen dressers whose drawers were crammed with exquisite silk clothing, and a nine-foot-tall sculpted bottle of purple liquid, which Ivy explained was an extract from a ferocious ant that, when taken internally—the extraction, not the ant—would give one an added fifteen years of good health, barring accidents, war, and unnatural stress.

Gideon couldn't help the itching of his palms. "You mean to tell me these people brought all this here voluntarily?"

"I said your way was quaint," she told him as she adjusted a ruby necklace around her throat. "I didn't say this way was smart."

The urge to take some of it with him was strong, but he resisted, knowing that he didn't need the extra weight, nor the possible complications of having his pockets jammed with gems when he had to fight again.

Which he did on the next floor.

When they came through, there were fourteen Moglar sitting on pillows, listening to a fifteenth singing them a song from the days when Moglar were Moglar and the Wamchu was only a small child's nightmare. It was very touching. It gave the scruffy giant dwarves an added dimension, until the singer came to the part about having the child for breakfast

because the Wamchu gave him nightmares. That was when
Red came through the floor, saw the Moglar just lying around
waiting to be trampled, and trampled them. While Tag bashed
them, the walls, the pillows, and nearly Vorden Lain.

The noise was horrendous because the warriors, possibly
anticipating the band's arrival, and possibly because they
knew the singer's reputation, were already armed. And they
fought fiercely, bravely, and only their sheer superiority in
numbers enabled them to last as long as they did. Which, in
the lifetime of a lorra, wasn't that long at all.

The Moglar were good, but Gideon and his band had more
incentive than most, struggling as they were to prevent the
end of the world; and ultimately, though not without a number of close shaves, which Gideon suspected would not be
written in his memoirs because no one would believe them,
they prevailed.

And when the fight was over and Ivy was tending a small
cut on Gideon's left arm with sufficient solicitation to get
her arrested in his old world, he noted the remarkable similar-
ity between the structure of this tower and the Trail of Stairs,
saving of course the fact that the spiral staircase didn't move.

"Not so odd, really," said Lain, recovering his arrows
from the various Moglar who were holding them for him.
"Thazbinn was created hundreds of years ago as a city to
which all the villages on the Upper Ground could send their
products and services for a decent price. It didn't work, alas.
The fact that it was built here was a major factor—the
Scarred Mountains, and Shashhag, as you have already seen,
make the trip rather a lengthy and unprofitable one."

He pulled up a pillow and sat.

"So it remained virtually empty for centuries, until the
Wamchu found a back way to this world and decided to place
his own stamp on it. This tower. And the others."

He smiled.

"Okay," Gideon said. "But what does that have to do
with the tower looking like the Trail of Stairs?"

"Well," the greenman said, "to explain that we shall have
to go back even further in time. Back to the era when the
Wamchu was still a prophesy, and his wives were not even in

the dreams of their ancestors. It was a time,'' he said with a sweep of his arm, "when the lorra were the rulers, and the pacchs, deshes, magrows, and ekklers were part of a vast army of—''

"Vorden," Gideon said.

The greenman frowned at the interruption.

Gideon pointed up to the next floor.

"Well," Lain said, struggling to his feet. "I would have thought at least Red would be interested in—''

"The goat," Gideon said, "is interested. The man would like to get on with it, if you don't mind.''

On the seventh floor they encountered a complete kitchen, and they voted to rest a bit while they filled their stomachs, checked what wounds they had, and debated whether or not they should move as rapidly as they had.

"They know we're coming," Ivy said, "so what's the problem?''

"Caution," said Lain. "We know they know, and they know we know, but we don't know how many more of them there are to know if you get my drift.''

"Stop," said Gideon before Ivy answered again. "I know this part, and I'll be damned if I'm going to sit here and listen to you two drag it on forever.''

He stood, unholstered his bat, and made for the staircase. Tag followed with his pike and asked if he couldn't go first this time.

"It's only logical, when you think about it," the boy argued. "If there are more and more of them each time we meet some, it makes sense that this thing can soften them up before you get there. Then you won't die, and I won't have to be the leader, which I'd kind of like, see, but not when you're not around.''

Gideon wondered if the lad's vest was too tight, smiled instead of shaking his head, and waved him on. Tag had to become a man sometime, he reasoned, and this was as good a time as any, if only to keep him quiet.

Tag hefted the pike to his shoulder and began the ascent, using one hand to grip the railing, the other the weapon. Gideon had no idea how balance was maintained, but the lad was getting the hang of it, no question about it, and he followed Tag with something akin to eagerness. And when he recognized that, he nearly stopped and went back down—that way, beginning to enjoy himself, was tantamount to suicide, since it would only lead to overconfidence and a false sense of his heroic worth. He told himself sternly that something soon was bound to screw things up, and thus make him more secure in his scheme of these things.

He did stop then, and looked up at Tag, down at Ivy on the step below him, and blinked at the revelation that not only was he here to stay, as the Bridge had already proven, but he was now beginning to think like them.

Oh god, he thought, and thought no more when Tag shouted, the shout became more like a scream, and boy and pike were snatched up from the next floor as if they weighed no more than a feather.

TWENTY-EIGHT

He heard Tuesday call a warning and felt Ivy reach for him as he ran up after the boy, but he ignored both, wishing only that the staircase were straight so that he could build up some decent momentum when he shot out onto the eighth floor.

"Gideon!" Tag called.

He looked side to side frantically, heard his name again and looked up. Tag was dangling from a snare that had closed around his chest and snapped him up to a beam that spanned the ceiling. The pike was entangled with him, and every time he moved the mace swung on its chain and added a lump to his shin.

"Hang on," Gideon said. "I'll get you down."

"Gideon!" Tag called again.

"I said—"

And grunted when something smashed across the back of his shoulders, driving him to the floor on his hands and knees. The bat skittered away. He heard Ivy's war cry. Another blow caught him in the same place, and though it wasn't as forceful as the first one, he still went down to his chest, arms splayed, forehead striking stone and stunning him into a field of pinwheels and fire that stuck around just long enough for him to get used to before it faded to a gentle black that seemed like a good place to be at the time since his back didn't hurt anymore and his forehead didn't ache, and when he rolled over and saw Lain staring worriedly into his eyes, he made it a point not to throw up his supper on the man's stomach.

"How are you feeling?" the greenman asked.

"Like I was hit with a club."

"Fine. You were."

He reached down and helped Gideon sit up, holding him until the dizziness passed. Gideon saw Ivy across the room, standing over two Moglar who were larger than normal and who were also either dead or unconscious. She was looking at her dagger, at their greasy hair, and back to her dagger.

"Don't," Gideon said weakly.

Lain let him go just as Ivy looked up.

The pinwheels were still lovely, but the stars lacked a certain warmth he had seen in them before, and it was less time therefore before he was sitting up again, waving off Lain's apologies. Ivy was still standing over the Moglar. The dagger was still in her hand.

"Hey!" Tag called from the beam under the ceiling.

"Thanks," Gideon said, blinking the pain away.

"No problem," she told him. "The thing is, you see, do I kill them or not?"

"They're not dead?"

"I just hit them, that's all."

He looked at her fist; there was no club in it.

Red was at his side, and when he managed a smile, the lorra began licking his face as gently as he could. Gideon laughed and hugged him, using the grip to haul himself to his feet.

"Hey!"

His head had somehow stayed on his neck, and his neck didn't protest more than a stab or two when he rubbed his nape in an effort to spread the pain around to diffuse it. And when he thought he could walk, he let go of Red, swayed, grabbed the animal's neck again and decided that Ivy could come to him for her thank-you kiss.

"I don't know," she said. "It would be like murder now. They can't fight back."

"It's a problem," Lain agreed. "And we can't wait for them to wake up so you can kill them, because time is running out."

Tuesday flew up to the beam, walked around, flew down.

"If you don't want them to follow us," Gideon said, "why don't you just tie them up? That way you won't have to worry about murder, or about them stabbing you in the back."

Lain nodded agreeably, and Ivy volunteered him to return to the kitchen to find something to use as binding; she did it, however, less than gracefully, and her expression left no doubt as to what her final decision would have been had she worked on it long enough.

"Hello?"

Gideon knew there was a lot about that woman he still didn't understand, and wondered if he would ever really understand once he thought he did. It was not a situation likely to clear up soon, however, so he beckoned his sister over and asked her if she wouldn't mind nipping up the stairs to see what was up there. Just a quick look, nothing permanent.

"I want the goat with me," she said.

"The goat is holding me up."

"So are you, unless you let me take the goat."

They left it up to Red, who was on the stairs before Gideon hit the floor again; this time, Ivy came over to help him, holding him so closely, so snugly, that he wondered if he could get away with a mild swoon just to make it last.

He couldn't.

The Moglar woke up, and Ivy regretfully rushed over and ended their doubts about the ambiguous Other Side.

"Oh," said Lain, who was left holding the rope.

"Goddamnit to hell, anyway! I'm getting airsick up here!"

Gideon looked up, regretted it when his head and shoulders rather pointedly reminded him that he shouldn't look up, and crawled over to the staircase. "Hey, Sis!"

All he could see was Red's tail, Red's rump, and the way his clawed hooves were digging into the stone to keep him from sliding back down to the ground floor.

"Hey! Sis!"

Her "What?" was muffled by the screen of Red's long hair.

"We need you to help get the kid down."

"I'm busy!"

"Save it. The kid needs help now."

Then he heard Red's growling and saw the claws dig in for a charge, and before he could get to his feet and find his bat, Ivy had shoved him aside and was racing up the stairs just as the lorra vanished through to the next floor.

By the sound of it, there was a lot of fighting.

Lain, who was halfway up the wall, asked if he should turn around and go to their assistance.

Tag's vote was ignored, though Gideon surmised from Red's cheerful bellows that no help was needed. Lain shrugged, lost a few feet in the shrugging, and made his way back up. When he reached the beam, he swung hand over hand to where the snare had been anchored, and began to saw at it with a knife.

"Wait a minute!" Gideon said. "He'll fall!"

"Well, he certainly can't fly, can he?" the greenman reminded him.

And Tag fell. Not as fatally as Gideon would have imagined, since the other anchor of the snare was still tied around the beam, which allowed Tag a drop of some distance before he was jerked up short and swung into a spinning imitation of a vested pendulum. When Lain cut the other end, he fell again, this time to the floor, where he landed neatly on his feet, grinned, and stepped nimbly to one side as the pike speared the floor where his left foot had been.

It would have been perfect had not the pike, its shaft supple as fiberglass, thwacked him a fair one in the middle of his pate. But to his credit, the boy didn't cry out; he merely rubbed his head, grabbed the pike when it sprang back, and broke it in half.

"There," he said.

"Jesus," Gideon said, and went up after his sister, who was, when he arrived, standing on a refectory table in the middle of a huge bowl of iceberg lettuce, chewing thoughtfully, while Red and Ivy finished off the last of twenty-three Moglar and a half-grown magrow.

"You have no idea," the duck said, "how symbolic this all is."

Gideon shrugged. He was looking up again and wondering how much farther they had to go. It was all right knocking off the Moglar guards as they were, and it was certainly no skin off his back that Agnes seemed to think she had an unlimited supply of them. But the effects were beginning to show on him and his friends—Lain was puffing, Tuesday wasn't gorging herself, Red was shaking his head slowly in an effort to fill his great lungs again, and Ivy was leaning heavily against the wall, not bothering to check to be sure the bodies at her feet were all she would have desired.

Sooner or later, he thought, they were going to drop.

And when they did, Agnes was going to make her move.

The bat slipped into its holster, and he walked gingerly across the corpse carpet until he reached Ivy's side. So weary was she that she didn't object when he put an arm around her waist and led her to the bench by the table; so weary was she that she didn't protest when he poured her a cup of water from a pewter jug and held it to her lips; so weary was she that when she passed out, she trusted him enough to catch her before she hit the floor.

"Jesus!" he exclaimed. "Tuesday, help me."

The duck didn't answer.

As he lowered Ivy to the bench, adjusting her legs so she wouldn't roll off, he saw that his sister was slumping in the lettuce bowl, eyes closed, wings draped limply over the sides. A foot twitched; otherwise, she didn't move.

"A drug," Lain offered when he sniffed the jug and the leaves. "Ah, she's a clever bitch, that one."

Gideon looked down at the unconscious woman, at the way her face was determined even in repose, and impulsively leaned over to kiss her lightly on the lips. It wasn't honey, he thought, but it wasn't diet soda, either.

A loud exhalation, and he rubbed his hands over his chest, down his jeans, and pointed to the stairs. "We can't wait for them to wake up. Let's go, old friend. If she's waiting, I don't want to disappoint her.''

Red attempted a purr of encouragement that sounded more like a belch, but he made it to the stairs just as Tag staggered up from below, complained about having a pip of a headache, and fell in a heap of discarded Moglar armor. Neither of the men bothered to go over to see if he was all right. They only passed a glance between them, checked their weapons for suitability for Armageddon, and followed the lorra up.

"What floor is this?" Gideon asked when they checked yet another empty room.

"Lost count," Lain panted. "Why?"

"I was just wondering if there wasn't some sort of significance to the number of the floor she's waiting on. I mean, if it's thirteen, that might be considered bad luck.''

The greenman nodded sagely. "I suppose that would be true, if that's where they killed you.''

Again they reached a deserted room, though they spotted a pile of desert-bleached pacch bones against the wall, and a rotted wineskin beside them; and again Gideon could not help but think that there was a purpose behind this, other than to drive them into a stupor to make them helpless against assault.

Agnes, though her Day had not yet dawned, was not so without armament that she couldn't have met them on the first floor and saved them all a lot of trouble.

It was wrong.

It was all wrong.

"Rest," Vorden gasped then, and with a look of dismal apology, he sat down where he stood and put his hands over his face. "Not as young," he said ruefully. "Away from the trees, I'm not as young.''

Gideon sat beside him, his legs dangling over the edge of the staircase opening. "You know," he said, "it's a shame we had to leave Whale's mead behind. I sure could use some of it now.''

Red wandered over, curled up, and went to sleep.

"Indeed, Gideon, I know what you mean.''

Five minutes later: "Y'know, Vorden, I must be more

tired than I thought. I'm sitting down, and I feel like I'm on the deck of a ship.''

Lain removed his hands, exposing a dangerously flushed face and feverishly bright eyes. "It's the wind.''

"Huh?''

"The wind, Gideon. We're so high up the wind is making the tower sway.''

"Oh.''

"Yes.''

"I hope it doesn't fall.''

"Never has.''

"There's always a first time.''

"Oh.''

And yet another five minutes during which Gideon wanted nothing more than to lie down and sleep the way Red was doing. But if he did, he'd never get up, and so thinking he nudged the lorra's side. Frowned. Nudged him again, prodded him, took out the bat and shoved it into his ribs.

"Shit,'' he said.

Red snored, unperturbed and unoffended.

Finally, Vorden Lain toppled onto his back. Without a sound. Without blinking his eyes. Gideon twisted around to kneel beside him, take off his hat and loosen his green jacket, his green vest, his pale green shirt.

"I'm not dead, you know,'' the man said with a trembling smile.

"But you will be if you try to go any higher.''

Vorden's eyes closed slowly, and opened again. "Lord, I feel as if I've been climbing for days.''

"I know just how you feel. As a matter of fact, I was just saying to myself that—''

He stopped. Rocked back on his heels. Looked down at the floors they had climbed thus far. Set into motion a slide show of each room, and what had happened there. Measured the distance between floor and ceiling with an inexpert eye. Squinted as he tried to recall how long he'd been unconscious.

"Damn,'' he said at last.

Red snored.

Vorden laughed, but it didn't last. "I was wondering when you'd notice."

Gideon grabbed his bat and went to the wall. He pressed a hand against it and felt the cold stone; he stood sideways to it and put the bat on his shoulder; he heard Vorden whisper a word of support, and swung the bat against the wall, bracing himself for the stinging impact, and ignoring it when it came as a piece of brick powdered his feet.

He swung again, and worked himself into a rhythm that banished time and pain and the dust that gathered around him like a cloud; he let his mind roam from Rayn to Harghe the Giant to the deserted village of Kori to the awesome evil of the flying deshes to the deserted city of Thazbinn; he choked on the clogged air and coughed and gagged and didn't stop until there was a hole in the wall and he was driven back by the fist of the wind that punched in from the night he saw before he fell.

He knew then why Agnes had picked one of the towers.

Time.

She was throwing meaningless obstacles at them, just in order to gain time.

"No," he said, staggering to his feet.

It wasn't possible that they had taken three days to get this far.

But how long had he been unconscious?

They had started out close to midafternoon on the third day before the Day. They had fought their way up the tower, and he figured an hour each time, more for the skirmishes, less for the empty rooms. He had been knocked out. Could he have then fallen into a sleep? Wouldn't they have awakened him? Or were they so tired themselves by that time that they had used his unexpected lapse as an opportunity to regain some of their strength?

He shaded his eyes and looked into the wind again.

He saw the night, saw the constant display of lightning, and felt without knowing how the sheer power that shimmered around the outside of the tower.

Three days.

One day left.

He was so sure of it that he turned his back on the hole and hurried over to Lain, to tell him what had happened, to tell him he was right and there was no time left.

Vorden's eyes were closed.

When he knelt, and put an ear against the man's chest, tried to find the man's pulse in his wrist and in his neck, he heard and felt nothing.

"Well, damn," he said. "Well, goddamnit!"

TWENTY-NINE

Gideon could barely see where he was going.

It wasn't the light; it was his temper.

Somewhere between pulling Vorden away from the stairwell and being unable to wake an exhausted Red up, his temper had snapped, and he'd made no effort to control it. That, he knew even as he climbed, was foolish, not to mention lethal; it would prevent him from thinking clearly about what he had to do, planning, checking, and checking again. But he'd been known for his sporadic temper ever since he was a kid, except that he always lost it for what he thought were the wrong reasons, either for things over which he had no control or for things about which he could do nothing.

This time, however, he could do something.

This time he would do something.

And by god and all the saints, he was going to do it even if it killed him.

Oh wrong, he told himself then, only barely refraining from slapping himself; not the most practical way to look at things, Gideon, old son. At least have the kindness to give yourself the benefit of the doubt and have some hope that you'll make it through at the end.

The tower swayed more alarmingly.

The wind he had released into it howled along the stairs, reminding him uncomfortably of a wolf that had scented its prey and was hunting it down, slowly.

Wrong again; bad attitude.

He smiled and shook his head, once. Even alone, he was having behavioral arguments with his sister, and while he figured it wouldn't exactly prove his sanity to the outside world, it permitted his temper to reduce itself from a boil to a patient simmer.

But while it had lasted, it had propelled him up another three stories, through empty rooms whose light had faded to a spectral green. It did nothing at all for his complexion when he looked at the back of one hand, but it served to guide him up the last set of steps.

He knew it was the last because it ended at a small landing, and off the landing was a door.

When he reached it, he saw there was neither knob nor latch, and guessed that all he had to do was push and it would open. Onto the roof, most likely, putting him between the five fingers, which were, from the sound of it, still attracting lightning.

Now, he thought, is the time to gird your loins, psych yourself up, direct your energies toward the woman who is waiting on the other side to kill you. And not just a swift and true murder either, but one that promises to give you so much pain you'll beg for the release of all-encompassing death.

"Ugh," he said, for the first time in his life.

He gave his bat the once-over-lightly with the palm of his hand, pulled at his jeans to be sure they wouldn't fall down at a moment of crisis, smoothed his shirt down over his chest, raked a hand through the beard he swore he was going to shave off whether he was dead or not, pushed his hair behind his ears, and thought about checking his boots for pebbles in case he had to run and didn't want to cripple himself.

He thought about it.

He didn't do it, and congratulated himself.

Instead, he called himself any number of impolite names, and four kinds of an idiot, and pushed open the door.

* * *

His mother, when she was speaking to him, which wasn't often because he was seldom home and wasn't really there when he was there, had taught him that first impressions were often the most important because they set in a person's mind the way they looked at another person, or thing, or group of things if you were talking about nouns.

Even as a child he had never argued that first impressions were often wrong if you caught a person, or a noun, at the wrong time, in the wrong place, under the wrong circumstances, because she was, at the end, usually right. And that lesson had stayed with him into his adult years, standing him in good stead in every instance save on the gridiron where he tended to think good of all men until they put him on his back and took the ball away.

Thus, his first impression upon walking out to the roof was that he was a flaming jackass.

The reasoning, which he didn't bother to analyze, was simple enough—if he were back in the tower, he wouldn't be out here, and if he wasn't out here he had a good chance of living five minutes longer than he knew he would if he stayed out here, gaping at the scene before him like the aforementioned flaming jackass.

Nevertheless, he had to admit it was impressive in a dour and unhealthy sort of way.

The air was cold, pluming his breath as if he were a racehorse in the dead dawn of winter, though he did not shiver and he did not feel the cold as much as he sensed it.

The wind swept visibly around the building, a cyclone of entrapped spirits laughing manically as it sought to tear the bricks from their mortar one by one.

And from it also came a flickering brilliant light, casting shadows which wove each other into patterns of obscenities best left to the imagination, though he noted a few of the more interesting ones stuck around longer when he stared at them for more than a few seconds at a time.

The five gnarled supratowers were at least forty feet high in their convoluted reach for the clouds so black they blacked out the night, and they had been seared to mere shadows of themselves by the constant battering of the lightning that struck them, in orderly sequence left to right, at least two or three times every five minutes; great chunks of them were scattered around the roof, smoldering, charred, powdered.

At first he thought he was alone.

Then, with a startled gasp he'd only heard before in the movies, he knew he was wrong again.

At the base of each of the towers he could see a figure, and when he took a step farther away from the door, which slammed behind him in so familiar a fashion that he didn't bother to turn around, he knew them: Ivy, bound by a silver rope; Lain, propped up by a webbing of copper; Tuesday, held in check by a gold belt with a sparkling neon buckle; Tag, virtually cocooned in mauve silk sparkling with dancing sequins; and Red, hobbled by a chain thick enough to sink a battleship.

Each of them looked at him with varying expression of relief, of horror, of gratitude for his presence, and of despair that their last hope of salvation had walked boldly into a trap where no man had ever gone before, and wouldn't have done had he two brains to rub together.

Then, one by one, each of them looked away, embarrassed that they should be so naked before him, and focused their attention on the simple raised platform in the center of the roof.

Gideon did, as well.

And Agnes bowed her head ever so slightly.

"You see," she said, with a nod toward her prisoners, "how I have prevailed."

"I see," he answered, "how you have wasted an awful lot of good rope and stuff for nothing."

She laughed gaily, and the top of one of the towers broke off with a thunderous roar and plunged down into the street.

"You think that's funny?" he said.

"I find it amusing," she told him. "And I find it rather touching that you have gotten this far, suffered so much, endured travail for so long, only to have it snatched away from you at the last moment."

He smiled; there wasn't much else he could do.

"What time?" he asked.

"I don't know," she said sadly. "I have been unable to keep a watch running for more than five minutes before it rots and falls off."

"No. I mean, what time does the Day begin."

There was thunder like a cannonade in the center of a great hall, and the wind increased its spin.

He began a slow movement toward her, knowing she would stop him with a look just before he reached the spot where he would be able to lunge at her wi the bat.

She did.

He stopped, but cheated by keeping one foot in front of the other.

"Soon," she said finally. "Soon, Gideon Sunday, I will be the One you've been afraid of all your life."

The lightning was giving him a headache; the wind was spinning so rapidly now that it was a wall of flickering whites and greens that dared him to stare at it without losing his mind.

Then she lowered herself into a crouch, hiking up her dress to expose her knees. "Do you remember the Hold, Gideon Sunday?"

His right hand took the bat from its holster and swung it like a cat's tail low and in front of him.

He remembered.

And when her eyes flared blue he felt the heat in his veins, and the pressure in his skull, and the slow birth of an agony that would tear off his legs if she didn't look away.

She did.

He staggered, but remained on his feet.

"I believe," she said, "my husband's exact words were: 'Fry the little prick.' Is that right?"

Again he had no choice; he nodded.

Her eyes, a limpid and deceptive brown, shifted to look at him sideways, and he grunted at the burning fist that struck his abdomen and brought him to his knees, brought a cascade of perspiration down his brow to sting and blind him, touched each of his internal organs and set them afire until she looked away again, and he dropped forward, catching himself with his hands before he collapsed on his face.

She laughed at him, and a corner of the platform broke off and spun over his head and through the door, through the wall behind, and over the rooftops toward the Scarred Mountains.

Slowly, swallowing bile and shaking away tears, he swayed to his feet and managed to stagger forward before stopping, the bat loose in his hand, but in his hand nonetheless.

"Soon," she said, turned her back to him and stood, arched her spine and looked over her shoulder.

The volcano erupted in the center of his brain, making him scream, making him fall, making him roll helplessly on the roof until he was stopped by the platform's base. Which he used when she looked away again to bring himself to his feet.

His legs were quivering, his arms were filling with lead; and it took him several seconds before he stopped seeing double.

"Very soon," she crooned.

And he brought the bat up over his head, aimed at the center of her spine, and missed.

The platform cracked, Agnes screamed a curse as she was thrown off balance, and he swung again, gasping, catching her on the left ankle and grinning when he heard the bone crack like her lightning.

She screamed and jumped down, whirled and faced him, her hands on the platform's surface and her eyes flickering so wildly from one color to another that the worst he felt was a series of childlike punches to his jaw.

"You can't," she said, struggling to regain control.

"I can," he said, struggling to find the strength to lift the bat again.

She shook her head, and the towers began to split, fragments of stone spilling over the side, spilling around his tied friends, some taken by the wind and hurled over Thazbinn to level homes and shops and slam trenches in the streets.

The wind increased again, and something made him look up, up into the funnel of a tornado to a distant black light that was descending on a black cloud.

Agnes laughed, and the tower just behind them crumpled to rubble before the wind took her laugh away.

"Come on, Gideon Sunday," she taunted. "You murdered my sisters, didn't you? You murdered Chou-Li, and you murdered Thong. What's the matter, hero, can't you do the same to me?"

They circled the platform in spurts of speed, in gasps, in stumbles. The pain in her ankle still forbade her the full use of her eyes, but he had no intention of attempting a brave leap over the stone only to be felled by a giggle.

"Gideon," she said, and chuckled loud enough to bring down both the tower that rose above Tag and the supratower that rose above Lain.

He swung the bat one-handed, and didn't laugh when he hit her shoulder and she dropped out of sight.

And rose again, hair torn by the wind, eyes wild as they kept checking the descent of the black light on the black cloud.

A laugh, and the pillar that held Red shattered to dust.

A cackle, and he heard the last two fall to wind-driven debris.

And he lost his temper again.

He didn't give a damn about the howling in his ears or the thundering that shook the roof under his feet or the lightning that sprayed around himself and Agnes, now the two highest points on the tower. All he needed was one glimpse of the rubble where his friends and sister used to be, and he sprang onto the platform with a mindless shriek of anger.

Agnes backed away.

Gideon marched toward her.

Agnes flashed blue again, and he felt the fire, the cold, the expanding pressure, the contracting iron, and he lifted Whale's bat over his head, grinned, and dropped as the lightning sought to strike it.

It missed the bat.

It didn't miss Agnes.

THIRTY

"You know," Gideon said wearily, "my mother didn't raise me to be a hero. Really she didn't. She always wanted me to be something like a shoe salesman or the owner of the corner luncheonette so she could get a free meal once in a while."

It was dawn, and the sky had cleared, most of the clouds had vanished, and the wind had softened to a cool autumn breeze.

"Your mother was right," answered Lu Wamchu. "A shoe salesman wouldn't have caused me all this trouble."

Gideon grinned and touched the man's shoulder with the bat, spurring him on to complete his work before the sun rose much higher.

It had taken Gideon hours to recover from the battle with Agnes, and five minutes of trying to move stone and brick to realize he couldn't do it by himself. So he had done something he'd always wanted to do ever since he was a kid—he'd straddled the staircase banister and ridden down to the floor where the Wamchu had been imprisoned. A quick one-two with the bat, and the man was free; a little prodding, a little persuasion, a little food from the kitchen after dragging him up there, and a little reminder that magic, when it works, can

241

work wonders, and the tall blond man with no shoes was soon busily excavating what was left of the tower.

"If I were myself, you wouldn't be able to do this, you know," Lu complained.

"Shut up," Gideon said politely. "You're on the last one, so why bitch?"

Then he looked at Tag, who was lying beside him, battered and scratched all to hell, but definitely alive. Lain was beside the lad, covered with dust, and beside him was the lorra, and the lorra was snoring.

Tuesday was on the platform. She had been caught in an open space between two large blocks and was perfectly well save for a lost feather or two. She hadn't said a word since her rescue, but Gideon thought it was enough, for now, that she was alive.

Then the Wamchu grunted, and Gideon dropped the bat and shoved the man aside. Lu looked at him, looked at the bat, shrugged and groaned to stand tall, his hands rubbing the small of his back and his shoulders working to drive the stiffness away.

Then he looked at the bat again.

Gideon saw the look and ignored it. Instead, he concentrated on tossing aside the last bits of debris that had fallen on Ivy. And when he saw her face he touched it tenderly, brushing the dust from her cheek, blowing the dust from her hair, flicking pebbles and shards from her breast until she opened her eyes with a great deal of fluttering and told him to keep his goddamned hands to himself.

He kissed her.

She shoved him away and tried to sit up, fell back with a moan, and he kissed her again.

"Gideon," she said, "three times will get you a kick where you don't want it."

He didn't care, not until she kicked him and he rolled onto his side, rolled up to his haunches and grinned at her again. "Tough jeans," he said, tapping the material. "They've been through a lot."

"I'll bet," said Ivy, though she said it with a smile.

* * *

By midafternoon he had gotten them all down the steps and into the street. Thazbinn looked as if it had been through a week-long bombardment, and he saw, in the distance, a few people making their way through the destruction, signaling, getting work crews together, ignoring the battered, limping band that eventually passed by them, though a few of the more feminine inclined wondered who that delicious naked blond guy was, holding the duck.

By nightfall they were clear of the city, Gideon insisting that they get out in the open before he let them stop.

And when they did, and when Lain's body had been placed beneath the tallest tree in a stand that topped a rise overlooking a slow-moving river, he dropped to his knees and began to weep. He didn't want to, not now that it was all over, but he hadn't had the time before to really say good-bye to his friend, and he had all the time he wanted now.

He wept until he couldn't find another tear, and when he rose and walked down to the grassy plain again, a firepit had been dug, and a fire brought them warmth, and he was mildly surprised to see the Wamchu still there.

"I thought you'd be gone," he said, taking a mug from Tag and a piece of cooked meat from Ivy.

"With no clothes, where would I go?" the man said. "And besides, it isn't going to be the same at home without Agnes." He allowed himself a chuckle. "Quieter, for one thing. And safer, for another."

"She tried to take over more than once?"

"No, but every time I told her a joke, I had to build her a new house. It got pretty grim there for a while when I ran out of things to build with."

Gideon watched him across the flames, trying to read his mind. This man, the Wamchu, had attempted to murder, pillage, subjugate, destroy, and cause havoc; now he was sitting there wrapped in a tattered cloak and not making a move to get rid of the only people left who could ruin his ambitions forever. And he could do it, easily—they were still shaken by the fight, still aching from their injuries, and every so often couldn't help looking back to the city as if Agnes would rise again from the ashes the lightning made her.

It didn't make sense.

"Right," said the Wamchu, and winked at him.

Gideon didn't respond.

"And I bet the fighting's over, too."

"Really?" said Tag, sounding disappointed.

"Would you fight if you knew you were going to die for a lost cause?"

"But is it really lost?" Gideon whispered.

The Wamchu winked again. "For the time being. Maybe for quite a while." He sobered then, and stared for a long time at the fire. "In a way, you know, you saved my life."

"No 'in a way' about it," Tuesday snapped from beside Red. "He saved your ass, pal, and you owe him for that."

Gideon stiffened, thinking that his sister was going too far at last, and only relaxed when Ivy put a hand on his shoulder and whispered something so obscene in his ear that he had to think about it for a while before he decided that it was, in an odd sort of way, a hell of a compliment.

"Now, wait a minute," the Wamchu said to the duck. "I grant you he saved me, all right? But he also stopped me—more than once, may I remind you—from fulfilling a lifelong ambition."

She waddled up to him and flipped a wing in his face. "But you, you sonofabitch, stopped me from fulfilling my lifelong ambition."

He nodded after a moment's thought.

"Not to mention this," she said, and flipped her wing at him again.

"Oh," he said, "well, I suppose I do owe you that."

Tuesday looked over her shoulder. "He does?"

Gideon nodded, not knowing what he was nodding for but not wanting her to take another chunk out of his leg.

"Okay," she said. "You do."

At which point he grabbed her by the neck, stood up, and held her over his head.

Instantly, Red growled dangerously to his feet, Gideon grabbed up the bat, and Ivy reached into the fire and pulled out a brand she prepared to toss at the man's head.

Until the duck stopped squawking, and the orange feet

stopped kicking, and the wings stopped flapping, and the Wamchu lowered Gideon's sister to the ground.

"My god," Tag said. "She's naked!"

"Jesus," Ivy said, "she's . . . she's beautiful!"

"Not too shabby, I admit," said Vorden Lain, close enough to make Ivy shriek, Red run a hundred yards into the dark, and Gideon grab his chest where he last knew his heart to be.

"What," he said then, "the hell are you doing here?"

"I'm cold," the greenman said. "And I'm hungry, if it's all the same to you."

"But you're dead!"

"I was not."

Gideon clenched a fist; this was really too much. "You were too. I checked. Didn't I check him, Ivy? Of course I checked him. Your heart had stopped, and you'd stopped breathing."

"I stopped breathing because I was sleeping," Lain said, pushing him easily to one side and grabbing for a piece of meat. "And my heart stopped because I don't have one."

"You what?"

"I don't have one. A heart. In the literal sense. Here, in my body. Behind—"

Gideon stared at him, openmouthed, and then walked away, walked around the fire, and looked at his sister looking at the Wamchu.

"Hey," he said.

She looked back at him, and smiled. Ivy was right, he thought; she was beautiful. She was his sister, but she was the most beautiful woman he had ever seen in his life.

"You want a steak?" he said.

Tuesday turned to face him, hands on her hips, her long brown hair falling modestly over her breasts. "Gideon Sunday, I am standing here in the absolute altogether, with a man who is also in the absolute altogether, and you ask me if I want a steak?"

"Tuesday—"

She looked at Wamchu with a sigh. "When he gets like this, you have to ignore him."

"Tuesday, that man tried to pluck you, kill you, and bury you more times than I can count!"

"See what I mean?" she said.

Gideon grabbed for her arm, but Ivy grabbed his instead and pulled him away. He sputtered, he protested, he shook off her grip and was grabbed again, though not before he saw his sister and Lu Wamchu walking arm in arm away from the fire, heads together, his cloak rippling around them suggestively. And when Ivy tugged at him, nearly yanking him off his feet, he turned and glared into her innocently wide green eyes.

"This is ridiculous, you know," he said heatedly.

"I suppose," she said.

"I mean, I can't let that happen."

"Why not? She's a big girl, and I guess it beats dolphins all to hell, wouldn't you say?"

"But he's the bad guy, for Christ's sake!"

"And who are you, the hero?"

He thought about it. He looked at Red and thought about it; he looked at young Tag and Vorden Lain, and thought about it; he thought of what Whale and Glorian would say when he told them what had happened to Agnes and, as a muttered aside, the Wamchu and the duck, and thought about it; and he looked at Ivy, and he thought about it.

"Yeah," he said. "Goddamnit, yeah. I am."

She laughed, laughed again when he flinched, and threw her arms around him. "Then act like a hero, hero, and take the heroine off into the woods and do disgusting but perfectly natural things to her body."

"Ivy, please," he said. "This isn't the time."

She released him with an exaggerated groan, stood back, and pointed angrily at his chest. "Gideon Sunday, don't you ever say that to me again, you hear me? Never!"

"But—"

She hushed him with a look. "And as long as you're going around talking about who saved whose hide here, let me remind you about the time—"

He walked away.

"Gideon!"

He walked up the hill toward the grove.

"Gideon, don't you dare walk away from me when I'm talking to you!"

He walked through the grove, over the top of the rise, and down the other side.

He walked until he couldn't hear her anymore, and walked a little more just to be on the safe side. Then he waited, and, as he had known he would, Red came to him and let him onto his back without him saying a word.

He rode for some time, not knowing where he was going, trusting the lorra to find the right way. And as he went, he explained how it was, how he might really be a hero, but in his world heroes didn't take advantage of women, especially not women who were out of their minds with the pain of injury, and especially not women with whom, he might as well admit it, he was in love.

"Now I'm not saving myself or anything," he said when the lorra stumbled. "I don't mean that at all. But it's like a code, you know what I mean? A code of the Old West, so to speak. You do what you have to do because you have to do it, and that's an end to it. If the woman you love can't see that for the clothes on her . . . body, then there ought to be a little breathing space before they make a commitment that might make them sorry later. Do you understand what I'm trying to say, Red? It's simple enough in my head, but I'm not very good at putting it into words. She'll just have to understand, that's all, that I haven't really rejected her because god knows I want her, but there's—where are you going, Red?"

The lorra climbed back up the rise.

"Red?"

Red ambled into the grove and stopped.

Ivy was standing under a tree, the fire below giving her shadow and light.

Gideon scowled at the betrayal, but slid off, deciding that now was the time she had to understand him, or that time would never come again.

"Ivy," he said.

"Thanks," she said to the lorra.

"Don't mention it," Red answered. "But couldn't you shut him up for a while so some of us can get some sleep?"

Ivy laughed.

Gideon gaped.

And the lorra trundled back down the hill toward the fire, shaking his silken head as he heard Gideon ask her how she made the big goat talk, and shaking his head again when she told the goddamned hero to shut his goddamned mouth and take off his goddamned clothes before she showed him what else his bat could do.

Gideon stared down at the lorra, stared over at Ivy, stared at her again, and said, "Be gentle. I've had a rough day."

THE BEST IN FANTASY

ANDRÉ NORTON